JN011813

大修館
シェイクスピア双書
第2集

THE

TAISHUKAN

SHAKESPEARE

2nd Series

大修館書店

タイタス（ブライアン・コックス）とラヴィニア（ソニア・リッター）デボラ・ウォーナー演出、スワン劇場、ストラッ
トフォード・アポン・エイヴォン (1987) © Shakespeare Birthplace Trust.

ウィリアム・シェイクスピア

タイタス・アンドロニカス

William Shakespeare
TITUS ANDRONICUS

清水徹郎
編注

大修館シェイクスピア双書 第2集（全8巻）について

　大修館シェイクスピア双書 第1集（全12巻）の刊行が始まったのは1987年4月。その頃はシェイクスピア講読の授業を行う大学もまだ多く、双書はその充実した解説と注釈において（手頃な値段という点においても）、原典に親しむ学生の心強い味方となり、教員の研究・教育に欠かせないツールとなった。

　そうした時代に比べれば、シェイクスピアよりも実用英語という経済性偏重の風潮もあって、シェイクスピア講読の科目を有する大学は数えるほどになったが、双書が役割を終えたわけでは全くなかった。そのことは発行部数からもよくわかる。2010年代になっても双書のほとんどは継続的に増刷を続けており、例えば『ロミオとジュリエット』の総発行部数は15,000に届く勢いだ。英文学古典の注釈書としてはかなりの部数と言える。

　これは大学の教員や学生のみならず、多くの一般読者にも双書が届いているからに他ならない。実際、周囲を見回せば、通信教育、生涯学習講座、地域のカルチャー・センター、読書会や勉強会でシェイクスピアの原典を繙く人は少なくない。そういう読者に双書が選ばれているのだとすれば、その主な理由は第1集編集委員会の目指した理念が好意的に受け取られているからだろう。

　原文のシェイクスピアをできるだけ多くの人に親しみやすいものにすること。とは言え、入門的に平易に書き直したりダイジェスト版にしたりするのではなく、最新の研究成果に基づいた解説や注釈により、原文を余すところなく読み解けるようにすること。そのために対注形式を取り、見開き2ページで原文と注釈を収めて読みやすさを重視すること。後注や参考文献により学問的な質を高く保ちつつ、シェイクスピアの台詞や研究の面白さを深く理

解できるようにすること。こうした第1集の構想が、第2集においてもしっかりと受け継がれていることは言うまでもない。また、表記の仕方などを除いて、厳密な統一事項や決まりなどは設けず、編集者の個性を十分に発揮していただく点も第1集と同様である。

　一方、重要な刷新もある。第1集ではAlexander版（1951）のテクストを基本的にそのまま用いたが、当時と比べれば近年の本文研究は大きな進展をみせ、現在Alexander版は必ずしも使いやすいテクストではない。むしろ編者が初期版本の性質を見極めた上で、そこからテクストを立ち上げ、様々な本文の読みを吟味しつつ編集作業を行う方が（負担は増すものの）、意義ある取り組みになるのではないか。そうした考え方に基づいて第2集では大きく舵を切り、各編者がテクストすべてを組み上げた。そのため作品によっては本文編集に関する注釈を煩雑に感じる読者もおられようが、注釈に目を通していただくと、問題になっている部分が実は作品の読みを左右する要なのだとご納得いただけると思う。

　第2集の企画を大修館編集部の北村和香子さんにご検討いただいたのは2017年秋。無謀とも思える提案に終始にこやかかつ冷静沈着に耳を傾け、企画全体を辛抱強く推し進めて下さった。第2集8巻の作品選定は大いに悩んだが、第1集『ハムレット』で編者を務めた河合祥一郎氏からのご提言もいただき、喜劇・悲劇・歴史劇・ローマ劇・ロマンス劇からバランスよく作品を選ぶことができた。ご両名にこの場を借りて心から御礼を申し上げる。「さらに第2期、第3期と刊行をつづけ、やがてはシェイクスピアの全作品を網羅できれば」という初代の思いが次に繋がることを願いつつ、あとは読者諸氏のご支援とご叱正を乞う次第である。

　　大修館シェイクスピア双書　第2集　編集者代表　　井出　新

まえがき

　本書の主な目的は、シェイクスピアの専門家でない読者に、作品のテクストに関してできる限り詳細な注釈を提供することにある。そのために、理解しにくいと思われる言葉については詳細な語義を与え、それを含む表現全体の文意が明らかになるよう配慮した。ただしシェイクスピアに限らず優れた詩人の文章に広く言えることであるが、詩句の解釈は決して一様に定まったものではない。むしろ読む人によって、また読む時によって、多種多様な解釈が可能になることこそ魅力と言える。従って本書の註釈では可能な限り正確かつ適切な語義を示すことを心がけたが、それはあくまで可能な意味の一例に過ぎないことを読者は心に留めていただきたい。その意味を深く掘り下げ、あるいは別の解釈の可能性を探って、豊かな想像力の世界へ足を運ぶことは読者自身に任される。

　『タイタス・アンドロニカス』はシェイクスピアが書いた最初の悲劇作品と推定され、この時期に特徴的な古典文学への言及も多い。だがそれは世に言う衒学趣味とは違い、若き日に馴染んだ古代ローマの詩人たちのテクストが、詩人シェイクスピアにとっては、自由に想像力を広げるためのインスピレーションを与えてくれる豊かな源泉だったからである。大学へ行くこともなかったシェイクスピアは、確かに教養の幅が狭かったかもしれない。だが若き詩人は自分の手の内を惜しみなく曝け出すことから詩作と台本制作を始めた。そうして花開いたのが、『ヴィーナスとアドーニス』や『ルークリースの陵辱』という長編の物語詩であり、『タイタス・アンドロニカス』や『間違いの喜劇』という人気作の悲劇喜劇なのである。

　シェイクスピアがグラマー・スクールを卒業した後にどのような場所でどのように勉強し詩人としての教養と技術を磨いていったのか、それを推測する手がかりはほとんどなく全てが謎である。だが私たち読者には、とてつもない大志を抱いたであろう若き日の詩人の思いと情熱を自由に思い描く権利がある。だから本書に付した注釈では、個々の古代詩人のテクストにシェイクスピアが直接接触できた可能性の有無についてはあまり拘らず、詩人とともに古代を自由に想像する手助けとなるように配慮した。詩人はアナクロニズムの手法で、「どこにも存在しないが常に存在する」幻の古代ローマ像を一つの神話として残した。

　この拙い注釈を書く際に、常に脳裏にあったのはお茶の水女子大学の学生・卒業生たちと長年にわたり続けてきた読書会である。東北大震災の2年ほど前、当時の優秀な学生河野美帆さんに促されて始めたシェイクスピア読書会は、代々の学生・卒業生に受け継がれ今も続いている。彼らがぶつけてくる控えめながら鋭い疑問、豊かな想像力と知的渇望が、シェイクスピア悲劇の難解な語句・イメージの一つ一つに注をつける私の作業の励みになった。皆に感謝したい。さて浅学の私が問題作『タイタス・アンドロニカス』の注釈書を纏めるのは容易でなかったが、多くの先輩や友人たちから直接また間接に助言・励ましをいただけたことが実に幸せであった。当然ながら、注釈に予期せぬ不備があるとすれば、それはひとり清水の責任である。最後に、遅筆な私を辛抱強く見守り的確な助言で刊行まで導いてくださった、大修館書店の北村和香子さん、並びに本企画にご尽力くださったすべての方々に、心より御礼申し上げる。

　2022年秋

清水徹郎

目次

挿絵リスト

凡例・略語表

1. 本文・注釈

(1) 本文

　本書のテクストは現在出回っている複数の版を参照しつつ、主として第1四つ折り本（1594）と第1二つ折り本の2系統のテクストをもとに、両者を比較対照しながら編纂したものである。

(2) 注釈

　注は原則として本文の対向ページに収めたが、収まりきれず次ページにわたった箇所もある。特に長いものはスペースの関係上、「後注」として巻末に置き、「⇒後注」と指示した。いずれの場合も訳語（訳文）は「　」の中に入れられている。幕、場、行の表示にはアラビア数字を用いることとし、例えば「2幕1場15行」は「2.1.15」と表記する。本作品以外のシェクスピア戯曲に言及する場合は、版により行数が異なるのが常であるから行を表記せず、幕、場のみをアラビア数字で記す。シェイクスピア戯曲以外の作品に言及する場合は、参照した版の表記に従う。引用文の日本語訳は特に記さない限り編注者自身による拙訳。

2. 略語表

Bacon	Bacon, Francis. 'Of Revenge'. *The Major Works*, ed. with an introduction and notes by Brian Vickers. Oxford World's Classics (Oxford U P, 2002).
Bate	Bate, Jonathan. *Titus Andronicus*, Revised Edition. The Arden Shakespeare Third Series (Bloomsbury, 2018).
Berthoud	Berthoud, Jacques. Introduction and Commentary. W. Shakespeare, *Titus Andronicus*, ed. by Sonia Massai. The New Penguin Shakespeare (Penguin Books, 2001).
Dessen	Friedman, Michael D. and Alan Dessen. *Titus Andronicus*. Shakespeare in Performance. Second Edition. (Manchester U P, 2013).
Burrow	Burrow, Colin. *Shakespeare and Classical Antiquity*. Oxford Shakespeare Topics (Oxford U P, 2013).
F1	The First Folio (1623).
Gk.	Classical Greek　古典ギリシャ語
Hoffman	Hoffman, S. F. W. *Bibliographisches Lexicon der gesammten Litteratur der Griechen*. 3 vols. (Leipzig: A. F. Böhme, 1839/ Amsterdam: Hakkert, 1961).

Hughes	Hughes, Alan, ed. *Titus Andronicus*. Updated Edition. The New Cambridge Shakespeare (Cambridge U P, 2006).
Lat.	Latin　古典ラテン語
Leedham-Green	Leedham-Green, E. S. *Books in Cambridge Inventories: Book-Lists from Vice-Chancellor's Court Probate Inventories in the Tudor and Stuart Periods*. 2 vols. (Cambridge U P, 1986).
Maxwell	Maxwell, J. C., ed. *Titus Andronicus*. The Arden Shakespeare (Methuen, 1968).
OED	*Oxford English Dictionary Online* (Oxford U P).
OLD	Glare, P. G., ed. *Oxford Latin Dictionary* (Oxford U P, 1982).
Partridge	Partridge, Eric. *Shakespeare's Bawdy* (Routledge & Kegan Paul, 1968).
Q1	The First Quarto (1594).
Rubinstein	Rubinstein, Frankie. *A Dictionary of Shakespeare's Sexual Puns and their Significance*. Second Edition (Macmillan, 1989).
Rudd	Niall Rudd, '*Titus Andronicus*: The Classical Presence' *Shakespeare Survey*, 55 (2002), 199-208.
SD	stage direction　ト書き
Taylor et al.	Taylor, Gary, John Jowett, Terry Bourus, Gabriel Egan, et al., eds. *The New Oxford Shakespeare the Complete Works*, Modern Critical Edition (Oxford U P, 2017).
Theobald	Lewis Theobald, *The Works of Shakespeare* (London, 1733).
Tilley	Tilley, Morris Palmer. *A Dictionary of the Proverbs in England in the Sixteenth and Seventeenth Centuries* (Michigan U P, 1950 / 名著普及会, 1985).
Vickers	Vickers, Brian. *Shakespeare, Co-Author: A Historical Study of Five Collaborative Plays* (Oxford U P, 2002).
Waith	Waith, Eugene, ed. *Titus Andronicus*. Oxford World's Classics (Oxford U P, 1994).
Williams	Williams, Gordon. *A Glossary of Shakespeare's Sexual Language* (Athlone, 1997).
逸身	逸身喜一郎『ギリシャ・ラテン文学 ― 韻文の系譜をたどる15章』(研究社, 2018)
松岡	松岡和子訳『タイタス・アンドロニカス』シェイクスピア全集 12 (筑摩書房, 2004)

大修館シェイクスピア双書　第2集

タイタス・アンドロニカス

TITUS ANDRONICUS

解　説

1. 作品

　悲劇『タイタス・アンドロニカス（*Titus Andronicus*）』は、謎の多いシェイクスピア（1564-1616）若き日の著作中でもとりわけ問題の作品である。一見シェイクスピア作とは信じ難いほどに残忍な流血劇という印象を与えがちだが、その残忍さ、センセーショナルな暴力の問題と我々はどう向き合えばよいのか。記録に残るこの芝居の最初の上演時 1594 年 1 月には詩人がすでに 29 歳のはずだから、単なる「若書き」という言い逃れは通用しないだろう。若い日の修行・研鑽の成果と新しい時代の悲劇詩人たろうとする希望を抱え、政治的宗教的不安、ペスト蔓延、劇場封鎖といった困難な時代を生き抜いてロンドンの観客にぶつけた問題作だったと思われる。

　後のシェイクスピア作品ではあまり見られなくなる古代ローマ詩人への明白な言及も気になる。近い時期にオウィディウス（Publius Ovidius Naso）風の物語詩（epyllion）『ヴィーナスとアドーニス（*Venus and Adonis*）』（1593）と『ルークリースの陵辱（*The Rape of Lucrece*）』（1594）、あるいはプラウトゥス（Titus Maccius Plautus）のローマ喜劇を大胆に改作した『間違いの喜劇（*The Comedy of Errors*）』（1594）などを集中して書いていることを見ても、この頃のシェイクスピアが手持ちの知識と教養と想像力を生かし、独自の「古代」表象の構築を野心的に試みていた様子が窺える。それが詩人 20 代後半のこの時期に集中し、以後少なくとも表面的には古典言及があまり表れなくなるのはなぜだろうか。この期を境にした思想的成熟の過程が気になるところ

だ。

　この芝居がどのような意味で悲劇なのか、あるいはそもそも悲劇なのかという疑問も大きい。この芝居の初版すなわち第1四つ折り本（First Quarto, 1594）に記されたタイトルは『タイタス・アンドロニカスの悲嘆極まりないローマの悲劇（*The most Lamentable Romaine Tragedie of Titus Andronicus*）』であり、悲劇として打ち出した芝居であることは間違いない。問題は悲劇（tragedy）という概念の定義で、この時代にはただ漠然と「ヒロイックな作品」という程度の意味でしかなかった。曖昧なまま「悲劇」の名を冠した作品が多く創作され、その成功した芝居が新しい時代の悲劇の定義とテーマを形成していったと考えるべきだ。初めてブランクヴァース（blank verse 弱強五歩格の無韻詩）で書かれた本格的な芝居『ゴーボダック（*The Tragedie of Gorboduc*）』がロンドン法学院インナーテンプルで、さらにホワイトホールにおける女王御前公演でかかったのが1561年。ロンドンで最初の本格的な大衆劇場となるシアター座（The Theatre）が建設されたのが1576年。『タイタス・アンドロニカス』が書かれたのはその後15年余り経ってからだが、その間が英国悲劇創造の時代と言える。手本となったのはまず古典古代の悲劇だが、当時はまだギリシャ悲劇の直接的受容がわずかしか進んでおらず、主に古代ローマ経由であった。すなわちギリシャ悲劇をもとに書き換えられたセネカ（Lucius Annaeus Seneca）の悲劇作品のテクストが中心だった。シェイクスピアもグラマー・スクールの教育で培われたラテン語力を頼りに、当時入手可能だったセネカ悲劇のテクストを読み漁り手本にしたものと推測される（Burrow）。

　セネカのテクストと並んで、シェイクスピアの悲劇創造の過程で重要な手本であり刺激となったのは、同時代の先輩劇作家であ

るピール（George Peele, c1556-96）、キッド（Thomas Kyd, 1558-94）、マーロウ（Christopher Marlowe, 1564-93）らの実作品であったことが推測される。ピールは『タイタス・アンドロニカス』の共作者と推定される詩人で、教養もあり、シェイクスピアが共同作業を通して彼から多くの知識と技術を学んだ可能性が高いと思われる（Burrow）。悲劇関係の作品としては『アルカサルの戦い（*The Battle of Alcazar*）』が知られる。キッドの『スペインの悲劇（*The Spanish Tragedy*)』は英国復讐悲劇の代表的作品で、『タイタス・アンドロニカス』とともに「25年か30年もの長期にわたり」ロンドンの劇場で観客の人気を集め続けたと、後にベン・ジョンソン（Ben Jonson, 1572-1637）の残したテクスト（*Bartholomew Fair*, Induction, 79-82）が証言している。またキッドの失われた芝居で通称『前ハムレット（*Ur-Hamlet*)』は、シェイクスピアの悲劇『ハムレット』の元になった作品とされる。

　しかしシェイクスピア悲劇の形成に最も強い影響を与えたのがマーロウの作品であろうことは疑いの余地がない。凱旋将軍タイタスのローマへの入場シーンが『タンバレン大王の悲劇的物語二部作（*Tamburlaine the Great, divided into Two Tragical Discourses*)』でのタンバレン入場シーンに比せられたであろうことは、多くの批評家が指摘するところだ。『カルタゴの女王ダイドーの悲劇（*The Tragedie of Dido Queene of Carthage*）』もウェルギリウスの『アエネーイス（*Aeneis*）』1巻〜6巻への関心において、『タイタス』と共通する。皇后となった愛人タモラの権勢を称えるエアロンの台詞には『フォースタス博士の悲劇（*The Tragical History of Doctor Faustus*)』のエコーが感じられるし、「神を恐れぬ信心深さ（irreligious piety）」が際限のない流血を呼ぶドラマという点では、やはりマーロウが近い時代の出来事を

4

扱った『パリの大虐殺（*The Massacre at Paris*）』（断片）が連想される。また強烈な個性を持つ悪党エアロンの手本として最も近いのはマーロウの『マルタ島の富豪ユダヤ人の有名な悲劇（*The Famous Tragedy of the Rich Jew of Malta*)』のバラバスだろう。

　エリザベス朝悲劇創造過程の末端近くに位置し、マーロウ劇の影響を強く受けながら誕生したシェイクスピアの悲劇『タイタス・アンドロニカス』の顕著な特徴は、ヒロイズムではなく、むしろその社会性にあった（Berthoud）。タンバレンを彷彿とさせるタイタスの英雄像は第1幕のアクションの急展開で脆くも崩壊し、娘の結婚話のもつれと息子たちの離反、そして父の権威に固執したタイタスによる発作的な子殺しなど、最悪の家庭内暴力といった観を呈する。家族への想いと理解、さらには社会的責任という問題が、新しい悲劇の重要なテーマとして浮かび上がった。この芝居が扱う暴力、レイプ、殺人、裏切り、復讐と怨恨、政治的無能といった事柄は、いずれもいつの世にもある社会的問題に通じる。若き日のシェイクスピアがピールとの共作において生み出した悲劇は、残忍な暴力と流血、そしてそれを清算する詩的正義（poetic justice）をエンターテインメントとして提供する見世物ではない。むしろそのような不幸に巻き込まれた人間の苦悩・苦痛を描き、それを悲劇として提示して社会的政治的責任を問う近代的ドラマだと言えよう。

　『タイタス・アンドロニカス』は近代悲劇が扱うべきテーマを明確に決定づけた、シェイクスピアの野心的な問題作である。

2. テクストと作者

　『タイタス・アンドロニカス』に関する最も古い上演記録は劇場経営者ヘンズロウ（?-1616 Philip Henslowe）の日記に記されたもので、1594年の1月24日（「23」は誤りと推定される）と

28 日、2 月 6 日。おそらくローズ座（the Rose）で上演。興行は
成功で大入りだったが、そのすぐ後にペスト（plague）の流行
で同劇場が封鎖された。劇団はおそらく封鎖で興行収入が途絶え
ることを見込み、時を移さずそのテクストを印刷して売りに出し
た。『タイタス・アンドロニカス』の第 1 四つ折り本（First
Quarto 1594: Q1）である。印刷に付されたシェイクスピアの戯
曲台本として残る、最も早いものとして知られる。執筆時期は不
詳だが、おそらくそれ以前の数年以内で 1592 年〜 94 年あたりか。
さらに早い時期の作と考える批評家も多い。

　『タイタス・アンドロニカス』の底本として主に使用されるシ
ェイクスピア同時代の印刷本には、第 1 四つ折り本（Q1）、第 2
四つ折り本（Second Quarto 1600: Q2）、第 3 四つ折り本（Third
Quarto 1611: Q3）、全戯曲を収める第 1 二つ折り本（First Folio
1623: F1）の 4 種類が知られる。そのうち Q1 が作者の手書き原
稿（foul paper）に最も近く、Q2 は Q1 を元にした再版、Q3 は
さらに Q2 を元にした再再版であると見做されている。シェイク
スピアの死後に出版された全集版 F1 のテクストは、Q3 を元に、
それまでにない 1 シーン（3 幕 2 場）と多くのト書き（stage
directions）を新たに付け加えたものと考えられる。Q1 が作者
の執筆時の意図を多く窺わせる版である一方で、F1 が劇団によ
る実際の上演を多く反映した版であると考えられている。現代の
テクストのほとんどは、Q1 と F1 の両テクストを中心に取捨選
択し、さらに必要な修正等を加えた形で編纂される折衷版であり、
本書もその例に倣う。

　Q1 が作者の手書き原稿に最も近いと推定される根拠としては、
「入退場に関する不正確なト書き」「発話者名表記（stage
prefix）の不統一」と並んで、台本原稿執筆時に作者が行った推
敲の痕跡、すなわち書き直しの際の古い文言の消し忘れ（false

図1　第1四つ折り本（First Quarto, 1594）タイトルページ

図2　第1二つ折り本（First Folio, 1623）タイトルページ

start と呼ばれる）かと疑われる箇所、が複数見られるという事実などが古くから批評家によって指摘されている（Bate 94-103）。例えば1幕1場のマーカスの台詞で、Q1 では 35 行以下に「そして今日、アンドロニカス家の墓碑に償いの生贄を捧げ、ゴート軍の最も高貴な捕虜を処刑した」という文言が入り、同場の少し後で実際にアラーバスが生贄にされるアクションと矛盾するように見える。この部分について、作者が原稿執筆時に古い文案を消し忘れた痕跡だと推測される。ただし同じ台詞の別な解釈も可能で、断定はできない（⇒後注 1. 1. 35-38.）。他の例としては、4幕3場でタイタスとマーカスが道化と交わすやりとりにおける重複・混乱など。これも、道化との会話が常にジョークや言い間違えを伴うものであることなどを考えると、作者による消し損ないかどう

かの判断が難しいところではあるが（⇒後注 4. 3. 94-99）。テクストが抱える曖昧さの解釈は多様だが、最も早く出版された Q1 に現れる不安定さは、推敲・書き直しを繰り返しながら執筆を進めたであろう台本作者のオリジナルな原稿との近さを推測する上で有力な手がかりとされる。

　Q1 から Q3 までのいずれの版にも存在せず、F1 で初めて現れる 3 幕 2 場については、人気作『タイタス・アンドロニカス』が劇団によって長く上演される過程において、観客の嗜好や演劇状況の変化に応じて付け加えられた一場であると推測されている。同場はアンドロニカス家の食事のシーンで、蠅をエアロンに見立てて激しく襲いかかるタイタスの狂気（の演技？）が見せ場。早くはトマス・キッドの『スペインの悲劇（The Spanish Tragedy）』、後にはシェイクスピアの『ハムレット（Hamlet)』や『リア王（King Lear)』などからも想像されるように、舞台上で演じられる狂気は観客に人気の高いエンターテインメントであった。そのような観客の嗜好を反映した改作・加筆であった可能性は十分に考えられる。また、この加筆された 3 幕 2 場の終わりと続く 4 幕 1 場の初めの繋がり具合にも多少問題がある。3 幕の終わりでタイタス他の一行が揃って退場し（Exeunt)、続けてすぐ 4 幕 1 場冒頭で同じ人物たちが登場する。同じ人物が前の場の終わりに退場して続く場の冒頭で再入場するという入退場の仕方は、少なくとも 16 世紀の芝居においては行われなかった。それまで幕の切れ目において今日で言う「幕間」がとられなかったので、同一人物が退場してすぐに再登場するという演技は、観客の目に奇妙に感じられたからである。それが 17 世紀に入り、シェイクスピアの所属する劇団も屋内劇場のブラック・フライアーズ（Blackfriars Theatre）を取得するなどして幕間を設ける上演形式が広まり始めたことと関係したであろうと推測されている。

　次に作者について。

　この芝居の第1幕がシェイクスピア以外の詩人の手になるもの
であろうという推測が古くからあった。20世紀後半から発達し
た文体・語彙等の統計的分析の手法によって、第1幕の作者をシェイクスピアの先輩詩人ジョージ・ピールとし、残りをシェイクスピアの作と考える部分的共作説が有力になり、現在ではほぼ定
説化している。これは統計的文体分析の精度が上がったこともさ
ることながら、共作という台本制作の作業形態を重視する批評動
向の変化によるところも大きい（Vickers / Bate 121-36）。台本
作者として駆け出しの若い詩人が先輩作者と共同作業を行うとい
うことは、前者が後者の知識・技術を学ぶという面でも益すると
ころが大きかったであろうし、演劇という芸術がそもそも共同作
業に馴染む性質のものであるという事実も見逃せない。統計的文
体分析による作者判定の有効性については賛否両論さまざまだが、
デジタル・テクストの登場・普及に伴って分析の精度も高まって
きているとされる。精度を決める鍵の1つは比較対照するテクス
トの数と長さであろうが、『タイタス・アンドロニカス』の場合、
シェイクスピア以外の作者の手になると疑われる箇所のうちでも
1幕1場は約500行と長く、ピールの文体との比較対照による判
定にもそれなりの精度が期待できる。その一方で、比較的短い部
分の作者判定は精度が落ちることになろう。

　では「蠅殺しの場（fly-killing scene）」とも呼ばれる3幕2場
アンドロニカス家の食事シーンの作者はどうだろうか。85行の
短い場面で、苦境に立たされたアンドロニカス一家の寂寥とタイ
タス自身の狂気を視覚的に強調する。上述したように劇場で長期
にわたって上演される過程のどこかで、狂気の見世物を好む観客
の嗜好に訴えることを目的として付け加えられたものと推測でき
る。悲劇のプロット上は特に必要のないシーン。作者については、

シェイクスピア自身によるもの、あるいはシェイクスピアの死後にトマス・ミドルトン（Thomas Middleton, c1580-1627）が加筆したもの（Taylor et al.）、など複数の候補が挙げられている。文体面でシェイクスピアのスタイルに近いこと、この劇全体のスタイルやプロットと矛盾しないことなどの理由からシェイクスピア作と推測することも可能だが、逆に見れば、劇場現場での改作に関わりかつ元の台本にも通暁した詩人であれば誰でも書くことが可能ということになる。この加筆が状況から見て17世紀初頭のものであるとするならば、『ハムレット』や『リア王』を書き、狂気の表象についても深い思索を巡らせていた詩人が、このような形で狂気を表現しようとするだろうか。直前の3幕1場で既に、苦悩する復讐者タイタスの狂気は心の奥深くから動き始めている。

3. アナクロニズム、神話、歴史

　この悲劇にはどこか帝政末期のローマ帝国を思わせる雰囲気があるが、時代設定は完全な虚構であり、歴史上のどの時代でもない。歴史のようでありながら歴史でない。初期近代に生きる英国詩人がその想像力によって描き出した「古代ローマ」のファンタスティックな絵柄である。とは言え、漠然とでも古代ローマのどこかを想定した芝居である以上は、「古代」という枠組みだけは外せないところだろう。だがそれすら不安なところがある。古代と初期近代の英国を混同させた時代錯誤、すなわちアナクロニズム（anachronism）が目に付く。

　この芝居のアナクロニズムとして頻繁に問題にされる例は、5幕1場で嬰児を連れてローマを逃れたエアロンがゴート族の一人に捕らえられるところだ。エアロンを捕縛したゴート人の報告では、「修道院の廃墟を眺めに行って荒れ果てた建物にじっと目を凝らしていると、突然、壁の下で赤ん坊の泣く声が聞こえた」（5.

1. 21-24）とある。シェイクスピアの同時代の英国人にとって「修
道院の廃墟（ruinous monastery）」と言えば、ヘンリー八世の
時代の宗教改革を経た英国の風景そのものだったはずで、古代ロー
ーマの風景ではない。この台詞を書いた詩人自身がその矛盾に気
づいていたはずだが、なぜわざわざこのように不合理な光景を選
んだのか。あるいは詩人の心情となにか関係があるのか。さまざ
まな空想を誘うテクストだが、作者の真意はわからない。

　本作のしばらく後、プルータルコスの影響を強く受けるように
なってから書かれたローマ史劇群『ジュリアス・シーザー（*Julius
Caesar*）』『コリオレイナス（*Coriolanus*）』『アントニーとクレ
オパトラ（*Antony and Cleopatra*）』などでは明確な時代設定が
なされるようになるが、それでも楽屋落ちのようなジョークとし
てのアナクロニズムは中期・後期の芝居でも時々見られる。有名
かつショッキングな例が『トロイラスとクレシダ（*Troilus and
Cressida*）』と『リア王（*King Lear*）』に現れる。

　　　　　　　　but superficially, not much
　Unlike young men, whom Aristotle thought
　Unfit to hear moral philosophy. 　　（*Troilus*, 2. 2. 165-67）
　　　　　　　しかし表面的においてのみだ。アリスト
　テレースが道徳哲学の話を聞くのに相応しくない
　と考えた若者たちとあまり変わらない。

This prophecy Merlin shall make, for I live before his time.
　　　　　　　　　　　　　　　　　　（*Lear*, 3. 2. 97）
以上の予言はマーリンがするだろう。なぜなら僕は彼の時代
より前に生きているのだから。

　前者はトロイアー戦争の真っ只中にいるヘクトール（Hector）が、アリストテレース（384-22 BC Aristoteles/Aristotle）の著作に言及するというもの。露骨なアナクロニズムだが、伝説上のトロイアー戦争がアリストテレースの時代よりはるかに昔であるという事実を知らないほどシェイクスピアが無知であったとは考えられない。芝居であればこそ許されるジョーク。後者はリアに付き従って荒野を彷徨した道化が退場前に言う台詞である。自分は昔の有名な預言者よりもさらに昔に生きているのだと言う。つまり、自分の存在そのものがアナクロニズムだと主張する道化特有のパラドックスである。要するに多くの場合、シェイクスピアのアナクロニズムの例は「錯誤」であるよりも、むしろなんらかの演劇的効果を狙ったアイロニーの類であったと考えるべきだろう。

　さて『タイタス・アンドロニカス』で気になるのは、幾人かの登場人物たちの行動と意識だ。ヒロインの名前ラヴィニア（Lavinia）がローマ建国伝説の英雄アエネーアースがイタリアに着いてから妻にする女性（*Aeneis*, 6. 764）と同じ名前であることは、シェイクスピア時代の少なからぬ観客にはおそらく明白で、古代ローマの伝説と歴史を漠然とイメージしたこの芝居では国の命運に関わる女性として象徴的な存在に見えるが、ラヴィニア自身は特にそのことを意識しているようにも思えない。問題なのは登場人物の中にローマ建国伝説と神話を強く意識し、自らの存在と行動を伝説上の人物に擬えようとしている者が少なくない点だ。例えばタイタスは自分を、時としてアエネーアースに（1. 1. 23 /4. 1. 104）、あるいは妹ピロメーラ（Philomela）をレイプした夫テーレウス（Tereus）に復讐するプロクネー（Procne）に（5. 2. 195）、そして名誉のために自分の娘ウィルギーニア（Virginia）を殺すウィルギーニウス（Virginius）（5. 3. 36-38）などに擬える。

タイタスの長男ルーシアスはルクレーティア伝説でタルクィニウ
ス（Tarquinius）の王族を追放し、共和政を樹立して初代執政
官（consul）になったブルートゥス（Lucius Junius Brutus）（4.
1. 88-90）などに自らを擬える。また長男アラーバスを殺害した
アンドロニカス一族への恨みと復讐の念に燃えるタモラは、息子
ディミートリアスによってギリシャ悲劇のヘカベー（Hekabe）/
ヘキュバ（Hecuba）に（1. 1. 136-38）擬えられる。そして最も
悪質な例は、エアロンに唆されてオウィディウス『変身物語
（*Metamorphoses*）』が伝えるピロメーラ伝説のレイプ犯テーレ
ウスを手本にして、それ以上に狡猾なレイプを実行しようとする
カイロンとディミートリアスの兄弟だろう。

　注意したい点は、これらの人物たちが先例とする詩や伝説が、
次節で記すように、シェイクスピアの時代の初等中等教育機関で
あるグラマー・スクールの古典語教育とその周辺の文化で馴染み
のテクストに関わるものばかりだというところだ。これらの登場
人物が伝説・先例を手本にしてそれぞれの思いと計画をやり遂げ
ようとする様子は、どことなくグラマー・スクールの生徒や卒業
生たちの姿を思わせる。カイロンが聞き覚えのあるラテン語の断
片を聞いて「それはホレイス（＝ホラーティウス）だ。むかし文
法教科書で読んだぞ」（4. 2. 23）と思わず叫ぶ場面などは、その
最も露骨な一例だろう。この劇中の古代ローマの現在は、シェイ
クスピアの同時代のグラマー・スクール文化の現在と頻繁に逆転
する。

　また厳密に言うならば、4幕1場でラヴィニアがオウィディウス
『変身物語』の頁を口でめくってレイプの事実を暴露するとい
う場面で小道具として使用する書物も、『トロイラスとクレシダ』
でユリシーズがアキリーズの気を引くために小道具として用いた
書物（3. 3. 69ff.）と同様に、実際にはどちらかと言うとシェイク

スピアの同時代的風景だろう。しかしこれらを不注意なアナクロニズムとして非難するのは適当でないかもしれない。限られた資料を手がかりに想像力で古代詩人たちの世界を再現しようと試みていたルネサンス詩人たちにとって、多少形態は変わっても本は常に重要な媒体だったからだ。

　ではなぜ「歴史のようでありながら歴史でない」芝居を書いたのだろうか。一つには神話創造に近いものが詩人の発想にあったのかもしれない。神話とは「どの時代にも存在せず、なおかついつつの時代にも常に存在するもの」（Georges Dumézil）だという。この芝居においてシェイクスピアは、昔の詩人の残した詩と書物を手がかりに、どの時代にも存在せずいつの世にも存在するような神話を、古代ローマのイメージとともに作り出していた。『タイタス・アンドロニカス』は新たに生み出された神話という側面を持つ。

　シェイクスピアの時代の歴史と古典文学は、その時代に生きる人々がそこから現代に生きるための教訓を掘り出すためのものとされた。関心はあくまで初期近代の現在にある。「歴史から現在に通用するモラルを学ばせる」ことが教育の重要な目的だったわけだが、現実にはその前に、現在のイデオロギーを古代の事例に読み込んで「歴史」を新たに書き編纂するというプロセスが存在する。つまり「歴史から知恵・教訓を学ぶ」という方向とともに、「現在のイデオロギーや信念で歴史を作り上げる」という逆方向の営みが必ず見られる。その意味で歴史記述にもアナクロニズムの側面が必ずやある。『タイタス・アンドロニカス』は詩的想像力によって新しいローマ神話を作るプロセスを示すとともに、上記のような歴史記述が孕むイデオロギー絡みのアナクロニズムを客観化し、メタ演劇的なアイロニーという形で劇場のエンターテインメントに仕立て上げたものだったのかもしれない。

　終局で娘ラヴィニアを殺すタイタスは、歴史の伝えるウィルギーニウスの先例から教訓を学んでそれを思い立ったのではなく、復讐のためにまず娘を殺した上で皇后タモラを殺害するという自分の戦略のイデオロギー的正当性の根拠を、ウィルギーニウスとその娘ウィルギーニアの伝説に読み込もうとした。

4．古典文学の受容

　『タイタス・アンドロニカス』は、物語詩『ヴィーナスとアドーニス』『ルークリースの陵辱』や喜劇『間違いの喜劇』とともに、シェイクスピア初期作品群における古代ローマ文学の代表的受容例である。この作品中で言及されている、あるいは影響を受けた可能性のある古典テクストの大半は、シェイクスピアが学んだグラマー・スクールで、すなわちエリザベス朝の人文主義教育理念に基づく初等中等教育の教科書として使用されていたものであることが知られている。具体的にはウェルギリウス（70-19 BC Publius Vergilius Maro、英 Virgil / Vergil）、オウィディウス（43 BC-AD 17 Publius Ovidius Naso、英 Ovid）、ホラーティウス（65-8 BC Quintus Horatius Flaccus、英 Horace）、キケロー（106-43 BC Marcus Tullius Cicero、英 Tully / Cicero）、セネカ（*c*4 BC-AD 65 Lucius Annaeus Seneca）、リーウィウス（59/64 BC-AD 1 Titus Livius Patavius、英 Livy）などが挙げられる。また『間違いの喜劇』の場合は、プラウトゥス（*c*254-184 BC Titus Maccius Plautus）のローマ喜劇『メナエクムス兄弟（*Menaechmi*）』他からの翻案である。

　またグラマー・スクールのテクスト以外でも、さまざまな場所・機会での読書や伝聞などを通して、直接・間接に古典の知識を得たものと推測される。例えば『ジュリアス・シーザー』以降のシェイクスピア作品においてギリシャ人思想家プルータルコス

（AD *c*45-*c*120 希 Plutarkhos、英 Plutarch）の影響が顕著になるが、シェイクスピアはトマス・ノース（Sir Thomas North）がフランス語版から英訳した『対比列伝（*The Lives of the Most Noble Grecians and Romans, Compared Together by that Grave Learned Philosopher and Historiographer Plutarch of Chaeronea*)』（1579/94）をどこかで読んだものと推測される。ただし『タイタス・アンドロニカス』執筆時にすでにそれに接していたかどうかは不明。

　第1二つ折本シェイクスピア全集（*Mr William Shakespeares Comedies, Histories, and Tragedies*, 1623）（First Folio）に添えられたベン・ジョンソンの有名な哀歌中の曖昧な1行 And, though thou hadst small Latin and less Greek なども原因の1つとなって、従来長期間にわたってシェイクスピアのラテン語力はかなり低いものと誤解されてきた。しかしながら近年の批評では、学歴がグラマー・スクール卒業に留まるシェイクスピアも相当なラテン語力を有したものと評価が修正されている。再評価の根拠の1つとしては、シェイクスピアの時代のグラマー・スクールのカリキュラムや使用テクストの詳細がわかるにつれ、そこで終始徹底したラテン語教育が行われていたことが明らかになってきたことがある（Baldwin）。また衒学的な引用の少ないシェイクスピア的作風も、新興大衆劇場の台本作家として同時代の状況を正確に捉えた上での微妙で独特なスタイルであると解釈できる。それも再評価の1つの根拠となる。古典文学・哲学に関する読書と教養の幅は限られていたであろうが、詩人自身が興味を持ったテクストへの理解は鋭く、詩人独自の思想となって深く自作中に織り込まれ、新しい時代の詩・演劇として開花している。

　グラマー・スクールでは新約聖書を原語（ギリシャ語共通語コイネー）で読むことを目標にギリシャ語も教えられた。シェイク

スピアにも多少ギリシャ語の知識（less Greek）があったと思われるが、ギリシャ悲劇や詩あるいは歴史書・哲学書を原語で読むという状況は想像し難い。その一方で、16世紀には大陸を中心にギリシャ文学のラテン語訳や近代各国語訳が次第に多く出回るようになっている。グラマー・スクール卒業程度の外国語力でも、翻訳・対訳あるいは翻案・断片的言及などを通して間接的にギリシャの詩文に触れる機会はあったであろう。またギリシャ悲劇は、主としてセネカによるラテン語への翻訳・改作である古典ローマ悲劇を通してルネサンス期の英国で受容されたが、ルネサンス期に直接ギリシャ語原文からラテン語に翻訳されたテクストも出回り始めていた（Hoffman / Leedham-Green）。

　さて悲劇『タイタス・アンドロニカス』、物語詩『ヴィーナスとアドーニス』、同『ルークリースの陵辱』、喜劇『間違いの喜劇』などのシェイクスピア初期作品群における古典受容の特徴として、グラマー・スクールで詰め込まれた古代ローマ文学の知識が、顕著にまた独特な形で現れている。『ヴィーナスとアドーニス』はオウィディウス『変身物語』からの200行あまりのエピソード（10.519-739）を、エラスムス流のレトリック他を交えて1,194行の豊かでエロティックな小叙事詩（epyllion）に発展させている。『ルークリースの陵辱』もオウィディウスの『祭暦（*Fasti*）』2.685-852とリーウィウスの『ローマ建国史（*Ab Urbe Condita*）』I.57-60の両エピソードを主要な材源とし、叙事詩の手法も取り入れて性暴力被害女性の苦悩と葛藤の過程を、1,855行の小叙事詩にしている。いずれもグラマー・スクールの教育で養った知識と修辞の技法を自在に活用し、古典のテクストを模倣するのみでなくさらに大きく発展させたものだ。

　『タイタス・アンドロニカス』について言えば、芝居のストーリーの明確な材源が見当たらない一方で、主要登場人物たちの台

詞・言動に、独特な形で時に乱暴にまたアイロニックに、グラマー・スクールでお馴染みだったはずの古典文学のテクストが言及される。中心となるのはオウィディウスが記述する２つのレイプ伝説、すなわちピロメーラ伝説とルクレーティア伝説、およびウェルギリウスの叙事詩『アエネーイス』の特に最初の６巻、すなわちトロイアー落城伝説とカルターゴーの女王ディードー（Dido）の物語。他にセネカ、ホラーティウス、キケローなどの断片的記憶が登場人物たちの台詞にふと現れる。極端な例としては、前の節でも触れたように、「それはホレイス（＝ホラーティウス）だ。むかし文法教科書で読んだぞ」（4.2.23）などと同時代観客の笑いを誘う楽屋落ちまでも見られる。『タイタス・アンドロニカス』では時代を架空の古代ローマに設定しながら、おかしなことに、登場人物たちがまるでエリザベス朝期のグラマー・スクールの生徒か卒業生のような話し方をする。台詞とアクションを支える古典文化のテクストがグラマー・スクールの教科書レベルであることを、若い詩人はあえて隠そうとしない。前の節でも記した通り、アイロニックで、一種の意図的なアナクロニズム（時代錯誤）の手法と言える。

　この劇でのオウィディウス、ウェルギリウス、ホラーティウス、キケロー、セネカなどの受容は、上述のようにグラマー・スクールにおける人文主義教育のパロディー的な性質のものから、悲劇に深く底流するポエティックな思想に至るまで、いくつかの層を成している。前者の例を挙げるならば、オウィディウス『変身物語』第６巻のピロメーラ／プロクネー神話は、ラヴィニアを襲った愚かなレイプ犯兄弟にとって、さらなる暴行を加えるための手本・口実にすぎなかった。それに対してタイタスもプロクネーの神話を、比類なく残忍な自分の復讐を進めるための先例として利用する。

　　For worse than Philomel you used my daughter,

　　And worse than Progne I will be revenged.　　　(5. 2. 194f.)

　カイロン、ディミートリアス、タイタスによるオウィディウス
詩の解釈はいずれも恣意的で、詩の思想を完全に無視したもの。
ただ形だけ古典を利用して詩を理解しない愚かな例が一種のパロ
ディーとして提示される。

　その一方でこの悲劇は、オウィディウスの詩が伝えるレイプ神
話の真の思想と問題点を演劇的に追求し、終始観客に問いかける。
例えば、レイプの後に舌を抜かれ両手を切り刻まれたラヴィニア
が、無言の痛々しい身体として、タイタスとともに終幕まで長く
舞台上に存在し続ける。観客はラヴィニアの苦痛と苦悩を生々し
く感じ取り、オウィディウス詩のピロメーラの苦悩も思いつつ、
共感のうちに復讐劇の行方を追うようにと仕向けられる。すなわ
ちこの悲劇には、オウィディウスの詩行の誤読・乱用と詩想への
深い共感とが２つながらに存在し劇的世界を構成する。

　２幕１場でエアロンにラヴィニアへの暴行を教唆された兄弟の
一人ディミートリアスが、次のようなラテン語引用混じりの台詞
を叫びながら退場する。

　　Sit fas aut nefas, till I find the stream

　　To cool this heat, a charm to calm these fits,

　　Per Stygia, per manes vehor.　　　　　　(2. 1. 135-37)

135 行の *Sit fas aut nefas* はホラーティウス『歌章（*Carmina*）』
1. 18. 10-11、ウェルギリウス『農耕詩（*Georgica*）』1. 505、オ
ウィディウス『変身物語』6. 585-56 のいずれかから好加減に引い
た句。ディミートリアス自身も引用句のもとの文脈は憶えていな

いはずだ。ホラーティウスの場合であれば、ケンタウロス族が酒に酔って欲情に駆られ「善悪の区別がつかなく」なってラピタイ人と凄惨な戦いを始めた伝説を引いて、過度の飲酒による酩酊と情欲を戒める文脈。ウェルギリウスの文脈であれば「善悪の転倒」の意味になる。いずれにしても、グラマー・スクールで憶えさせられたラテン語のフレーズが、記憶が曖昧なままふと思い浮かんで、それを威勢良く叫んだというような状況であろう。またオウィディウスの場合であれば、夫のテーレウスが妹のピロメーラに暴行したことを知ったプロクネーが復讐を決意した瞬間に叫ぶ台詞であり、その台詞をこれから強制猥褻を実行しようとするチンピラのディミートリアスに叫ばせるのは、辛辣なアイロニー。演劇的ジョークという観点から考えるならば、立身出世のために否応なくラテン語を詰め込ませるグラマー・スクールの慣習とその出来の悪い卒業生たちのパロディーのように思われる場面だ。

　『タイタス・アンドロニカス』における古代ローマ詩受容の重層構造は、セネカ悲劇の詩行などについても見られる。セネカ悲劇で復讐劇として思い浮かぶのは『テュエステース（*Thyestes*）』や『メーデーア（*Medea*）』であろうが、『タイタス』で気になるテクストの１つが『ヒッポリュトゥス（*Hippolytus*)』別名『パイドラー（*Phaedra*）』である（Burrow）。注目したいのは、原典の詩的世界の風景が作品の重要な背景として観客と詩人の脳裏に見えているであろうという点である。37 行の *Per Stygia, per manes vehor*「私はステュクスを抜け、影の国を抜けて運ばれる」は『ヒッポリュトゥス』1180 からのやはり不正確な引用。セネカの原文は「私はステュクスを抜け、燃える数々の川を抜け、狂乱してあなたを追いかけよう（Per Styga, per amnes igneos amens sequar）」で、自分の虚言が元で斃れたヒッポリュトゥスの死骸を前にして、パイドラーが叫ぶ台詞。セネカの悲劇ではこ

の台詞の後18行ほどでパイドラーも自殺する。セネカ悲劇の詩句はしばしば芝居から切り離され、名文句集・金言集の類に入れられて暗記に供されたという。ここでのディミートリアスもそのような形で、悲劇の文脈を理解せぬままにセネカのラテン語断片をがむしゃらに憶えていた当時の文化の戯画であったかもしれない。

　しかしこの芝居を書いた詩人にとって重要な問題は、さらにその先の深いところにある。コリン・バロウの言葉を借りて言うならば、『ヒッポリュトゥス』は「セネカのどの劇よりも、そして他の作家のどの劇よりも、深くかつ恒常的・持続的な影響をシェイクスピアに与えた」作品であった（Burrow 178）。ボールドウィン（T. W. Baldwin）によれば、セネカ悲劇のテクストが戯曲としてそのままグラマー・スクールの教材として使われることはなかったようだが、そこで徹底したラテン語教育を受けた若い詩人・台本作者シェイクスピアが、自分の語学力で十分に読める数少ない古典悲劇作品のテクストを読まずにいたとは想像しがたい（Burrow 177）。シェイクスピアが詩人・台本作者としてデヴューするよりも早い時代に、セネカ悲劇のテクストとは掛け離れた演劇作品である「英国セネカ（English Seneca）」が英国の劇場に上演され始めていたが、シェイクスピアはその「英国セネカ」とは別に、グラマー・スクールで培ったラテン語力を自分なりに駆使して、当時入手できたセネカ悲劇のラテン語テクストを読みあさっていたと考えるのが蓋然性の高い推測であろうと思われる。その中で最も詩人の関心を引いた悲劇作品の1つが『ヒッポリュトゥス』だったであろう。作劇法においても、言語・イメージの点においても、芝居のテーマとプロットにおいても、セネカ悲劇の読書から若い詩人シェイクスピアは多くを学び取ったに違いない。

　『タイタス・アンドロニカス』における古典受容の重層性は、台本作者と詩人という2つの顔を同時に持っていた作者の微妙な立場と関係するかもしれない。同時代の証言やその後の上演史を見ても明らかなことだが、記録に残る最初期の作品を書いた頃からシェイクスピアは、劇場で多くの観客を惹きつける演じて面白い芝居を書く才能を備えていた。例えば『ヘンリー六世・3部作（*Henry VI, Parts 1-3*）』、『リチャード三世（*Richard III*）』、『間違いの喜劇』、『じゃじゃ馬ならし（*The Taming of the Shrew*）』、『ヴェローナの二紳士（*The Two Gentlemen of Verona*）』などのシェイクスピア初期の作は、現代でも上演すればまず楽しい芝居になる。面白い台本作りの才能は初めから備わっていたと考えるべきだろう。その後経験を積み勉強と読書で、思想性・社会性・人の心を読む共感力・洞察力を深めていったと推測できる。

　悲劇『タイタス・アンドロニカス』は、純粋に詩人として生きようとする真剣な野心と同時代の人間模様を面白い芝居にしてしまう才能に恵まれた演劇人の興行精神と、その両方の影を同時に垣間見ることのできる興味深いテクストと言える。古典文学の受容という点に関して言うならば、立身のための教養としてあるいは世俗的権威・階級的特権の根拠として乱用される古典語の教育とその空虚な文化を突き放し客観化して軽妙なエンターテインメントに仕立て上げると同時に、その一方で詩人自身は手に入りうる範囲のごく限られた古代詩人と心の会話を愉しんでいたということか。その成果がやがて『ソネット集（*The Sonnets*）』（1609）や後期の成熟した芝居の数々となって実を結ぶことになるのは、周知の通り。

5.　復讐と狂気とレイプ

　『タイタス・アンドロニカス』はしばしば「復讐悲劇（revenge

tragedy)」という呼び名で分類されるが、ジャンルの名称としては曖昧である。そもそも「復讐」の概念そのものが曖昧であったことも理由と言えよう。復讐は、例えば、公的な権力によって行われるものと、私的な恨みに基づいて行われるものとの2種類に分類されることが多く、後者は狂気として扱われる（Bacon）。『タイタス・アンドロニカス』の悲劇ではその両者がそれぞれのプロットをなして絡み合い、問題を複雑にしている。

　主人公タイタスはその2つの復讐プロットに関わり、破局の原因となる致命的な誤り（ハマルティアー）も2つ犯している。1つには、第1幕でタモラの嘆願を退けてその子アラーバスを人身御供にしたこと。それがタイタスとタモラとの間の、復讐が復讐を呼ぶ恐怖の因縁の始まりである。これが私的復讐のプロット。もう1つは、皇帝選出に際して、ローマ民衆から支持されて皇帝指名の権限を得たにもかかわらず、民衆の期待を裏切ってサターナイナスを皇帝に指名してしまったこと。その悪政を正そうとするのが「政治的」すなわち「公的」な復讐のプロット。その2つの復讐プロットの絡み合ったところに復讐者として立つのが主人公タイタスである。

　アラーバスを犠牲にしたことに起因する私的な復讐の連鎖に巻き込まれていることにタイタス自身は初め気づいていないが、その流れの中で起こるのが、タモラの2人の息子によるラヴィニアのレイプと舌・両手の切断である。自分が皇帝にしたサターナイナスの悪政を正すべき使命を自覚した公的復讐者であるはずのタイタスだが、娘のレイプや息子たちの処刑という事態に直面する過程で、次第に狂気を帯びた「私的」復讐者としての面が強くなる。

　二重の復讐者であることによって、狂気と正気の区別そのものが困難になる。その復讐者の狂気の複雑さ曖昧さを滑稽に演劇化

するのが、タモラが後段で仕掛ける奇妙な仮面劇（マスク）の罠である。つまり客観的には劇中劇だが、その劇中劇を演じるタモラとタイタスがそれぞれ別様に自分の復讐の演劇性を自覚している点で極めて手の混んだメタドラマになっている。しかもその２人が争うのは復讐者の「狂気」を巡ってだ。この劇中劇はキッドの『スペインの悲劇』に代表される復讐悲劇の、特にその擬人化された「復讐」が外側からドラマを支配するという枠構造の、滑稽なパロディにもなっている。そしてその滑稽なイリュージョンからさめた瞬間に突きつけられる恐怖の場が問題である。佯狂を解いたタイタスは、カイロンとディミートリアスのレイプ犯２人を屠ってパイに調理し、それを母親のタモラに食わせるという復讐計画を冷静に実行し始める。観客に突きつけられるのは、正気を自認して平然と演じ実行する「復讐の正義」こそ、実は最も恐ろしい狂気ではないかと思わせる衝撃のタブロー。『タイタス・アンドロニカス』という手の混んだ芝居は、同時代に始まり急速に成長した復讐悲劇の伝統の中に身を置きながら復讐の演劇性そのものを自己言及的に問いかける、初期近代に相応しいメタ演劇としての特徴を持つ。

　このメタ演劇的な復讐プロットの流れの中で忘れてはならないもう１つ重要な点が、ラヴィニアのレイプとそれを隠蔽するための暴力が復讐の中核に置かれている点だ。正義の復讐をメタの視点で、すなわち批判的分析的に観るように導かれる観客の眼前に、同時にそしてほぼ恒常的に曝されるのがレイプという人格否定の暴行の傷跡と苦痛に耐える被害者の姿である。復讐の狂気と暴力がレイプと同列に提示されることの意味は何か。それらの現実から社会が目を逸らすことを禁じる、そのようなリアリズムと社会性への訴えを新しい悲劇のテーマとしたとまで言っては時代錯誤だろうか。

　そしてエアロン。「子供を助けろ。…嫌なら、みな復讐で滅ぶがいい。」これからローマ社会の新しい支配者・政治家になろうとするルーシアスに、この劇最大の悪党が叫ぶ。舌を切り取られた女性の声と同様に、異邦人エアロンの訴えの成否はわからない。あるいは復讐の狂気を凌ぐのが政治だろうか。

6.　受容・上演史と批評の問題

　20世紀半ば以降、にわかに重要視されるようになった研究分野に受容・上演史がある。『タイタス・アンドロニカス』も、幾度も形を変えて繰り返される舞台上演が作品の評価に大きな影響を与え続けてきた。それは同時に、受容する側のローカルな文化状況やイデオロギーによってテクストが書き換えられ、時にラヴィニアの身体のように切り刻まれ、傷と苦悩を隠し美化され、そして再び暴かれて蘇り、新たな価値を発見される歴史でもあった。

　先に触れたように（5頁）、『タイタス』の最も古い上演記録はヘンズロウの日記中の「新作：『タイタス・アンドロニカス』1594年1月2[4]日（木）、収入3ポンド8シリング（New: Titus Andronicus, Thursday 2[4] January 1594, receipts three pounds eight shillings）」という記載。売り上げはシーズン最高の1つで、同月29日と翌月6日に再演された。同7日からローズ座劇場が封鎖されることになるが、おそらく劇場での興行成功からその台本の売れ行きを見込んで、時を置かず同じ6日に印刷業者ダンター（John Danter）がこの戯曲の出版登録を行っている。初めて印刷されたシェイクスピアの戯曲、第1四つ折り本（Q1）である（Bate 68-69）。『タイタス』は早くから劇場の人気作品だった。そしてジョンソンの皮肉な証言が示すように、人気は同時代のロンドンで長く続く。『タイタス』の上演についてはまた、「現存唯一のシェイクスピア同時代舞台画」（Chambers）と見做さ

れる資料が残る（図8）。ヘンリー・ピーチャム（Henry Peacham）による二つ折りサイズ1ページの手書き文書で、挿絵の下に『タイタス』からの引用が記されている。描かれた年代は不明（1595年から1623年の間）だが、上演から同時代の観客が受けたであろう印象を知る手がかりとなる。タモラによる嘆願、エアロンの不気味な存在感、古代風衣装と同時代風衣装の混在などの特徴が指摘されている。

　その後の『タイタス』上演史についてはフリードマンとデッセン（Michael D. Friedman and Alan Dessen）の解説書（2013）とベイト版（2018）の序文が詳しく記しているので、特に前者を一読されたいが、ここでは影響の大きかった数例を拾い手短に概観する。

　初期の重要な改作例としては、ラヴェンズクロフト（Edward Ravenscroft）による *Titus Andronicus, or the Rape of Lavinia*（1686）が知られる。改作の特徴の1つは、エアロンの描き方にある。劇前半でエアロンの計略家としての役割が拡大し、後段では、父親として助命を要求した愛児が母親のタモラに殺されるという筋書きに。18世紀にラヴェンズクロフト版が復活された時は、名優クウィン（James Quin）がエアロン役を演じ成功している（Bate 53）。ラヴェンズクロフトによる改作時においてすでに、流血他、後々まで残るこの芝居の扱いにくさが浮き彫りになっている。

　その後20世紀までシェイクスピアが残した形で『タイタス』がまともに上演されることはまずなかった。その間に演じられた重要な改作の1つは、黒人俳優アイラ・オルドリッジ（Ira Aldridge, 1807-67）と劇作家サマセット（C. A. Somerset）によるもので、1849年から1860年にかけて上演された。この改作ではエアロンがオセローのように高潔なキャラクターとして美化さ

れる一方で、ラヴィニアへのレイプ、舌と両手の切断、さらに数多くの殺人など、原作にあったほとんどの暴力的なシーンと言葉が削除された。原作とはかけ離れた作品だが、このような削除と改作が歓迎されたという事実が、逆にレイプ・暴力・人種差別などの問題に対するヴィクトリア朝社会の道徳的姿勢あるいは嗜好と不安を如実に映し出している（Bate / Dessen）。

　シェイクスピアの作品が原作通りのテクストで上演されるようになるのは、主に 20 世紀になってからである。中でも『タイタス』は、原作テクストにある流血やレイプ、そして露骨にオウィディウス風な詩的台詞などが障壁や躊躇（とまど）いのもととなって本格的な作品評価が遅れ、シェイクスピアらしからぬ稚拙で悪趣味な作品として誤解される時代が長く続いた。そのような偏見と思い込みを正し、作品のテクストと演劇的価値の客観的評価を加速させることになったのは、テクストの特徴を生かし工夫したいくつかの優れた上演の成功であった。中でも特に影響が大きかったのが、ピーター・ブルック（Peter Brook）、デボラ・ウォーナー（Deborah Warner）、ジュリー・テイマー（Julie Taymor）それぞれの演出による舞台上演および（テイマーの場合の）映画化である。他にも現代社会の問題や政治状況を鋭く反映させた、シルヴィウ・プルカレーテ（Silviu Purcarete）やグレゴリー・ドーラン（Gregory Doran）それぞれによる演出作品他、優れた上演が続いた。また日本を含めたアジアの劇団による各国の文化・特性を生かした多様な上演も注目されるようになっている。

　ブルックの演出によるストラットフォード（Stratford-upon-Avon）での公演（1955）（図 5・7 参照）は、流血と暴力の様式化（stylization）と台詞の大胆なカットが特徴であったとされる。ブルック演出がレイプ・殺人・暴力等の表現を様式化したことは、シェイクスピア作品の重要な特徴である社会問題へのリアルな視

点とその社会的責任の問題を回避したものとも言える。しかしながら従来評価の低かった『タイタス』という作品が稚拙でも単なる悪趣味でもなく、舞台で演じられれば見事な花を咲かせ得る優れた戯曲・台本であることを実践で証明した功績が大きい。ブルック演出を機にこの悲劇の価値を改めて評価する本格的な研究が始まったと言っても過言ではない。またブルック演出による『タイタス』のもう1つの特徴である台詞の大幅なカットについて、「不自然なオウィディウス風の台詞を切り捨てた」と評価される場合が多いが、これは少し違うように思う。台詞を極限まで切り詰めて演劇の本質的なものを浮かび上がらせるというやり方は、他の多くの作品に関しても用いているブルック独特の手法だからだ。

ウォーナー演出によるローヤル・シェイクスピア劇団（The Royal Shakespeare Company）の『タイタス』公演（1987-88）（口絵参照）では、「原作のテクストを全面的に信頼する」という方針のもと、削除を一切せずに演じられた。役者たちの優れた演技力にも恵まれ、苦悩も狂気じみた笑いの恐怖も、すべて見事に表現されたとのこと（Dessen）。「英語至上主義」と非難するのは的外れだろう。シェイクスピア劇はもともと台本としてよくできているのだ。

テイマー演出『タイタス』は、初めオフ・ブロードウェイの劇団（Theater for a New Audience）のために制作され（1994）、後に映画版として制作し直された。1999年公開。特徴はブルックの様式性とウォーナーの原作テクスト重視との両特徴を取り入れたものと評価される（Friedman）。映像を見てまず気付かされる特徴は、古代風の衣装とムッソリーニの時代を思わせるイメージとの混在で、映像を駆使した意図的なアナクロニズムである。先に記したように、アナクロニズムは「古代」を表象しつつ同時

にその現代的意味を問うシェイクスピアの特徴的技法の1つで、特に『タイタス』において顕著。演出はそれを鋭く再現している。隠れていたこの作品の魅力を映画化で世界に広めた功績も大きい。

　純粋な文献批判や実証的歴史研究は別として、近年のシェイクスピア批評が上演から多くの刺激を受けて進展したことは明らかだ。特に『タイタス』において著しかった。「共作」が重視されるようになった流れも、共同作業を旨とする劇場現場の問題をシェイクスピア劇に通じるものとして考えられるようになったことと関係があるだろう。受容・上演史の研究は受容者側の文化研究であるが、それが古いテキストのうちに隠れていた密かな魅力を発見し、シェイクスピア時代の文化の歴史的研究に新たな刺激を与えることが、そして私たちの後に続く世代へその遺産を伝えて行くことが理想である。『タイタス・アンドロニカス』を書いた若いシェイクスピアは、古代詩人たちへの深い思いを抱くと同時に、同時代社会が抱える問題をリアルな眼差しで眺め、後に続く人類へ深い愛を抱いた。悪党エアロンでさえ我が子に希望を抱いたのだから。

参考文献解題

1. シェイクスピアの同時代作家等

Bacon, Francis. 'Of Revenge' (1625). *The Major Works*, ed. with an introduction and notes by Brian Vickers. Oxford World's Classics (Oxford U P, 2002). 私的復讐を野蛮な愚行とし、法の裁きあるいは公的復讐のみをよしとする。

Henslowe, Philip. *Henslowe's Diary*, ed. by R. A. Foakes. Second Edition (Cambridge U P, 2002). 劇場経営者による興行関係の記録。

Jonson, Ben. *Bartholomew Fair. The Cambridge Edition of the Works of Ben Jonson*. Vol. 4 (Cambridge U P, 2012). 芝居の序 (Induction) に『タイタス』の長期にわたる人気について言及がある。

Kyd, Thomas. *The Spanish Tragedy*, ed. by Clara Calvo and Jesus Tronch. Arden Early Modern Drama (Bloomsbury Publishing, 2013). 復讐悲劇の代表的作品。『タイタス』と並び人気芝居。

Lily, William. *A Short Introduction of Grammar to Be Generallie Used* (Geneva, 1557). グラマー・スクールのラテン語文法入門書。

Marlowe, Christopher. *The Complete Works of Christopher Marlowe*, 5 vols. (Oxford U P, 1987-95). マーロウはシェイクスピアが最も強い影響を受けた詩人・劇作家。エアロンの造形など。

Peacham, Henry. 'Henry Peacham's drawing', now stored at Longleat House, Wiltshire. 同時代の『タイタス』上演シーンのスケッチ。この芝居から観客の受けた印象を推測させる資料。

Peele, George. *The Life and Works of George Peele*, 3 vols. (Yale U P, 1970). 『タイタス』での共作者と推測される。第1幕はピールが書いたとする説が有力。シェイクスピアが技術的に学ぶところ

も多かったと考えられる（Burrow）。

Ravenscroft, Edward. *Titus Andronicus, or the Rape of Lavinia* (London, 1687). Facsimile Edition (Cornmarket Press, 1969). 王政復古期の改作。これ以後、書き換えと削除の歴史が続く。

Shakespeare, William. *King Lear*, ed. by Jay L. Halio. A new introduction by Lois Potter. Textual Introduction, edited, with a new preface, by Brian Gibbons (Cambridge U P, 2020).

——. *Mr. WILLIAM SHAKESPEARES COMEDIES, HISTORIES, & TRAGEDIES Published according to the True Originall Copies*. (London, 1623).［第1 二つ折り本（The First Folio）F1］Bodleian Library Arch. G c.7. シェイクスピア没後に編纂された全集。オンラインで読める。https://firstfolio.bodleian.ox.ac.uk/

——. *The Complete Poems of Shakespeare*, ed. by Cathy Shrank and Raphael Lyne. Longman Annotated English Poets (Routledge, 2018). シェイクスピアの詩が『タイタス』理解の参考になる。

——. *The most Lamentable Romaine Tragedie of Titus Andronicus* (London, 1594)［第1四つ折り本（The First Quarto）Q1］作者原稿に近いとされる。

——. *The most lamentable Romaine Tragedie of Titus Andronicus* (London, 1600)［第2 四つ折り本（The Second Quarto）Q2］Q1に修正を加えた再版。

——. *The most lamentable Romaine Tragedie of Titus Andronicus* (London, 1611)［第3四つ折り本（The Third Quarto）Q3］再版回数の多さはその本の需要の多さを示す。上記3つの版は現在いずれもオンラインで読むことが可能。
https://www.bl.uk/treasures/shakespeare/homepage.html

——. *The New Oxford Shakespeare the Complete Works, Modern Critical Edition*, ed. by Gary Taylor, John Jowett, Terry Bourus, Gabriel Egan, et al. (Oxford U P, 2017). 新しいテキスト学の成果を反

映させているシェイクスピア全集。併行して *The New Oxford Shakespeare: Authorship Companion*, ed. by Gary Taylor and Gabriel Egan (Oxford U P, 2017) も出ている。

——. *Titus Andronicus*, ed. by Eugene Waith. Oxford World's Classics (Oxford U P, 1994)。初版は1984年。P・ブルック演出『タイタス』(1955) 他の影響で、にわかに起こった再評価の流れを反映する。

——. *Titus Andronicus*, ed. by Sonia Massai. Introduction and Commentary by Jacques Berthoud. The New Penguin Shakespeare (Penguin, 2001)。ベルトゥーは悲劇の社会性を指摘する。近代社会での悲劇の役割を考察する上で参考になる。

——. *Titus Andronicus*, ed. by Barbara A. Mowat and Paul Werstine. Folger Shakespeare Library (Washington Square Press, 2005) 初学者に使いやすい。

——. *Titus Andronicus*, ed. by Alan Hughes. Updated Edition. The New Cambridge Shakespeare (Cambridge U P, 2006)。

——. *Titus Andronicus*, ed. by Jonathan Bate. Revised Edition. The Arden Shakespeare Third Series (Bloomsbury, 2018)。初版 (1995) では『タイタス』1幕1場のシェイクスピア単独作を主張しているが、その後修正し改訂版 (2018) でピールとの共作説を受け入れている。上記 Hughes と Bate は両者とも上演史の記述が詳しい。Friedman and Dessen と併せて読んでおきたい。

——. *Troilus and Cressida*, ed. by David Bevington. Revised Edition. The Arden Shakespeare Third Series (Bloomsbury, 2015)。シェイクスピア円熟期における意図的アナクロニズムの作品例。

——.(松岡和子訳)『タイタス・アンドロニカス』シェイクピア全集 12 ちくま文庫(筑摩書房 2004) 現場の役者にも一般読者にも想像力を広げさせる、癖のない優れた日本語訳。英語原文に通じた読者にも翻訳の違和感を感じさせない。

2. 古典作家

ウェルギリウス（Publius Vergilius Maro, 70-19 BC 英 Virgil / Vergil）

――．（岡道男・高橋宏幸訳）『アエネーイス』西洋古典叢書（京都大学学術出版会 2001）［*Aeneis*］『タイタス』では最初の 6 巻への言及が多い。ただし Lavinia の名が現れるのは第 6 巻以降の後半。

――．（小川正廣訳）『牧歌 / 農耕詩』西洋古典叢書（京都大学学術出版会 2004）［*Georgica / Eclogae*］

Vergil. *Eclogues, Georgics and Aeneid 1-6,* translated by H. R. Fairclough and revised by G. P. Goold. Loeb Classical Library (Harvard U P, 1976). ロウブ古典叢書は以下すべて古典語と英語の対訳。同出版局のウェブサイトでオンラインで読むことも可能。

――．*Aeneid 7-12 and the Minor Poems*, translated by H. R. Fairclough. Loeb Classical Library (Harvard U P, 1986).

エウリーピデース（Euripides, *c*485-406 BC）

――．（丹下和彦訳）『エウリピデス 悲劇全集 2』西洋古典叢書（京都大学学術出版会 2013）『ヘカベー（*Hekabe*）』他を収録。

オウィディウス（Publius Ovidius Naso, 43 BC-AD 17 英 Ovid）

――．（高橋宏幸訳）『祭暦』（国文社 1994）［*Fasti*］

――．（中村善也訳）『変身物語 上・下』岩波文庫（岩波書店 1981-84）［*Metamorphoses*］

Ovid. *Fasti*, translated by Sir James George Frazer. Loeb Classical Library (Harvard U P, 1976).

――．*Metamorphoses,* 1- 2, translated by Frank Justice Miller. Loeb Classical Library (Harvard U P, 1968).

キケロー（Marcus Tullius Cicero, 106-43 BC 英 Tully / Cicero）

――．（大西英文訳）『弁論家について 上・下』岩波文庫（岩波書店 2005）［*De Oratore*］

セネカ（Lucius Annaeus Seneca, *c*4 BC-AD 65）

——.（高橋宏幸訳）「倫理書簡集 I・II」『セネカ哲学全集 5・6』（岩波書店 2005-06）

——.（小川正廣・高橋宏幸他訳）『セネカ悲劇集 1・2』西洋古典叢書（京都大学学術出版会 1997）

Seneca. *Tragedies*, 1, translated by John G. Fitch. Loeb Classical Library（Harvard U P, 2002）. [*Troades* /*Phaedra* (=*Hippolytus*)] シェイクスピアはセネカ悲劇を原語で読んだと推測される。

プラウトゥス（Titus Maccius Plautus, *c*254-184 BC）

——.（鈴木一郎他訳）『古代ローマ喜劇全集 2』（東京大学出版会 1976）『メナエクムス兄弟（*Menaechmi*)』他を収録。

Plautus. *Casina; The Casket Comedy; Curculio; Epidicus; The Two Menaechmuses*, translated by Wolfgang de Melo. Loeb Classical Library（Harvard U P, 2011）.

プルータルコス（Plutarkhos, AD *c*45-c. 120　羅 Plutarchus 英 Plutarch）

Plutarch. *The Lives of the Most Noble Grecians and Romans, Compared Together by that Grave Learned Philosopher and Historiographer Plutarch of Chaeronea*, translated by Sir Thomas North from the French version（1579/94）.

フロールス（Publius Annius Florus, AD c. 70-c. 140）

Florus. *Epitome of Roman History*, translated by E. S. Forster. Loeb Classical Library（Harvard U P, 1929）.　リーウィウスの簡略版。

ホメーロス（Homeros, a. 800 BC 羅 Homerus 英 Homer）

——.（松平千秋訳）『イリアス 上・下』岩波文庫（岩波書店 1992）[*Ilias*] 16世紀後半にはホメーロスの両叙事詩の複数種類のラテン語訳が学生向けに多く出版されていた。伊・仏他の近代語訳も多い。Hoffman, Vol. 2. 314-58参照。

ホラーティウス（Quintus Horatius Flaccus, 65-8 BC 英 Horace）

——.（藤井昇訳）『歌章』古典文庫（現代思想社 1973）[*Carmina*]

Horace. *Odes and Epodes*, translated by C. E. Bennett. Loeb Classical Library (Harvard U P, 1968). [*Carmina*]

リーウィウス（Titus Livius Patavius, 59/64 BC-AD 17 英 Livy)

――. (鈴木一州訳)『ローマ建国史 上』岩波文庫（岩波書店 2007）長大な歴史記述。簡略にしたものがフロールス（Florus）。

Livy. *History of Rome, Books 1-2*, translated by B. O. Foster. Loeb Classical Library (Harvard U P, 1919). [*Ab Urbe Condita*]

3. 研究書・批評

Barber, C. L. *Creating Elizabethan Tragedy: The Theater of Marlowe and Kyd*, ed. with Introduction by Richard P. Wheeler（Chicago U P, 1988）．エリザベス朝悲劇草創期の演劇の社会的・心理的機能を論ずる。新歴史主義の批評家へも影響を与えた。三盃隆一の邦訳がある。

Baldwin, T. W. *William Shakespeare's Small Latine and Lesse Greeke*, 2 vols. (Illinois U P, 1944)．グラマー・スクールの教育課程・教科書他を詳細に記述。シェイクスピアの教養に関する誤解を修正する。

Bartels, Emily C. *Speaking of the Moor: From* Alcazar *to* Othello (Pennsylvania U P, 2008)．政治経済状況の文脈の中で人種とムーア人の演劇的表象のあり方を論じる。

Bate, Jonathan. *Shakespeare and Ovid* (Oxford U P, 1993)．詩人シェイクスピアのオウィディウスへの関心の深さを包括的に論じる。

Braden, Gordon. *Renaissance Tragedy and the Senecan Tradition: Anger's Privilege* (Yale U P, 1985)．ルネサンス演劇におけるセネカの重要性を捉え直す重要な一書。フランス古典劇までを扱う。

Burrow, Colin. *Shakespeare and Classical Antiquity*. Oxford Shakespeare Topics (Oxford U P, 2013)．シェイクスピアにとっての古代の意義と詩人成長過程での位置づけについて示唆に富

む。

De Grazia, Margreta. *Four Shakespearean Period Pieces* (Chicago U P, 2021).　アナクロニズムの問題を論じている。

Friedman, Michael D. and Alan Dessen. *Titus Andronicus*. Shakespeare in Performance. Second Edition.（Manchester U P, 2013).　デッセンがウォーナー演出（1987）まで、フリードマンがその後を加筆。上演が作品再評価につながる流れを重要視する。

Enterline, Lynn. *Shakespeare's Schoolroom: Rhetoric, Discipline, Emotion* (Pennsylvania U P, 2012).　人文主義教育の修辞法等が、劇作家では本来の目標とは異なる新しい実を結んだ状況を論じる。

Greene, Thomas M. *The Light in Troy: Imitation and Discovery in Renaissance Poetry* (Yale U P, 1982).　ルネサンス詩人の抱く古代詩人との断絶感と模倣（imitation）のあり方を分析する。

Kerrigan, John. *Revenge Tragedy: Aeschylus to Armageddon* (Oxford U P, 1996).　復讐悲劇の概念をめぐって幅広い角度から論じる。

Miola, Robert S. *Shakespeare and Classical Tragedy: the Influence of Seneca* (Oxford: U P, 1992).　セネカのシェイクスピアおよび同時代詩人・劇作家への影響を詳細に論じる。

Rudd, Niall. '*Titus Andronicus*: The Classical Presence', *Shakespeare Survey*, 55 (2002), 199-208.　古典の引用を客観的に分析している。

逸身喜一郎『ギリシャ・ラテン文学 — 韻文の系譜をたどる15章』（研究社 2018）　古代詩の系譜で、ホメーロス、ウェルギリウス、オウィディウス、ホラーティウス他の特色・位置づけが明瞭。

4. 基礎資料集・文献目録・辞典類

Bullough, Geoffrey, ed. *Narrative and Dramatic Sources of Shakespeare*. Vol. 6 (Columbia U P, 1966).　主な材源を収録。

Chambers, E. K. *The Elizabethan Stage*, 4 vols (Clarendon Press,

1923）． エリザベス朝期の演劇に関する膨大な資料を収録する。

Dent, R. W. *Shakespeare's Proverbial Language: An Index*（1981; California U P, 2020） 諺・格言的表現の集成。

Drummond, H. J. H. *A Short-title Catalogue of Books Printed on the Continent of Europe, 1500-1600, in Aberdeen University Library*（Oxford U P, 1979）． 大陸印刷本の流入状況を推測する手がかり。

Early English Books Online. The Open Source Version（English-Corpora.org ） 略称 EEBO. https://www.english-corpora.org/eebo/ 初期近代英国（1470s-1690s）の出版物のテクストを収録するデータベースの簡略版。完全版は国立国会図書館他でアクセス可能。

Hoffman, S. F. W. *Bibliographisches Lexicon der gesammten Litteratur der Griechen*. 3 vols（Leipzig: A. F. Böhme, 1839/ Amsterdam: Hakkert, 1961）． 古代ギリシャ文学の出版情報を収録する。

Leedham-Green, E. S. *Books in Cambridge Inventories: Book-Lists from Vice-Chancellor's Court Probate Inventories in the Tudor and Stuart Periods*. 2 vols（Cambridge U P, 1986）． 書籍リストはケンブリッジ大学関係に限られるが、16世紀英国で入手可能だった古典文学他のテクストを推定する手がかりに。

Oxford English Dictionary. Online（Oxford U P）. 略称 *OED*. https://www.oed.com 英文学の古典を読むために必須の辞典。

Oxford Latin Dictionary, ed. by P. G. W. Glare（Oxford U P, 1982）. 古典ラテン語の信頼できる辞典。

Partridge, Eric. *Shakespeare's Bawdy*（Routledge & Kegan Paul, 1968）． Rubinstein、Williams とともに、性的隠語表現の辞書・語彙集。

Rubinstein, Frankie. *A Dictionary of Shakespeare's Sexual Puns and their Significance*. Second Edition（Macmillan, 1989）． 同上。

Tilley, Morris Palmer. *A Dictionary of the Proverbs in England in the*

Sixteenth and Seventeenth Centuries (Michigan U P, 1950 / 名著普及会 1985)． 初期近代の英語の諺を集めた基本文献。

Traub, Valerie, ed. *The Oxford Handbook of Shakespeare and Embodiment: Gender, Sexuality, and Race* (Oxford U P, 2016)． フェミニズム批評の論集。レイプ表象の問題も扱う。

Williams, Gordon. *A Glossary of Shakespeare's Sexual Language* (Athlone, 1997)． Partridge と同様の趣旨の隠語集。

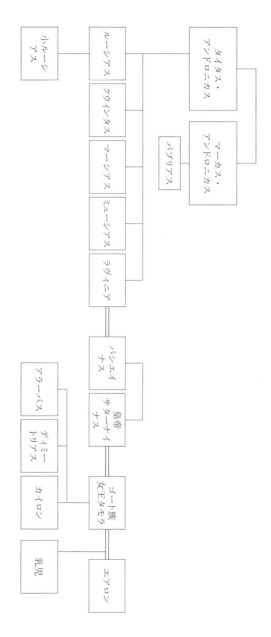

『タイタス・アンドロニカス』関係系図

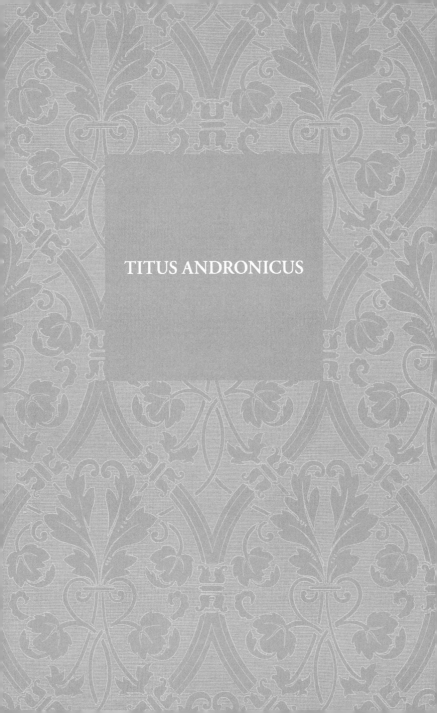

TITUS ANDRONICUS

THE PERSONS OF THE PLAY

SATURNINUS	eldest son of the late Emperor of Rome, afterwords Emperor
BASSIANUS	younger brother of Saturninus
TITUS ANDRONICUS	Roman general, victorious over the Goths
MARCUS ANDRONICUS	Titus' brother, a tribune
LUCIUS	
QUINTUS	
MARTIUS	Titus' sons
MUTIUS	
LAVINIA	Titus' daughter
YOUNG LUCIUS	a boy, son of Lucius
PUBLIUS	Marcus' son
SEMPRONIUS	
CAIUS	Titus' kinsmen
VALENTINE	
AEMILIUS	a noble Roman
TAMORA	Queen of the Goths, afterwards Empress
ALARBUS	
DEMETRIUS	Tamora's sons
CHIRON	
AARON	a Moor, Tamora's lover
Nurse	
Clown	
Messenger	

Senetors, Tribunes, Roman Soldiers, Attendants, Other Romans, The Goths

登場人物

サターナイナス	先のローマ皇帝の長男、後に皇帝
バシエイナス	サターナイナスの弟
タイタス・アンドロニカス	ローマの将軍、ゴート族との戦いの勝利者
マーカス・アンドロニカス	タイタスの弟、護民官

ルーシアス クウィンタス マーシアス ミューシアス	タイタスの息子たち

ラヴィニア	タイタスの娘
小ルーシアス	少年、ルーシアスの息子
パブリアス	マーカスの息子

センプロニアス カイアス ヴァレンタイン	タイタスの親戚

イミリアス	ローマ人の貴族
タモラ	ゴート族の女王、後にローマ皇帝の妃

アラーバス ディミートリアス カイロン	タモラの息子たち

エアロン	ムーア人、タモラの愛人
乳母	
道化	
使者	

元老院議員たち、護民官たち、ローマ兵たち、従者たち、それ以外のローマ人たち、ゴート人たち

登場人物表はシェイクスピアの同時代の版（Q/F）にはなく、後代に加えられたもの。

[ACT I SCENE I]

*Flourish. Enter the Tribunes and Senators aloft; and then enter
[below] Saturninus and his followers at one door, and Bassianus and
his followers at the other door, with other Romans, with Drum &
Colours*

SATURNINUS   Noble patricians, patrons of my right,
Defend the justice of my cause with arms.
And countrymen, my loving followers,
Plead my successive title with your swords.
I am his firstborn son that was the last   5
That wore the imperial diadem of Rome.
Then let my father's honours live in me,
Nor wrong mine age with this indignity.
BASSIANUS   Romans, friends, followers, favourers of my right,
If ever Bassianus, Caesar's son,   10
Were gracious in the eyes of royal Rome,
Keep, then, this passage to the Capitol,
And suffer not dishonour to approach
The imperial seat, to virtue consecrate,
To justice, continence, and nobility;   15
But let desert in pure election shine,
And, Romans, fight for freedom in your choice.

Enter Marcus Andronicus aloft with the crown

MARCUS   Princes that strive by factions and by friends
Ambitiously for rule and empery,
Know that the people of Rome, for whom we stand   20
A special party, have by common voice,
In election for the Roman empery,
Chosen Andronicus, surnamèd Pius
For many good and great deserts to Rome.
A nobler man, a braver warrior,   25

〔1.1〕**あらすじ**…………………………………………………………………

　架空の古代ローマ。先帝の２人の子サターナイナスとバシエイナスの兄弟が皇帝位を争い市民に支持を訴える。タイタス・アンドロニカスがゴート族との戦いから女王タモラ他を捕虜として凱旋し、戦死した自分の息子を埋葬する際、タモラの長男を人身御供に捧げる。タイタスはサターナイナスを皇帝に推挙するが、その際嫁として差し出した娘ラヴィニアをめぐる混乱の最中、行く手を遮って諫める息子を斬り殺す。サターナイナスはタモラと、バシエイナスはラヴィニアと、結婚する。⇒後注

…………………………………………………………………………

0 SD.　⇒後注

1. patricians　「貴族」(Lat. patrici)　　**patrons**　「支持者たち」

2. cause = ground of action; reason for action

4. successive title　ここでは皇帝位の「継承権」を指す。

5. his firstborn son that was the last　「先頃亡くなられた皇帝の長男」関係代名詞 that の先行詞は his。　　**last** = latest, the most recent

6. imperial diadem　「皇帝の冠」

7. my fathers' honours「父祖が代々受けてきた（皇帝としての）敬意と栄誉」

8. Nor　⇒後注　**wrong mine age with this indignity**「こうして兄の私を侮辱する」　**wrong** = treat unfairly or without due respect　　**mine age**　韻律(iambic pentameter）の関係で、母音の前では my が mine になる。

　　this indignity　帝位継承権を脅かされる事態を指す。

10. Caesar　⇒後注

11. gracious = enjoying grace or favour; acceptable

12. Keep = guard, defend　　**the Capitol**　(Lat. Capitolium) ローマの中心部に位置し、ユーピテル（ジュピター Jupiter）の神殿があるカピトーリウム（の丘）。シェイクスピアの時代にしばしば元老院 (Lat. senatus) の議場 Curia とも混同された。

13. suffer = allow, tolerate　　**dishonour** = a person who is not honourable　換喩。

14. consecrate　「神聖な」　　**15. continence** = self-restraint「節制」

16. desert = meritoriousness, worth　　換喩で a deserving person を指す。

　　in pure election　長子相続でなく純粋に人格・功績による選出を主張。

17. in your choice　「（皇帝にふさわしい人物を）あなた方が選ぶことにおいて」

19. empery = the status of an emperor (*OED* empery, *n*. 1.)

20. for whom we stand = whose tribunes we are

22-23. In election for ... Chosen = nominated as a candidate for ... (Bate)

23. surnamèd Pius　⇒後注

24. deserts　「報われるべき功績」

Lives not this day within the city walls.
He by the Senate is accited home
From weary wars against the barbarous Goths,
That with his sons, a terror to our foes,
Hath yoked a nation strong, trained up in arms.   30
Ten years are spent since first he undertook
This cause of Rome, and chastisèd with arms
Our enemies' pride. Five times he hath returned
Bleeding to Rome, bearing his valiant sons
In coffins from the field.   35
And now at last, laden with honour's spoils,
Returns the good Andronicus to Rome,
Renownèd Titus flourishing in arms.
Let us entreat, by honour of his name
Whom worthily you would have now succeed,   40
And in the Capitol and Senate's right,
Whom you pretend to honour and adore,
That you withdraw you and abate your strength,
Dismiss your followers and, as suitors should,
Plead your deserts in peace and humbleness.   45
SATURNINUS   How fair the tribune speaks to calm my thoughts!
BASSIANUS   Marcus Andronicus, so I do affy
In thy uprightness and integrity,
And so I love and honour thee and thine,
Thy noble brother Titus and his sons,   50
And her to whom my thoughts are humbled all,
Gracious Lavinia, Rome's rich ornament,
That I will here dismiss my loving friends,
And to my fortunes and the people's favour
Commit my cause in balance to be weighed.   55
                              Exeunt [Bassianus'] soldiers
SATURNINUS   Friends that have been thus forward in my right,
I thank you all and here dismiss you all,

27. accited = summoned

28. weary = fatiguing, toilsome

30. yoked = brought into subjection「(牛馬のように) 軛をかける」という視覚的イメージも強い。　　**trained up in arms**「鍛え上げた兵力を持つ」

32. cause　1. 1. 2 注参照。

35-38.　⇒後注

36. honour's spoils「名誉 (ある戦役 / 戦士たち) の戦利品」　honour は an honorable battle または honorable warriors の換喩。

39. his　誰を指すか曖昧で、「先帝」あるいは「あなた方が推挙したい皇帝候補者」の 2 通りの解釈が可能。後者の場合さらにタイタス、サターナイナス、バシエイナスのいずれもありうる。

41. in the Capitol and Senate's right「カピトーリウムと元老院の権限において」1. 1. 12 注参照。元老院は古代ローマの最高立法・司法組織。

42. pretend = assert, claim

43. withdraw you = withdraw yourselves

47. affy = trust; rely on

55. Commit my cause in balance to be weighed「私の主張・大義を秤にかけてもらう」　balance「天秤ばかり」　weigh「(秤で) 重さを計測する」

55 SD.　*Exeunt* [*Bassianus'*] *soldiers*　ラテン語のト書き *Exeunt* は複数の人物の退場を示す。1 人で退場する場合は *Exit* (1. 1. 301)。以下テクスト中の括弧 [　] は、シェイクスピアの同時代テクストになく、後代の編者が補った語句であることを示す。

56. forward = ready, eager

And to the love and favour of my country
Commit myself, my person, and the cause.

[Exeunt Saturninus' soldiers]

Rome, be as just and gracious unto me   60
As I am confident and kind to thee.
Open the gates and let me in.

BASSIANUS   Tribunes, and me, a poor competitor.

Flourish. They go up into the Senate House.
[Exeunt aloft] Tribunes and Senators

Enter a Captain.

CAPTAIN   Romans, make way! The good Andronicus,
Patron of virtue, Rome's best champion,   65
Successful in the battles that he fights,
With honour and with fortune is returned
From where he circumscribèd with his sword
And brought to yoke the enemies of Rome.

Sound drums and trumpets, and then enter two of Titus' sons; and
then two men bearing a coffin covered with black, then two other
sons [, Martius and Quintus]. After them Titus Andronicus, and
then Tamora the Queen of Goths and her [three] sons [Alarbus,]
Chiron and Demetrius, with Aaron the Moor, and others as many
as can be, then set down the coffin, and Titus speaks

TITUS   Hail Rome, victorious in thy mourning weeds!   70
Lo, as the bark that hath discharged his fraught
Returns with precious lading to the bay
From whence at first she weighed her anchorage,
Cometh Andronicus, bound with laurel boughs,
To resalute his country with his tears,   75
Tears of true joy for his return to Rome.
Thou great defender of this Capitol,

60. gracious = kind, benevolent

65. Patron = defender, protector; pattern, model (*OED* pattern, *n.* I.A.) (Hughes)

68. circumscribèd = confined, restrained　語末の母音èの重アクセント符号は、韻律（iambic pentameter）の都合上、そこが1音節として発音されることを明示するために便宜的に付せられる。強勢が置かれる訳ではない。

69 SD.　*After them Titus Andronicus* ⇒後注

70. weeds = garments

71-73. Lo, as the bark ... her anchorage　叙事詩的明喩（Homecric simile）。　**Lo** = Look! See! 感嘆詞。　**bark** = ship　**lading** = freight, cargo　**weighed** = hoisted up, lifted up

77. Thou　カピトーリウム神殿（Capitolium）に祀られている神ユーピテル（Jupiter）を指す。thou は、目下や親しい人の他に、神に対しても用いる二人称単数形の人称代名詞。

this Capitol　Lat. Capitolium　1. 1. 12 注に記したようにシェイクスピアの時代にしばしば元老院の所在地とも混同されたが、ここでは特にユーピテルを祀るカピトーリウム神殿とカピトーリウムの丘の両者を思わせる。後者にはもともと「城砦」の意味もある。語源はラテン語で「頭・頂（caput）」。（*OED* Capitol, *n.* 1.）

図3　対ゴート族戦争から凱旋するタイタス　デボラ・ウォーナー演出、バービカン劇場、ロンドン（1988）© Geraint Lewis/ArenaPAL

Stand gracious to the rites that we intend.
Romans, of five-and-twenty valiant sons,
Half of the number that King Priam had,   80
Behold the poor remains alive and dead.
These that survive let Rome reward with love;
These that I bring unto their latest home,
With burial amongst their ancestors.
Here Goths have given me leave to sheathe my sword.   85
Titus, unkind and careless of thine own,
Why suffer'st thou thy sons unburied yet
To hover on the dreadful shore of Styx?
Make way to lay them by their brethren.   *They open the tomb*
There greet in silence, as the dead are wont,   90
And sleep in peace, slain in your country's wars.
O sacred receptacle of my joys,
Sweet cell of virtue and nobility,
How many sons hast thou of mine in store
That thou wilt never render to me more?   95
LUCIUS   Give us the proudest prisoner of the Goths,
That we may hew his limbs and on a pile,
Ad manes fratrum, sacrifice his flesh
Before this earthy prison of their bones,
That so the shadows be not unappeased,   100
Nor we disturbed with prodigies on Earth.
TITUS   I give him you, the noblest that survives,
The eldest son of this distressèd queen.
TAMORA   [*Kneels*]   Stay, Roman brethren, gracious conqueror,
Victorious Titus, rue the tears I shed,   105
A mother's tears in passion for her son.
And if thy sons were ever dear to thee,
O think my son to be as dear to me.
Sufficeth not that we are brought to Rome
To beautify thy triumphs, and return   110

78. gracious = abounding in grace or mercy

80. King Priam 「プリアモス王」トロイアー戦争伝説でギリシャ軍に滅ぼされたトロイアー最後の王。50人の息子と多くの娘を持った。王子の1人パリスによるスパルタ王妃ヘレネーの誘拐が原因でギリシャの大群に攻囲され、長年の攻防戦の末に落城・滅亡したトロイアーの物語は、ホメーロス叙事詩『イーリアス (*Ilias*)』と『オデュッセイア (*Odysseia*)』を初め、現代に至るまで数々の西洋文学で言及される有名な古代伝説の1つ。この芝居では、しばしばタイタスがプリアモス王に、タモラがその王妃ヘカベー (Gk. Hekabe / Lat. Hecuba) に、擬えられる。ヘカベーについては 1. 1. 136-38 注参照。

81. Behold = give attention to; look at　　**remains**「残り」名詞。

86. unkind = unnatural; lacking normal human feelings or sympathies「親子の情を忘れた」この台詞は劇的アイロニー (dramatic irony)。終局で、逆にサターナイナスがタイタスを unkind と呼ぶことになる (5. 3. 47)。

87-88. suffer'st ... unburied / To hover「埋葬されぬままに浮遊させておく」suffer'st は suffer の二人称単数形。1. 1. 13 注参照。

88. Styx [stiks]「ステュクス」冥界の川。Vergilius, *Aeneis*, 6. 322-30.

90. greet「(先に葬られた死者たちの霊と) 挨拶を交わす」

wont = accustomed, used

92. receptacle = a containing vessel; repository　　**my joys**　息子たちを指す。

93. cell = a small apartment, dwelling; a monastery

virtue and nobility = the virtuous and the noble

95. render = return, give back; reproduce

96. proudest「最も高い地位・身分の」

98. *Ad manes fratrum*「兄弟たちの霊に」(Lat.)　　Livius, 1. 25. 12 'duos ... fratrum minibus dedi' (2人とも私の兄弟たちの霊に捧げた) ローマ史の伝説アルバ・ロンガの戦いで、ホラーティウスが敵方のクーリアーティウスに言う。ローマ方の勇士ホラーティウス (Horatius) 3兄弟とアルバ方の勇士クーリアーティウス (Curiatius) 3兄弟が決戦に臨み、どちらも2人の兄弟が斃れて残った2人の一騎打ちとなる。

100. shadows = ghosts　　前々行の *manes* の英訳に相当する。大衆劇場で観客に意味を類推しやすくさせる手法。

101. prodigies　不吉な前兆となる天変地異や異常な出来事を指す。

106. passion = overpowering emotion

107. thy　二人称代名詞として、タイタスがタモラへ呼びかける際に丁寧な you を用いるのに対して、タモラは目下の者へ呼びかける際に用いる二人称 thou を使用する。両者の立場と力関係は微妙で、後者は捕虜ながらゴート族の女王。

109. Sufficeth not = Doesn't it suffice　　-eth は三人称単数現在形の語尾。

109-11. brought to Rome ... thy Roman yoke　⇒後注

Captive to thee and to thy Roman yoke,
But must my sons be slaughtered in the streets
For valiant doings in their country's cause?
O, if to fight for king and commonweal
Were piety in thine, it is in these!   115
Andronicus, stain not thy tomb with blood.
Wilt thou draw near the nature of the gods?
Draw near them then in being merciful.
Sweet mercy is nobility's true badge.
Thrice-noble Titus, spare my first-born son.   120
TITUS   Patient yourself, madam, and pardon me.
  These are their brethren whom your Goths beheld
  Alive and dead, and for their brethren slain
  Religiously they ask a sacrifice.
  To this your son is marked, and die he must,   125
  T' appease their groaning shadows that are gone.
LUCIUS   Away with him, and make a fire straight,
  And with our swords upon a pile of wood
  Let's hew his limbs till they be clean consumed.
                              Exeunt [Titus'] sons with Alarbus
TAMORA   O cruel, irreligious piety!   130
CHIRON   Was never Scythia half so barbarous!
DEMETRIUS   Oppose not Scythia to ambitious Rome.
  Alarbus goes to rest and we survive
  To tremble under Titus' threat'ning look.
  Then, madam, stand resolved, but hope withal   135
  The selfsame gods that armed the Queen of Troy
  With opportunity of sharp revenge
  Upon the Thracian tyrant in his tent
  May favour Tamora the Queen of Goths
  (When Goths were Goths, and Tamora was queen)   140
  To quit the bloody wrongs upon her foes.

              Enter the sons of Andronicus again

117. draw near 「〜に近づく」　draw = move, proceed, come　自動詞。
　nature = the essential qualities or properties of a thing; the inherent and innate disposition or character of a person「本性、生まれながらの性質・性格」

118-19. merciful ... mercy *The Merchant of Venice*, 4. 1 ポーシャが裁判の場でシャイロックに語る台詞参照。　　**badge** = a heraldic symbol worn as an identifying mark by a knight and his retainers (*OED* badge, *n.* 1.a.)

122-23. their brethren whom your Goths beheld / Alive and dead 「お前らゴートの輩がその生死を目撃した者たちの兄弟」関係代名詞 whom の先行詞は their。人称代名詞の所有格形が関係代名詞の先行詞になる構文は、現代英語ではあまり見られないが、シェイクスピアの英語ではごく普通に使われる。

126. that 上記 1. 1. 122-23 と同様に、関係代名詞 that の先行詞は their。

130. irreligious piety ⇒後注

131. Scythia [síθiə]「スキュティア」黒海北岸一体の地域を漠然と呼んだ地名。現在のウクライナ共和国あたり。ここでは場所（Scythia）でその住人「スキュティア人（Scythians）」を指す換喩（metonymy）。同時代演劇でのスキュティア人のイメージとしては、シェイクスピアと同年生まれの人気作家マーロウ（Christopher Marlowe, 1564-93）の悲劇『タンバレイン』2 部作の主人公が有名。*Tamburlaine, Part 1*, 1. 1 'Tamburlaine, that sturdie Scythian thiefe ...'古代のスキュティア伝説の記録としては、ヘーロドトス（Herodotos, 紀元前 5 世紀）の『歴史（Historiai）』第 4 巻が知られる。

132. Oppose 「突き合わせる、比較する」

135. madam もともと高位の女性への呼びかけに使われた語。ゴートの女王であるため、ディミートリアスは自分の母親であるタモラに向かっても敬称で話しかける。

136-38. the Queen of Troy ... in his tent ⇒後注

141. quit = repay, avenge

LUCIUS   See, lord and father, how we have performed
Our Roman rites. Alarbus' limbs are lopped,
And entrails feed the sacrificing fire,
Whose smoke like incense doth perfume the sky.   145
Remaineth naught but to inter our brethren,
And with loud larums welcome them to Rome.
TITUS   Let it be so. And let Andronicus
Make this his latest farewell to their souls.

Flourish. Then sound trumpets, and lay the coffin in the tomb

In peace and honour rest you here, my sons,   150
Rome's readiest champions, repose you here in rest,
Secure from worldly chances and mishaps.
Here lurks no treason, here no envy swells,
Here grow no damnèd drugs; here are no storms,
No noise, but silence and eternal sleep.   155
In peace and honour rest you here, my sons.

Enter Lavinia

LAVINIA   In peace and honour live Lord Titus long;
My noble lord and father, live in fame.   *[Kneels]*
Lo, at this tomb my tributary tears
I render for my brethren's obsequies,   160
And at thy feet I kneel, with tears of joy
Shed on this earth for thy return to Rome.
O bless me here with thy victorious hand,
Whose fortunes Rome's best citizens applaud.
TITUS   Kind Rome, that hast thus lovingly reserved   165
The cordial of mine age to glad my heart.
Lavinia, live, outlive thy father's days
And fame's eternal date, for virtue's praise.   *[Lavinia rises]*

[Enter Marcus Andronicus]

147. larums = calls to arms

149. latest = last, final

150. rest you = rest yourselves

151. readiest = most willing 「(敵との戦いに) 最も積極的で勇敢な」

152. mishaps = bad luck; misfortunes

153. lurks no treason, here no envy swells　抽象名詞 treason「裏切り」と envy「悪意、妬み」は、それぞれ、擬人化した寓意 (allegory)、あるいは treason＝treasonable people; envy＝envious people のように換喩 (metonymy)、そのどちらにとることも可能。中世文学の一つの特徴であった寓意は初期近代のシェイクスピアでは次第に用いられなくなる傾向にある。ここは死者への祈りで、魔術的・象徴的な意味合いの強い言葉として使われている。

154. drugs　「毒草」

159-60. my tributary tears / I render　「私の涙を貢物として捧げる」tributary = paying tribute

obsequies = funerals

166. cordial = a medicine, food, or beverage which invigorates the heart and stimulates circulation「強心剤」

168. fame's eternal date　「永遠なる名声が続く限りの日々、時間」

for virtue's praise = for praiseworthy virtue　女性の場合 virtue「美徳」は一般に「貞節」「純潔」を指した。タイタスは、娘ラヴィニアの名声が純潔・貞節の美徳によって肉体の死後も永遠に残ることを願う。

MARCUS   Long live Lord Titus, my belovèd brother,
  Gracious triumpher in the eyes of Rome.   170
TITUS   Thanks, gentle tribune, noble brother Marcus.
MARCUS   And welcome, nephews, from successful wars,
  You that survive, and you that sleep in fame.
  Fair lords, your fortunes are alike in all,
  That in your country's service drew your swords;   175
  But safer triumph is this funeral pomp,
  That hath aspired to Solon's happiness,
  And triumphs over chance in honour's bed.
  Titus Andronicus, the people of Rome,
  Whose friend in justice thou hast ever been,   180
  Send thee by me, their tribune and their trust,
  This palliament of white and spotless hue,
  And name thee in election for the empire
  With these our late deceasèd emperor's sons.
  Be *candidatus*, then, and put it on   185
  And help to set a head on headless Rome.
TITUS   A better head her glorious body fits
  Than his that shakes for age and feebleness.
  What, should I don this robe and trouble you?
  Be chosen with proclamations today,   190
  Tomorrow yield up rule, resign my life,
  And set abroad new business for you all?
  Rome, I have been thy soldier forty years,
  And led my country's strength successfully,
  And buried one and twenty valiant sons,   195
  Knighted in field, slain manfully in arms,
  In right and service of their noble country.
  Give me a staff of honour for mine age,
  But not a scepter to control the world.
  Upright he held it, lords, that held it last.   200
MARCUS   Titus, thou shalt obtain and ask the empery.

170. Gracious = beautiful, graceful; generous

171. gentle 「高貴な生まれにふさわしい、立派で温厚な」

175. That 先行詞は前行の your。1. 1. 122-23 注参照。

177. Solon's happiness 栄光のうちに死ぬ若者などのように、最期まで神々に愛された人こそ最も幸せであるとする死生観を指す。 Cf. Plutarchus (Plutarkhos), 'Solon'.

182. palliament 1. 1. 185 で言う「白い衣」に相当する衣。pallium（= a rectangular piece of material worn draped mainly by men as an outer garment）と paludamentum（= a military cloak fastened with a brooch at the shoulder, the typical garment of generals and others of high rank）（*OLD*）の 2 つのラテン語から作られた珍しい語。共作者ジョージ・ピールによる造語とも推測されるが、諸説分かれる。

184. With these ... sons 「ここにいる亡き先帝の遺児たちと並んで」マーカスは護民官として平民（plebes）のタイタス支持を伝え、サターナイナスおよびバシエイナスと並んでタイタスに次期皇帝候補者の一人として立つことを勧めている。

185. *candidatus* 「白い衣を纏った」（Lat.）古代ローマで皇帝候補者の出で立ち。英語 candidate の語源。

189. What, should I ... 「なんだね、私に…しろと言うのか」What の後のコンマは Theobald による修正の読み。Q1 では What should I ... となっており、その場合は意味を What = What ... for; Why のようにとる。

don = put on

191. yield up = return; hand over, give up

192. set abroad = set (a matter) on foot; initiate（*OED* set, *v.¹* PV2. set abroad, 2.）

196. Knighted in field 「戦場で騎士に任ぜられた」古代ローマを想定する芝居の文脈で中世の騎士道風のイメージに言及するのはアナクロニズムだが、それによって、タイタス自身の古い騎士道的価値観・倫理観を印象づける。

197. In right and service of 「～ の権利を守り、奉仕するため」（Waith）

198. mine age 1. 1. 8 注参照。

200. that 関係代名詞。先行詞は he。

201. obtain and ask 予弁法（*prolepsis*）と呼ばれる修辞の一種（Hughes）。聞き手への効果を狙う修辞だが、同時に話し手マーカス自身の動揺や焦りを示すようにもとれる。伝統的修辞（rhetoric）すなわち説得の技法を使用する場合も、相手を説得するという目的にとどまらず、同時にその台詞の話し手自身の性格や心理を表わす機能があることが重要。後者は伝統的修辞法の演劇的・近代的な応用例。

SATURNINUS   Proud and ambitious tribune, canst thou tell?

TITUS   Patience, Prince Saturninus.

SATURNINUS   Romans, do me right.
    Patricians, draw your swords and sheathe them not   205
    Till Saturninus be Rome's emperor. —
    Andronicus, would thou were shipped to hell
    Rather than rob me of the people's hearts.

LUCIUS   Proud Saturnine, interrupter of the good
    That noble-minded Titus means to thee.   210

TITUS   Content thee, prince. I will restore to thee
    The people's hearts and wean them from themselves.

BASSIANUS   Andronicus, I do not flatter thee,
    But honour thee, and will do till I die.
    My faction if thou strengthen with thy friends,   215
    I will most thankful be, and thanks, to men
    Of noble minds, is honourable meed.

TITUS   People of Rome, and people's tribunes here,
    I ask your voices and your suffrages.
    Will you bestow them friendly on Andronicus?   220

TRIBUNES   To gratify the good Andronicus
    And gratulate his safe return to Rome,
    The people will accept whom he admits.

TITUS   Tribunes, I thank you, and this suit I make:
    That you create our emperor's eldest son,   225
    Lord Saturnine, whose virtues will, I hope,
    Reflect on Rome as Titan's rays on Earth
    And ripen justice in this commonweal.
    Then, if you will elect by my advice,
    Crown him and say 'Long live our emperor!'   230

MARCUS   With voices and applause of every sort,
    Patricians and plebeians, we create
    Lord Saturninus Rome's great emperor,
    And say 'Long live our Emperor Saturnine!'

207. would = I wish; O that (*OED* will, *v.*¹ 36.)

shipped to hell = sent off to hell; damned

209-10. the good / That noble-minded Titus means to thee　ここでタイタス
の長子ルーシアスは父の決断を事前に仄かす。アラーバス人身御供の件（1. 1.
96-129）と並び、タイタスが犯す2つの致命的誤り、すなわちギリシャ悲劇
の場合で言えばハマルティアー（άμαρτία）となる行為を最初に示唆するの
はいずれもルーシアス。

212. wean them from themselves　「彼らを彼ら自身（の望み）から引き離す」
現状ではローマ市民の支持がタイタス自身にある。wean　原義「（乳幼児を）
乳離れさせる」の視覚的印象が強いメタファーで、ローマの平民に対するタイ
タスの意識と彼自身の性格を感じさせる。

217. meed　「報酬、報奨」

219. suffrages = help, support

222. gratulate = express joy at; greet, salute

223. whom = the candidate whom

224. suit ... make　make suit = make an entreaty or petition

225. create = constitute (a personage of rank or dignity); invest with rank
or dignity (*OED* create, *v.* 3.)「（皇帝に）任じる」

227. Titan's rays　「太陽光」　Titan　英詩でしばしば太陽の意味に用いられ
る。ギリシャ神話で太陽神ヒュペリオーンは、天空ウーラノスと大地ガイアの
間に生まれた子たちティーターネス（the Titans / Gk. Titanes）の一人。

228. commonweal = the whole body of the people, the body politic;
commonwealth

229. Then, if you will elect by my advice　「では、あなた方は私の助言によっ
て（皇帝を）選ぶわけだから」if に始まる条件節の動詞 elect は直接法。タイ
タスはすでに自分に皇帝指名の全権が与えられたも同然と自認しているが、平
民たちの意向として護民官がタイタスに伝えたのは、タイタス自身が次期皇帝
候補として立つようにということであった。自分の奉じる価値観だけで突き進
む性急さが、破局に繋がる致命的誤ち（ハマルティアー）を印象づける。

A long flourish till they come down

SATURNINUS Titus Andronicus, for thy favours done   235
   To us in our election this day,
   I give thee thanks in part of thy deserts,
   And will with deeds requite thy gentleness.
   And for an onset, Titus, to advance
   Thy name and honourable family,   240
   Lavinia will I make my empress,
   Rome's royal mistress, mistress of my heart,
   And in the sacred Pantheon her espouse.
   Tell me, Andronicus, doth this motion please thee?
TITUS It doth, my worthy lord, and in this match   245
   I hold me highly honoured of your grace;
   And here in sight of Rome to Saturnine,
   King and commander of our commonweal,
   The wide world's emperor, do I consecrate
   My sword, my chariot, and my prisoners,   250
   Presents well worthy Rome's imperious lord.
   Receive them, then, the tribute that I owe,
   Mine honour's ensigns humbled at thy feet.
SATURNINUS Thanks, noble Titus, father of my life.
   How proud I am of thee and of thy gifts   255
   Rome shall record. — And when I do forget
   The least of these unspeakable deserts,
   Romans, forget your fealty to me.
TITUS Now, madam, are you prisoner to an emperor,
   To him that for your honour and your state   260
   Will use you nobly, and your followers.
SATURNINUS A goodly lady, trust me, of the hue
   That I would choose, were I to choose anew.
   Clear up, fair queen, that cloudy countenance.
   Though chance of war hath wrought this change of cheer,   265

236. us ... our 王・皇帝が自称として使用する人称代名詞の特殊な用法 royal plural。一人称複数形で王・皇帝である自分一人を指す。

237. in part of thy deserts 「そちの功績にふさわしい報奨の一部分として」

238. gentleness 「好意、親切、高貴な生まれにふさわしい判断・振る舞い」

239. onset 「手始め」

243. the sacred Pantheon 「聖なるパンテオン（万神殿）」古代ローマ最大の円蓋を持つ建築物。ここでは婚礼を挙げる教会のイメージとして。歴史的には609 年からキリスト教会 Santa Maria Rotonda として使用されている。

espouse ＝ marry

244. motion 「提案」

246. hold me ＝ consider myself

250. chariot 「戦車」Marlowe, *Tamburlaine, Part 2*, 4. 3 などを連想させる。マーロウの悲劇では、征服戦争で捕虜にした敵国の王たちに引かせた戦車に乗って主人公タンバレインが登場する場面が有名で、シェイクスピアの劇の舞台でもそれに倣って主人公タイタスが戦車に乗って登場したと想像することが可能。しかし芝居の台本は一般に柔軟で、台詞に合わせて大道具の戦車を舞台に持ち込むことも、台詞のみで観客に戦車を想像させることも、演出次第でどちらもありうる。劇場の立地や形状あるいは劇団の状況に応じて、どのようにでも上演しうる台本であったと考えられる。1. 1. 69 SD 後注参照。

251. imperious ＝ imperial

253. Mine honour's ensigns humbled at thy feet 「我が名誉の旗印として謹んで汝の足元に」タイタスが軍人としての功績と栄誉のすべてを新帝に捧げる象徴的シーン。

257. unspeakable ＝ inexpressible 「言葉では言い尽くせない」

258. fealty ＝ loyalty

260. for your honour and your state 「（ゴート族女王という）あなたの名誉と地位を重んじて」 for ＝ because of, on account of（*OED* for, *prep.* 20.）

262. hue ＝ appearance, complexion「容姿」

265. wrought work の過去分詞形。

change of cheer ＝ change of mood

Thou com'st not to be made a scorn in Rome.
Princely shall be thy usage every way.
Rest on my word, and let not discontent
Daunt all your hopes. Madam, he comforts you
Can make you greater than the Queen of Goths. 270
Lavinia, you are not displeased with this?
LAVINIA   Not I, my lord, sith true nobility
Warrants these words in princely courtesy.
SATURNINUS   Thanks, sweet Lavinia. Romans, let us go.
Ransomless here we set our prisoners free. 275
Proclaim our honours, lords, with trump and drum.
BASSIANUS   Lord Titus, by your leave, this maid is mine.
TITUS   How, sir? Are you in earnest then, my lord?
BASSIANUS   Ay, noble Titus, and resolved withal
To do myself this reason and this right. 280
MARCUS   *Suum cuique* is our Roman justice.
This prince in justice seizeth but his own.
LUCIUS   And that he will and shall, if Lucius live!
TITUS   Traitors, avaunt! Where is the Emperor's guard?
Treason, my lord. Lavinia is surprised. 285
SATURNINUS   Surprised? By whom?
BASSIANUS   By him that justly may
Bear his betrothed from all the world away.
MUTIUS   Brothers, help to convey her hence away,
And with my sword I'll keep this door safe.
        [*Exeunt Bassianus, Lavinia, Marcus, Lucius, Quintus, and
        Martius*]
TITUS   Follow, my lord, and I'll soon bring her back. 290
        [*Exeunt Saturninus, Tamora, Demetrius, Chiron, Aaron,
        and Guards*]
MUTIUS   My lord, you pass not here.
TITUS   What, villain boy,
Barr'st me my way in Rome?

269. Daunt ＝ discourage, overcome

270. Can make ＝ Who can make　関係代名詞主格形 who が省略されている。先行詞は前行の he ＝ Saturninus.

272. sith ＝ since; seeing that

272-73. true nobility / Warrants these words in princely courtesy　これを言うラヴィニアの心理は不明。　warrants ＝ guarantees; authorizes

276. trump ＝ trumpet

279. resolved withal ＝〔I am〕resolute moreover　withal ＝ in addition

280. reason ＝ justice

281. *Suum cuique* （Lat.）キケロー『神々の本性について』からの引用。Cicero, *De natura deorum*, 3. 38 'Nam iustitia, quae suum cuique distribuit, quid pertinet ad deos?'（さて<u>それぞれにその応分のものを</u>分け与えるという正義についてだが、神々に関してはどうなるだろうか？）古典ラテン語の問題については⇒解説 15-22 頁。

283. that he will and shall ＝ he will and shall seize her as his own「バシエイナス自身ラヴィニアを自分のもの（＝妻）として摑みたいと思っているし、実際そうさせてやる」

if Lucius live　「この俺が生きている限り」

284. avaunt ＝ begone! be off! away!（*OED* avaunt, *int.*）

285. surprised ＝ seized by force

286-87. him that justly may / Bear ... ＝ the man who is entitled to bear ... lawfully

288. help to convey ＝ help Bassianus to convey

289. safe ＝ not exposed to danger; secure

290. Follow, my lord　解釈の分かれる台詞。「陛下、（私の後に）付いて来てください」「陛下、そのままお先へどうぞ」の両方が可能。臣下のタイタスが皇帝に付いて来るように命じるという状況（前者）は普通には考えにくいが、動揺故の混乱と解釈することも可能であり、決め手はない。

292. villain boy　「この出来損ないめ」villain には「悪党の」の他に low in respect of birth の意味もある。この瞬間タイタスは、ミューシアスが自分の子であることを認めない（*OED* villain, *adj*. 4.b.）。

MUTIUS Help, Lucius, help!   *Titus kills him*

Enter Lucius

LUCIUS My lord, you are unjust, and more than so!   295
  In wrongful quarrel you have slain your son.
TITUS Nor thou nor he are any sons of mine.
  My sons would never so dishonour me.
  Traitor, restore Lavinia to the Emperor.
LUCIUS Dead if you will, but not to be his wife   300
  That is another's lawful promised love.   *[Exit]*

Enter aloft the Emperor with Tamora and her two sons,
and Aaron the Moor

SATURNINUS No, Titus, no, the Emperor needs her not,
  Nor her, nor thee, nor any of thy stock.
  I'll trust by leisure him that mocks me once,
  Thee never, nor thy traitorous haughty sons,   305
  Confederates all thus to dishonour me.
  Was none in Rome to make a stale
  But Saturnine? Full well, Andronicus,
  Agree these deeds with that proud brag of thine
  That said'st I begged the empire at thy hands.   310
TITUS O monstrous! What reproachful words are these?
SATURNINUS But go thy ways. Go give that changing piece
  To him that flourished for her with his sword.
  A valiant son-in-law thou shalt enjoy,
  One fit to bandy with thy lawless sons,   315
  To ruffle in the commonwealth of Rome.
TITUS These words are razors to my wounded heart.
SATURNINUS And therefore, lovely Tamora, Queen of Goths,
  That like the stately Phoebe 'mongst her nymphs
  Dost overshine the gallant'st dames of Rome,   320
  If thou be pleased with this my sudden choice,

297. Nor thou nor he = Neither thou nor he

300. Dead if you will = She shall be dead if you want

301. That = who　関係代名詞。先行詞は Dead の前に動詞とともに省略されている主語 She。

302. the Emperor　サターナイナスは「皇帝」と自称している。

303. stock　「家族、一族」

304. by leisure = slowly, barely

307. to make a stale　「（人を）だしに使う」　stale = a person or thing made use of as a means or tool for inducing some result, as a pretext for some action, or as a cover for sinister designs (*OED* stale, *n.³* 5.)

312. changing piece　「浮気な小娘」と「小銭、やすもの」の二重の意。

319. Phoebe 'mongst her nymphs　ウェルギリウスではカルターゴーの女王ディードー (Dido) の比喩（*Aeneis*, 1. 498-502）。Phoebe [ffːbi] = Diana ギリシャ神話の神々は出自が複雑多様で、ポイベーはもともとティーターネス (the Titans / Gk. Titanes) の一人。後にディアーナと同一視された。1. 1. 227 注参照。

図 4 《たいまつを振りかざすポイベー》ペルガモン大祭壇南側フリーズ
（紀元前 2 世紀）ペルガモン博物館、ベルリン（Claus Ableiter）

Behold, I choose thee, Tamora, for my bride,
And will create thee Emperess of Rome.
Speak, Queen of Goths, dost thou applaud my choice?
And here I swear by all the Roman gods,   325
Sith priest and holy water are so near,
And tapers burn so bright, and everything
In readiness for Hymenaeus stand,
I will not resalute the streets of Rome
Or climb my palace till from forth this place   330
I lead espoused my bride along with me.

TAMORA   And here in sight of heaven to Rome I swear,
If Saturnine advance the Queen of Goths,
She will a handmaid be to his desires,
A loving nurse, a mother to his youth.   335

SATURNINUS   Ascend, fair queen, to Pantheon. Lords, accompany
Your noble emperor and his lovely bride,
Sent by the heavens for Prince Saturnine,
Whose wisdom hath her fortune conquerèd.
There shall we consummate our spousal rites.   340

Exeunt omnes [except Titus]

TITUS   I am not bid to wait upon this bride.
Titus, when wert thou wont to walk alone,
Dishonoured thus and challengèd of wrongs?

Enter Marcus and Titus' sons Lucius, Martius and Quintus

MARCUS   O Titus, see! O, see what thou hast done!
In a bad quarrel slain a virtuous son.   345

TITUS   No, foolish tribune, no; no son of mine,
Nor thou, nor these confederates in the deed
That hath dishonoured all our family.
Unworthy brother and unworthy sons!

LUCIUS   But let us give him burial as becomes,   350

326. sith　1. 1. 272 注参照。

328. Hymenaeus ＝ Hymen「結婚」「結婚の神」ギリシャ神話でヒュメーン
（Hymen）/ ヒュメナイオス（Hymenaios）は結婚の神の名。さらに結婚あ
るいはそれを言祝ぐ歌を意味した。

329. resalute ＝ salute or greet again

332. in sight of heaven　劇場で「神（god/God）」の語をみだりに使用するこ
とを憚り、代わりに「天（heaven）」と言う場合が多い。

334. will a handmaid be to ...　不自然な語順でぎこちない響きの台詞が、時と
して、話し手の心理やその場の微妙な状況を映し出すことがある。

　　handmaid「侍女、小間使い」ここでは捕囚の身からにわかに皇后の権力を
手中にできることになったタモラの、緊張した心理を映すものか。

336. fair ＝ beautiful

338. the heavens ＝ the seat of the celestial deities of heathen mythology
「（異教の神々の）天上の御座処」転じて「神々」（*OED* heaven, *n.* 5.d.）。上
記 1. 1. 332 注参照。

341. bid ＝ asked to come; invited

342. wont　1. 1. 90 注参照。

343. challengèd ＝ accused　語末の重アクセント符号については 1. 1. 68 注参
照。

350. as becomes ＝ in such a way as it becomes　関係代名詞 as で始まる関
係詞節内ではしばしば主語が省略される。　becomes ＝ is suitable, fitting

Give Mutius burial with our brethren.
TITUS   Traitors, away! He rests not in this tomb.
This monument five hundred years hath stood,
Which I have sumptuously reedified.
Here none but soldiers and Rome's servitors   355
Repose in fame, none basely slain in brawls.
Bury him where you can. He comes not here.
MARCUS   My lord, this is impiety in you.
My nephew Mutius' deeds do plead for him.
He must be buried with his brethren.   360
MARTIUS   And shall, or him we will accompany.
TITUS   And shall? What villain was it spake that word?
MARTIUS   He that would vouch it in any place but here.
TITUS   What, would you bury him in my despite?
MARCUS   No, noble Titus, but entreat of thee   365
To pardon Mutius and to bury him.
TITUS   Marcus, even thou hast struck upon my crest,
And with these boys mine honour thou hast wounded.
My foes I do repute you every one.
So trouble me no more, but get you gone.   370
QUINTUS   He is not with himself; let us withdraw.
MARTIUS   Not I, till Mutius' bones be burièd.

The brother and the sons kneel

MARCUS   Brother, for in that name doth nature plead —
MARTIUS   Father, and in that name doth nature speak —
TITUS   Speak thou no more, if all the rest will speed.   375
MARCUS   Renownèd Titus, more than half my soul —
LUCIUS   Dear father, soul and substance of us all —
MARCUS   Suffer thy brother Marcus to inter
His noble nephew here in virtue's nest,
That died in honour and Lavinia's cause.   380
Thou art a Roman; be not barbarous.

355. servitors = servants; those who serve in war（*OED* servitor, *n.* 1. and 4.）

356. brawls 「騒々しい喧嘩」自ら我が子を斬り殺した件を喧騒と見做している。

358. impiety 1. 1. 130 後注参照。

363. vouch = assert, affirm（*OED* vouch, *v.* 5.）

364. in my despite = in open defiance of me

365-66. entreat of thee / To = entreat you to

367. crest 「兜の羽飾り」武人・名士としての誇りを表わす。近接・連想するものに擬える換喩で「兜」を、さらには「頭」をも指す。

369. repute = consider, reckon

371. not with himself = beside himself「正気でない、逆上して」

372. burièd 語末の母音の重アクセント符号は韻律（iambic pentameter）の都合上、独立した音節であることを示すもの。-i・èd のように弱強の 2 音節に数える。1. 1. 68 注参照。

373. nature = the inherent dominating power or impulse（in men）by which action or character is determined, directed, or controlled; natural feeling or affection「（人間 / 肉親としての）決定的な情」（*OED* nature, *n.* 9.a. and e.）寓意的な人格化は嘆願を強調するための因習的文飾。

375. speed = press or urge on （*OED* speed, *v.* 11.）ここは曖昧な一文。あるいは speed = prosper ととり「他の皆さえ良ければ」のように読むことも可能。

376. more than half my soul Horatius, *Carmina*, 1. 3. 8 'animae dimidium meae'（私の魂の半分）から。ウェルギリウスへの呼びかけ（Rudd）。

378. Suffer 1. 1. 13 注参照。

379. virtue's nest 「美徳の巣」美徳・武勇を持って死んだ者は、死後も美徳によって育まれ名声のうちに生き続けることになるという信念（Berthoud）。1. 1. 394 参照。

381. be not barbarous 誰をまた何を「野蛮」とするかは、この劇で終始疑問のまま。文明の進んだローマ人から見て非ローマのゴート人は夷狄・野蛮人であろうが、地勢的には北方民族であるゴート人の方がシェイクスピアの英国に近いのが微妙なところ。 barbarous = speaking a foreign language; uncivilized; savage

The Greeks upon advice did bury Ajax,
That slew himself, and wise Laertes' son
Did graciously plead for his funerals.
Let not young Mutius, then, that was thy joy,   385
Be barred his entrance here.

TITUS   Rise, Marcus, rise.   [*They rise*]
The dismall'st day is this that e'er I saw,
To be dishonoured by my sons in Rome.
Well, bury him, and bury me the next.   390

They put him in the tomb

LUCIUS   There lie thy bones, sweet Mutius, with thy friends',
Till we with trophies do adorn thy tomb.

They all [except Titus] kneel and say

No man shed tears for noble Mutius.
He lives in fame, that died in virtue's cause.

Exeunt [all but Marcus and Titus]

MARCUS   My lord, to step out of these dreary dumps,   395
How comes it that the subtle Queen of Goths
Is of a sudden thus advanced in Rome?

TITUS   I know not, Marcus, but I know it is.
Whether by device or no, the heavens can tell.
Is she not then beholding to the man   400
That brought her for this high good turn so far?
Yes, and will nobly him remunerate.

Flourish. Enter the Emperor, Tamora and her two sons, with Aaron
the Moor, Drums and Trumpets, at one door. Enter at the other
door Bassianus and Lavinia, and others

SATURNINUS   So, Bassianus, you have played your prize.
God give you joy, sir, of your gallant bride.

BASSIANUS   And you of yours, my lord. I say no more,   405

382-84. The Greeks ... his funerals　トロイアー戦争において英雄アキレウスの死後、アイアースは、亡きアキレウスの武具が自分でなくオデュッセウスに与えられたことに怒ってギリシャ軍総大将アガメムノーン他を襲おうとするが、ことを事前に察したアテーナー女神に狂気を吹き込まれ、多数の羊をギリシャ軍の大将たちと思い込んで殺戮する。その後狂気から覚めたアイアースは真相を知り自刃する。ソポクレース（Sophokles）の悲劇では、アガメムノーンは初めアイアースの埋葬を禁じるが、オデュッセウスの説得を受けて埋葬を許す（*Aias*, 1319-1416）。シェイクスピア自身は、当時のグラマー・スクールの教科書に載録された Lambinus' commentary on Horace, *Saturae*, 2. 3. 187 'Ulysses ... Agamemnonem ... exoravit ut Aiacem sineret sepeliri'（ウリュセースは…アヤクスを墓へ埋葬するようにとアガメムノーンを説得した）でその話についての知識を得たであろうとされる（Maxwell/Rudd）。

　なお古代末期以来、『アイアース』はソポクレース悲劇の中でも最もよく読まれたテクストであり、さまざまな形で引用・翻訳（ラテン語訳）・翻案がなされていた。この場の作者が何らかの形で悲劇『アイアース』に由来する物語あるいは直接にラテン語訳テクストに馴染んでいた可能性も考えられる。

382. advice ＝ weighing of opinions; deliberation（*OED* advice, *n.* 4.）

　Ajax　ギリシャ語ではアイアース（Aias）。

383. Laertes's son ＝ Odysseus

388. dismall'st ＝ most unlucky, most disastrous

392. trophies　武功を称える記念碑あるいは戦利品。

394. He lives in fame, that died in virtue's cause.　格言的。Tilley V74 "Only virtue / True fame never dies." in virtue's cause　「美徳という大義のもとで」

395. dumps ＝ heaviness of mind; mournful melody

400. beholding to ＝ beholden to, obliged to「…の恩義を受けて」

　the man　タイタス自身を指す。

402. remunerate ＝ reward

403. played your prize　「競技して賞品（の女）を手に入れた」フェンシングの用語。ここでサターナイナスは、バシエイナスが腕ずくで取り戻した恋人ラヴィニアを、喧嘩騒ぎを起こす無頼漢の情婦かなにかのように言う（Berthoud）。

404. gallant ＝ gorgeous or showy in appearance; fine-looking, handsome　ここではあてこすり。

405-06. I say no more, / Nor wish no less ＝ I neither say nor wish any more　過剰な否定辞の連続は話し手の動揺・上気した心理の表れ。

Nor wish no less, and so I take my leave.

SATURNINUS   Traitor, if Rome have law or we have power,
Thou and thy faction shall repent this rape.

BASSIANUS   'Rape' call you it, my lord, to seize my own,
My true betrothèd love and now my wife? 410
But let the laws of Rome determine all.
Meanwhile am I possessed of that is mine.

SATURNINUS   'Tis good, sir, you are very short with us.
But if we live, we'll be as sharp with you.

BASSIANUS   My lord, what I have done, as best I may, 415
Answer I must, and shall do with my life.
Only thus much I give your grace to know:
By all the duties that I owe to Rome,
This noble gentleman, Lord Titus here,
Is in opinion and in honour wronged, 420
That in the rescue of Lavinia
With his own hand did slay his youngest son,
In zeal to you, and highly moved to wrath
To be controlled in that he frankly gave.
Receive him then to favour, Saturnine, 425
That hath expressed himself in all his deeds
A father and a friend to thee and Rome.

TITUS   Prince Bassianus, leave to plead my deeds.
'Tis thou, and those, that have dishonoured me.
Rome and the righteous heavens be my judge 430
How I have loved and honoured Saturnine.   [*He kneels*]

TAMORA   My worthy lord, if ever Tamora
Were gracious in those princely eyes of thine,
Then hear me speak indifferently for all,
And at my suit, sweet, pardon what is past. 435

SATURNINUS   What, madam, be dishonoured openly,
And basely put it up without revenge?

TAMORA   Not so, my lord; the gods of Rome forfend

409. 'Rape' ... to seize my own　ここでの rape は「強奪、誘拐」。一般に他人の娘を不当に奪う場合がレイプで、結婚を約している相手を連れて行くのは正当な行為だという主張。　rape = the act of taking something by force; *esp.* the seizure of property by violent means; robbery　古くはその意味合いでの rape の語の使用が多かった。(*OED* rape, *n.*³ 1.)

412. am I possessed of = I am in possession of

that = that which; what

413. 'Tis good = very well (Bate)　'Tis = it is

short = rudely brief or curt「物言いが無礼でぶっきらぼうな」(*OED* short, *a.* 10.)

414. if we live, we'll　自分が皇帝であることを強調している。1. 1. 236 注参照。

sharp = severe, merciless　諺 'All that is sharp is short' にひっかけた皮肉。(Berthoud)

415. as best I may = in the best way that I can

420. opinion = reputation

423. zeal = love, devotion

424. be controlled = be rebuked; be held in check (*OED* control, *v.* 3.a. and 4.b.)

that　1. 1. 412 注参照。

frankly = freely, bountifully

425. to favour = to your favour

426. That　関係代名詞。先行詞は him = Titus。

428. leave to = cease to

plead my deeds　「(まるで私が罪を犯したかのように) 私の行為を弁護する」(*OED* plead, *v.* 8.)

429. those　「彼奴ら」タイタスの子たちを指す。

430. righteous heavens　「公正なる天の神々」

433. gracious = attractive, pleasing

438. forfend = forbid, prevent「(ローマの神々が) 禁じ給え」

I should be author to dishonuor you.
But on mine honour dare I undertake   440
For good Lord Titus' innocence in all,
Whose fury not dissembled speaks his griefs.
Then at my suit look graciously on him.
Lose not so noble a friend on vain suppose,
Nor with sour looks afflict his gentle heart.   445
[*Aside to Saturninus*]   My lord, be ruled by me; be won at last.
Dissemble all your griefs and discontents.
You are but newly planted in your throne.
Lest, then, the people, and patricians too,
Upon a just survey take Titus' part   450
And so supplant you for ingratitude,
Which Rome reputes to be a heinous sin.
Yield at entreats, and then let me alone.
I'll find a day to massacre them all
And raze their faction and their family,   455
The cruel father and his traitorous sons,
To whom I sued for my dear son's life,
And make them know what 'tis to let a queen
Kneel in the streets and beg for grace in vain.
Come, come, sweet emperor. Come, Andronicus.   460
Take up this good old man, and cheer the heart
That dies in tempest of thy angry frown.
SATURNINUS   Rise, Titus, rise. My Empress hath prevailed.
TITUS   [*Rises*]   I thank your majesty and her, my lord.
These words, these looks, infuse new life in me.   465
TAMORA   Titus, I am incorporate in Rome,
A Roman now adopted happily,
And must advise the Emperor for his good.
This day all quarrels die, Andronicus.
And let it be mine honour, good my lord,   470
That I have reconciled your friends and you.

439. author ＝ a person who causes an action, event, circumstance, state or condition of things (*OED* author, *n.* 1.c.)

442. fury not dissembled speaks his griefs 「(タイタスの) 激怒は、見せかけでなく真実彼の悲痛を表している」

dissembled＜dissemble ＝ disguise the semblance of (one's character, a feeling, design, or action) so as to conceal, or deceive as to, its real nature (*OED* dissemble, *v.¹* 1.) fury ... speaks は fury を擬人化した言い方、つまりタモラは寓意 (allegory) を用いる。シェイクスピア劇では助言役的な人物に、寓意を多く用いる傾向が見られる。⇒ 1. 1. 153 注参照。タモラはいま皇后となり、さっそく国政に関する皇帝の助言役を自任する。タモラの寓意依存癖はやがて劇の後段で自らの破滅を招くことになる。第 1 幕をジョージ・ピールの作とする共作説が現在有力となっているが、タモラの人物造形における言葉遣いには、他のシェイクスピア劇の助言役的人物の言葉遣いに通じるところがある。

443. graciously ＝ kindly, indulgently

444. on vain suppose 「根拠のない思い込みで」 suppose ＝ supposition

446. be won at last 「最後には私の言うことを聞きなさい」

450. survey ＝ the act of examining in detail

451. supplant 「(皇帝の) 地位から追い落とす」

452. Rome reputes 1. 1. 369 注参照。Rome は擬人化。

heinous [ˈheɪnəs] ＝ odious; highly criminal

453. Yield at ＝ yield to

entreats ＝ entreaties, supplications

455. raze ＝ erase, obliterate, remove completely

458. 'tis ＝ it is

461. Take up 「立ち上がらせる」この台詞から、タイタスはそれまで (1. 1. 430 前後から) 跪いていたものと考えられる。台詞に埋め込まれたト書き (embedded stage direction) として機能する。

466. incorporate ＝ incorporated; united in one body

468. must advise the Emperor for his good. 1. 1. 442 注参照。

469. This day all quarrels die 1. 1. 495 注参照。

470. mine honour mine の形については 1. 1. 8 注参照。

For you, Prince Bassianus, I have passed
My word and promise to the Emperor
That you will be more mild and tractable.
And fear not, lords — and you, Lavinia.   475
By my advice, all humbled on your knees,
You shall ask pardon of his majesty.

[*Marcus, Lavinia and Titus' sons kneel*]

LUCIUS   We do, and vow to heaven and to his highness
    That what we did was mildly as we might,
    Tend'ring our sister's honour and our own.   480
MARCUS   That on mine honour here do I protest.
SATURNINUS   Away, and talk not; trouble us no more.
TAMORA   Nay, nay, sweet Emperor, we must all be friends.
    The tribune and his nephews kneel for grace.
    I will not be denied. Sweetheart, look back.   485
SATURNINUS   Marcus, for thy sake, and thy brother's here,
    And at my lovely Tamora's entreats,
    I do remit these young men's heinous faults.
    Stand up.   [*They rise*]
    Lavinia, though you left me like a churl,   490
    I found a friend, and sure as death I swore
    I would not part a bachelor from the priest.
    Come, if the Emperor's court can feast two brides,
    You are my guest, Lavinia, and your friends. —
    This day shall be a love-day, Tamora.   495
TITUS   Tomorrow, an it please your majesty
    To hunt the panther and the hart with me,
    With horn and hound we'll give your grace *bonjour*.
SATURNINUS   Be it so, Titus, and gramercy too.

Flourish. Exeunt [*all but Aaron*]

476. all humbled on your knees 「皆謙虚に跪いて」我が子アラーバスの助命
を嘆願してタモラ自身がタイタスの前でとった姿勢（1. 1. 104-20）。 ⇒図版
8（p. 217）参照。

478-80. Q1, Q2 ではタモラの台詞とする。

479. mildly as we might ＝ as mildly as we could

480. Tend'ring ＝ caring for

483. Nay ＝ no

484. kneel for grace 「お慈悲を求めて跪く」

485. I will not be denied この場合 will は強い意志を表わす。

487. entreats ＝ entreaties

488. heinous ＝ hateful, odious

490. churl ＝ boor; base fellow

491. sure as death ＝ as surely as death「断じて、金輪際」 death は確実に来
るものの代表例。

492. would not part a bachelor 「独身のままでは帰らぬ」part は自動詞。

495. a love-day ＝ 1. a day appointed for a meeting with a view to the
amicable settlement of a dispute; 2. a day devoted to love（*OED* loveday,
n. 1. and 2.）1. の意味ではタモラの台詞（1. 1. 469）に応えるもの。しかし好
色なサターナイナスとしては 2. の意味合いが強いはず。

496. an ＝ if

499. gramercy ＝ thanks 古フランス語の grant merci（＝ may God reward
you greatly）から。

499 SD. Exeunt〔*all but Aaron*〕 次の場の冒頭でエアロンが独白で話し始
めるため、エアロン一人が舞台上に残るものと考えられる。16 世紀の芝居の
伝統として、同一の登場人物が退場してすぐ再登場することはなかった（the
law of re-entry）。エアロンが残るのは幕表示のない Q1 による。F1 では 1 幕
の終わりにエアロンも他の人物とともに一旦退場し、すぐに 2 幕 1 場の冒頭
で再登場することになる。F1 では 3 幕 2 場の終わりと 4 幕 1 場の間に同様の
現象が見られる。3. 2. 85 SD 参照。

[Act II Scene I]

AARON   Now climbeth Tamora Olympus' top,
　　Safe out of Fortune's shot, and sits aloft,
　　Secure of thunder's crack or lightning flash,
　　Advanced above pale Envy's threat'ning reach.
　　As when the golden sun salutes the morn　　　　　　5
　　And, having gilt the ocean with his beams,
　　Gallops the zodiac in his glistering coach
　　And overlooks the highest-peering hills,
　　So Tamora.
　　Upon her wit doth earthly honour wait,　　　　　　10
　　And virtue stoops and trembles at her frown.
　　Then, Aaron, arm thy heart and fit thy thoughts
　　To mount aloft with thy imperial mistress,
　　And mount her pitch whom thou in triumph long
　　Hast prisoner held, fettered in amorous chains　　　15
　　And faster bound to Aaron's charming eyes
　　Than is Prometheus tied to Caucasus.
　　Away with slavish weeds and servile thoughts!
　　I will be bright, and shine in pearl and gold
　　To wait upon this new-made emperess.　　　　　　20
　　To wait, said I? To wanton with this queen,
　　This goddess, this Semiramis, this nymph,
　　This siren that will charm Rome's Saturnine
　　And see his shipwrack and his commonweal's.
　　Holla! What storm is this?　　　　　　　　　　　25

Enter Chiron and Demetrius, braving

DEMETRIUS   Chiron, thy years wants wit, thy wits wants edge
　　And manners, to intrude where I am graced,
　　And may, for aught thou knowest, affected be.
CHIRON   Demetrius, thou dost overween in all,

〔**2. 1**〕あらすじ……………………………………………………………………

　タモラの愛人エアロンがひとり野望を語る。彼はラヴィニアに横恋慕して言い争うタモラの２人の息子ディミートリアスとカイロンを説得し、狩りの最中にラヴィニアを襲ってレイプするように唆す。

………………………………………………………………………………………

1-11. Now climbeth Tamora Olympus' top ... at her frown. ⇒後注

2. Fortune's shot 「運命（の女神）の射程」Cf. *Hamlet*, 1. 3 'Keep you in the rear of your affection / Out of the shot and danger of desire.'

3. Secure of = safe from

7. Gallops the zodiac「黄道を駆け抜ける」Cf. *Romeo and Juliet*, 3. 2 'Gallop apace, you fiery-footed steeds, / Towards Phoebus' lodging ...'

　　his glistering coach ギリシャ神話で太陽神が御する輝く馬車。

8. overlooks「上から見下ろす」　　**highest-peering**「最も高く山頂を覗かせる」（*OED* peer, *v*.³1.a.）

10-11. Upon her wit ... honour ... virtue ... frown この文脈で honour「名誉（ある人々）」および virtue「徳（の高い人々）」は、中世以来の文学に多い寓意（allegory）ではなく、性質あるいは性格を表わす語でそれを所有する人々を表わす換喩。

14. mount her pitch 「到達しうる限りの頂点まで飛翔する」もとは鷹狩りの鷹が飛翔するイメージ。pitch は鷹が上昇する最高点で、そこから獲物めがけて降下する。動詞 mount にはエロティックな響きもある。

16. charming 「魔力で魅了する」

17. Prometheus ギリシャ神話のプロメーテウス。ヤペトスとクリュメネーの子。プロメーテウスは、オリュンポスから火を盗み人類に与えるなどしてゼウスに逆らった罰として、コーカサス山脈中の岩山に縛られ毎日大鷲に内臓を食い破られる。アイスキュロス（Aiskhylos）の悲劇『縛られたプロメーテウス（*Prometheus Desmothes*)』など。　またプロメーテウスは、知性を持つ存在としての人類誕生そのものに深く関わる神格。Hesiodos, *Theogonia*, 507-616; Ovidius, *Metamorphoses*, 1. 76-88.　　**18. weeds** 「衣服」

22. Semiramis アッシリアの伝説上の女王セミーラミス。夫亡き後女王となり数々の武功を立て多くの国を征服したが、好色かつ残忍で最後は愛人である自分の息子に殺された。Dante, *Inferno*, 5. 52-57; Petrarca, *Triumphi*, 3. 67-76; Boccaccio, *De Mulieribus Claris*, 2.

23. siren ギリシャ神話のセイレーン。美声で船人を魅了し滅ぼす。*Odysseia*, 12. 39-54, 165-200.

26. wants 主語が三人称複数でも定動詞形語尾に -s が付く場合がしばしばあった。　　**27. graced** = favoured　　**28. affected** = fancied, loved

29. overween 「高望みしすぎる、自惚れる」

And so in this, to bear me down with braves.   30
'Tis not the difference of a year or two
Makes me less gracious or thee more fortunate.
I am as able and as fit as thou
To serve and to deserve my mistress' grace,
And that my sword upon thee shall approve   35
And plead my passions for Lavinia's love.

AARON   Clubs, clubs! These lovers will not keep the peace.

DEMETRIUS   Why, boy, although our mother, unadvised,
Gave you a dancing rapier by your side,
Are you so desperate grown to threat your friends?   40
Go to. Have your lath glued within your sheath
Till you know better how to handle it.

CHIRON   Meanwhile, sir, with the little skill I have,
Full well shalt thou perceive how much I dare.

DEMETRIUS
Ay, boy, grow you so brave?   *They draw*

AARON   Why, how now, lords?   45
So near the Emperor's palace dare you draw
And maintain such a quarrel openly?
Full well I wot the ground of all this grudge.
I would not for a million of gold
The cause were known to them it most concerns,   50
Nor would your noble mother for much more
Be so dishonoured in the court of Rome.
For shame, put up.

DEMETRIUS   Not I, till I have sheathed
My rapier in his bosom, and withal
Thrust those reproachful speeches down his throat   55
That he hath breathed in my dishonour here.

CHIRON   For that I am prepared and full resolved,
Foul-spoken coward, that thund'rest with thy tongue
And with thy weapon nothing dar'st perform.

31-32. 'Tis not the difference ... / Makes me ＝ The difference ... does not make me　文頭の 'Tis not は否定の文意を強調する。

32. gracious ＝ likely to find favour or grace（*OED* gracious, *adj.* 1.b.）

34. grace ＝ favour, mercy

35. approve ＝ prove「証明する、試す」

36. plead ＝ maintain（a plea or cause）by argument in a court of law「（法廷で）申し立てる、主張する」（*OED* plead, *v.* 2.b.）

37. Clubs, clubs!　街中での喧嘩の折などに役人や警備員を呼ぶ叫び声（Maxwell）。*Henry VI, Part 1,* 1. 3. 'I'll call for clubs, if you will not away.'　clubs ＝ truncheons「警棒」それを持って警備・治安維持にあたる人を指す換喩。

38. unadvised　「無思慮なことに」

39. dancing rapier　「踊り用の（飾りの）刀」

40. to ＝ as to

　　friends　「味方」「肉親」（*OED* friend, *n.* 2 and 3.）

41. Go to　「おいおい、いかんぞ」（*OED* go, *v.* PV go to 1.b.）

　　lath「木製の刀」

48. wot ＝ know（*OED* wit, *v.¹* 1.a.）

49-50. I would not ... The cause were known「動機を知られたくない」　I would ＝ I wish; O that（*OED* will, *v.¹* 36.）

53. put up　「（刀を）鞘に納める」

53-54. have sheathed / My rapier in his bosom　「あいつの胸に、俺の刀をぐさりと納める」sheathe は刀を「鞘に納める」が原義。剣先で突き刺す身体を鞘に擬えるメタファーとして慣用表現化していた。

58. Foul-spoken ＝ given to speaking in an offensive or disgraceful way「口汚い」（*OED* foul-spoken, *adj.*）

AARON Away, I say! 60
  Now by the gods that warlike Goths adore,
  This petty brabble will undo us all.
  Why, lords, and think you not how dangerous
  It is to jet upon a prince's right?
  What, is Lavinia then become so loose 65
  Or Bassianus so degenerate
  That for her love such quarrels may be broached
  Without controlment, justice, or revenge?
  Young lords, beware! And should the Empress know
  This discord's ground, the music would not please. 70
CHIRON I care not, I, knew she and all the world.
  I love Lavinia more than all the world.
DEMETRIUS Youngling, learn thou to make some meaner
    choice.
  Lavinia is thine elder brother's hope.
AARON Why, are you mad? Or know you not in Rome 75
  How furious and impatient they be,
  And cannot brook competitors in love?
  I tell you, lords, you do but plot your deaths
  By this device.
CHIRON   Aaron, a thousand deaths
  Would I propose to achieve her whom I love. 80
AARON To achieve her how?
DEMETRIUS   Why makes thou it so strange?
  She is a woman, therefore may be wooed;
  She is a woman, therefore may be won;
  She is Lavinia, therefore must be loved.
  What, man, more water glideth by the mill 85
  Than wots the miller of, and easy it is
  Of a cut loaf to steal a shive, we know.
  Though Bassianus be the Emperor's brother,
  Better than he have worn Vulcan's badge.

62. brabble ＝ brawl「諍い（いさか）」

64. jet upon「（他人の領分・財産）を侵害する」

66. degenerate「腑抜けな」

67-68. may be broached / Without ...　「口外して … せずに済まされる」

68. controlment「咎め、譴責（けんせき）」　**justice**「裁き、処罰」

69. And should the Empress know ＝ If the Empress should know

70. This discord's ground, the music ...　悪の芸術家エアロンが音楽的メタ
ファーで話す。　ground には「原因」の他に ground-base「基礎低音」の
意味もある。Cf. *Richard III*, 3. 7 'For on that ground I'll build a holy des-
cant.' (*OED* ground, *n*. 6.c.)

71. knew she and all the world ＝ even if she and all the world knew this

73. meaner ＝ poorer in quality; humbler

74. thine elder　韻律上、mine age (1. 1. 8) などの場合と同様に母音の前で
thy は thine になる。

79. device ＝ design「筋立て」

81. Why makes thou it so strange?「なにが意外なものか」
make ＝ consider

83. She is a woman, therefore may be won「あの人も女、だから手に入れら
れる」俗諺的。Tilley W681 'All women may be won.'
may ＝ can　初期近代では may を可能の意味で使う用法がまだ頻繁に見られ
た。英語法助動詞の意味は長い時間の経過とともに移り変わってきた。

85. man　軽蔑、苛立ち、忠告などを表わす呼びかけ。(*OED* man, *n.*[1] and *int*.
16.a.)

85-86. more water glideth ... miller of「粉屋の主人も知らぬほど多くの水が
水車小屋の脇を滑る」俗諺的。Tilley W99 'Much water goes by the mill
that the miller knows not of.'　glideth の -eth は 1. 1. 109 注参照。

86-87. easy it is / ... steal a shive「切り分けたパンから、ひとかけら盗むのは
たやすい」俗諺的。Tilley T34 'It is safe taking a shive of a cut loaf.'

89. Better than he ＝ those who are better than Bassianus
Vulcan's badge　寝取られ亭主 (cuckold) の頭に生えるとされた角のこと。
愛と美の女神ウェヌス (Venus / Gk. Aphrodite) は鍛冶（かじ）の神ウゥルカーヌス
(Vulcanus / Gk. Hephaistos) の妻だが、軍神マルス (Mars / Gk. Ares)
と逢い引きする。ウゥルカーヌスが浮気の現場に罠を仕掛けて両者の抱き合っ
ているところを捕縛し、そのまま神々の眼前に晒（さら）して笑い物にするという滑稽
なエピソードが伝えられている。*Odysseia*, 8. 266-366; Ovidius, *Metamorphoses*, 4. 169-89.

AARON [*Aside*]   Ay, and as good as Saturninus may.   90

DEMETRIUS   Then why should he despair that knows to court
   it

  With words, fair looks, and liberality?

  What, hast not thou full often struck a doe

  And borne her cleanly by the keeper's nose?

AARON   Why, then, it seems some certain snatch or so   95

  Would serve your turns.

CHIRON   Ay, so the turn were served.

DEMETRIUS   Aaron, thou hast hit it.

AARON   Would you had hit it too!

  Then should not we be tired with this ado.   100

  Why, hark you, hark you! And are you such fools

  To square for this? Would it offend you then

  That both should speed?

CHIRON   Faith, not me.

DEMETRIUS   Nor me, so I were one.

AARON   For shame, be friends, and join for that you jar.   105

  'Tis policy and stratagem must do

  That you affect, and so must you resolve

  That what you cannot as you would achieve,

  You must perforce accomplish as you may.

  Take this of me: Lucrece was not more chaste   110

  Than this Lavinia, Bassianus' love.

  A speedier course than ling'ring languishment

  Must we pursue, and I have found the path.

  My lords, a solemn hunting is in hand;

  There will the lovely Roman ladies troop.   115

  The forest walks are wide and spacious,

  And many unfrequented plots there are,

  Fitted by kind for rape and villainy.

  Single you thither then this dainty doe,

  And strike her home by force, if not by words.   120

90. Ay [ʌɪ] ＝ aye, yes　肯定・同意を表わす副詞。

as good as Saturninus　アイロニックな言い方。実は皇帝サターナイナスその人を指す。

92. liberality　「気前の良さ、贈り物」

93. doe　「雌鹿」つまり若い女性のこと（Partridge）。以下卑猥な含みの隠語が続く。

94. by the keeper's nose ＝ right in front of the keeper

95. snatch ＝ quick copulation (Rubinstein)

96. serve your turns ＝ satisfy your needs

turn ＝（used allusively for) copulation (Williams)

97. so ＝ so long as

98., 99. hit it ＝ understood it; hit the target　hit ＝ coit with (Williams)

100. tired ＝ satiated, exhausted　　**ado** ＝ concerns, trouble

101. hark ＝ listen

102. square ＝ fall out; quarrel

103. speed ＝ prove successful

104. Faith ＝ really, truly　間投詞。　　**so**　上記2. 1. 97 注参照。

105. that you jar ＝ what you quarrel about

106-7. 'Tis policy ... / That you affect　「欲しいものを手に入れるには、策略に限る」　policy ＝ a device, a contrivance; a trick (*OED* policy *n.¹*3.)

That you affect ＝ what you seek to obtain

109. perforce accomplish as you may　「自分にできるやり方で強引に仕遂げる」格言的。Tilley M554 'Men must do as they may, not as they would.' perforce ＝ by the application of physical force or violence「力尽くで」 may ＝ can

110. of me ＝ from me　　**Lucrece**　ローマ建国史に登場する伝説的貞女ルクレーティア（Lucretia）。タルクィニウス（Lucius Tarquinius Superbus）にレイプされて自殺し、ローマが王族を追放し共和政を樹立するきっかけとなる。この芝居で終始想起される主要な古代ローマ伝説の1つ。Ovidius, *Fasti*, II. 685-852; Livius, *Ab Urbe Condita*, I. 57-60; Shakespeare, *The Rape of Lucrece* (1594).　⇒解説15-22頁

112. than ling'ring languishment　「いつまでも満たされぬ想いに悩むより」

117. unfrequented plots　「人跡まばらな場所」

118. by kind ＝ by nature

119. Single　狙った獲物（鹿など）を群から引き離す　　**dainty** ＝ delicate

doe　上記2. 1. 93 注参照。

120. strike her home　「彼女の的を外さずに刺す」　home ＝ directly, effectively; at the mark aimed for (*OED* home, *adv.* 4.a. and b.)

This way, or not at all, stand you in hope.
Come, come, our empress, with her sacred wit
To villainy and vengeance consecrate,
Will we acquaint withal what we intend,
And she shall file our engines with advice   125
That will not suffer you to square yourselves,
But to your wishes' height advance you both.
The Emperor's court is like the house of Fame,
The palace full of tongues, of eyes, and ears;
The woods are ruthless, dreadful, deaf, and dull.   130
There speak and strike, brave boys, and take your turns.
There serve your lust, shadowed from heaven's eye,
And revel in Lavinia's treasury.
CHIRON   Thy counsel, lad, smells of no cowardice.
DEMETRIUS   *Sit fas aut nefas*, till I find the stream   135
   To cool this heat, a charm to calm these fits,
   Per Stygia, per manes vehor.

Exeunt

[ACT II SCENE II]

*Enter Titus Andronicus and his three sons, and Marcus, making a
noise with hounds and horns*

TITUS   The hunt is up, the moon is bright and gray,
   The fields are fragrant, and the woods are green.
   Uncouple here, and let us make a bay
   And wake the Emperor and his lovely bride,
   And rouse the Prince, and ring a hunter's peal,   5
   That all the court may echo with the noise.
   Sons, let it be your charge, as it is ours,
   To attend the Emperor's person carefully.
   I have been troubled in my sleep this night,
   But dawning day new comfort hath inspired.   10

122-23. with her sacred wit / To villainy and vengeance consecrate 「神聖な知恵を用いて、悪事と復讐心へと淨らかに身を捧げ」アイロニー。1. 1. 130後注参照。 consecrate = consecrated

124. acquaint 「知らせる」 **withal what we intend** = with what we intend

125. file 「滑らかにする、研ぎ澄ます」

engines = contrivances, plots (*OED* engine, *n.* 3.)

126. suffer = allow **square** = fall out; disagree or quarrel

128. the house of Fame 「噂の女神の館」狩りの途中で驟雨に襲われたアエネーアースとディードーが洞窟で実質上の夫婦になるが、2人の関係をすぐに噂の女神（Fama）が世界中に広める（Vergilius, *Aeneis*, 4. 173-92）。「館」はOvidius, *Metamorphoses*, 10. 39-63、Chaucer, *The House of Fame* 参照。

131. take your turns 「順番にやれ / 犯せ」猥褻語。

135. *Sit fas aut nefas* 「神の掟に叶おうが叶うまいが」(Lat.) *Metamorphoses*, 6. 585: 'sed fasque nefasque.' 夫テーレウスに自分の妹ピロメーラをレイプされたプロクネー（Procne）が復讐を決意して叫ぶ言葉。淫らな欲望に駆られるディミートリアスは、その文脈を忘れ、うろ覚えの詩句を口にする（dramatic irony）。復讐心と欲望が共に人間を滅ぼす狂気であり区別不可能だとする、オウィディウス的テーマを連想させる。5. 1. 58 注参照。

137. *Per Stygia, per manes vehor* 「私はステュクス川と死者たちの霊を通って運ばれる」(Lat.) 典拠は Seneca, *Hippolytus*, 1180 'Per Styga, per amnes igneos amens sequar' （私［＝パイドラー Phaedra］はステュクスを抜け、燃える数々の川を抜け、狂乱してあなた［＝ヒッポリュトゥス］を追いかけよう） Styx は冥界を流れる川の名。1. 1. 88 注参照。タモラの息子たちは、シェイクスピアの時代にはグラマー・スクールで習ったであろうラテン語のフレーズを、よく意味もわからずに振り回す。前項 *Sit fas aut nefas* などと並んで、劇中もっとも粗暴な人物たちにラテン語のフレーズを引用させるのは明白なアイロニー。古典ラテン語引用の問題については⇒解説 15-22 頁。

〔**2. 2**〕あらすじ……………………………………………………………
タイタスが新婚の皇帝夫妻とバシエイナス夫妻を起こし、狩りに出かける。
……………………………………………………………………………………

0 SD. *making a noise* 2. 2. 6 注参照。

1. up = into a state of activity「始まるところだ」

3. Uncouple 「（猟犬を）解き放つ」 **bay** 「（猟犬が獲物を追い詰めて襲いかかるときに発する）唸り声」タイタスは、自分ではユーモアのつもりで、新婚の皇帝夫妻を狩りの獲物に喩えている。

5. ring a hunter's peal 「狩り人の角笛を鐘のように高々と鳴り響かせる」

6. noise = sound 快い音やメロディーについても言った。(*OED* noise, *n.* 3.a.)

*Here a cry of hounds, and wind horns in a peal. Then enter
Saturninus, Tamora, Bassianus, Lavinia, Chiron, Demetrius, and
their Attendants*

TITUS   Many good morrows to your majesty;
   Madam, to you as many, and as good.
   I promisèd your grace a hunter's peal.
SATURNINUS   And you have rung it lustily, my lords,
   Somewhat too early for new-married ladies.   15
BASSIANUS   Lavinia, how say you?
LAVINIA   I say no.
   I have been broad awake two hours and more.
SATURNINUS   Come on, then. Horse and chariots let us have,
   And to our sport. Madam, now shall you see   20
   Our Roman hunting.
MARCUS   I have dogs, my lord,
   Will rouse the proudest panther in the chase
   And climb the highest promontory top.
TITUS   And I have horse will follow where the game
   Makes way and runs like swallows o'er the plain.   25
DEMETRIUS   *[Aside to Chiron]*
   Chiron, we hunt not, we, with horse nor hound,
   But hope to pluck a dainty doe to ground.

                                       Exeunt

[**ACT II SCENE III**]

Enter Aaron, alone

AARON   He that had wit would think that I had none,
   To bury so much gold under a tree
   And never after to inherit it.
   Let him that thinks of me so abjectly
   Know that this gold must coin a stratagem   5

11. morrows = mornings

22. Will rouse = That will rouse

    proudest 「立派な、堂々とした」

    chase = a hunting-ground; a tract of unenclosed land reserved for breeding and hunting wild animals（*OED* chase, *n.¹* 3.）

25. Makes way 「進む」

27. pluck a dainty doe 「甘味な牝鹿を（果物のように）摘む」レイプの比喩。
2.1.93 および 119 各注参照。

〔2. 3〕あらすじ…………………………………………………………………………

    森でタモラとエアロンが２人でいるところをバシエイナスとラヴィニアが目撃し、非難する。ディミートリアスとカイロンが登場し、バシエイナスを殺害した上、ラヴィニアを連れ去って暴行する。さらにエアロンがタイタスの２人の息子クウィンタスとマーシアスをその場所へ誘い込む。２人は罠に嵌まって、バシエイナスの死体が遺棄されている穴に落ちる。そこへ皇帝一行が登場し、タイタスの２人の息子をバシエイナス殺しの犯人として連行する。

■■

1. had wit had は仮定法。

2-3. bury so much gold under a tree / And never after to inherit it ⇒後注

4. thinks of ... abjectly 「… を見損なう、腑抜けだと考える」

5. coin = devise, produce また同時に計略の成功を金貨の流通にも喩える、含みの多いメタファー。

図5 エアロン（アンソニー・クウェイル）とタモラ（マクシン・オードリー）　ピーター・ブルック演出（1955）ⓒ RSC

Which, cunningly effected, will beget
A very excellent piece of villainy.   [*Hides gold*]
And so repose, sweet gold, for their unrest
That have their alms out of the Empress' chest.

Enter Tamora alone to the Moor

TAMORA   My lovely Aaron, wherefore look'st thou sad,   10
When everything doth make a gleeful boast?
The birds chant melody on every bush,
The snakes lies rollèd in the cheerful sun,
The green leaves quiver with the cooling wind
And make a checkered shadow on the ground.   15
Under their sweet shade, Aaron, let us sit,
And whilst the babbling echo mocks the hounds,
Replying shrilly to the well-tuned horns,
As if a double hunt were heard at once,
Let us sit down and mark their yellowing noise.   20
And after conflict such as was supposed
The wand'ring prince and Dido once enjoyed
When with a happy storm they were surprised,
And curtained with a counsel-keeping cave,
We may, each wreathèd in the other's arms,   25
Our pastimes done, possess a golden slumber,
Whiles hounds and horns and sweet melodious birds
Be unto us as is a nurse's song
Of lullaby to bring her babe asleep.
AARON   Madam, though Venus govern your desires,   30
Saturn is dominator over mine.
What signifies my deadly standing eye,
My silence, and my cloudy melancholy,
My fleece of woolly hair that now uncurls
Even as an adder when she doth unroll   35
To do some fatal execution?

6. beget 「(男親が) 子をつくる」

8. repose ... for their unrest 「奴らが面倒なことになるように、それまでおとなしく休んでいろ」Cf. Thomas Kyd, *The Spanish Tragedy*, 1. 3. 5 'Then rest we here a while in our unrest.' (Berthoud) their はこの計略に嵌(は)まる連中、つまりアンドロニカス一族を指す。

9. alms out of the Empress' chest 「皇后陛下の蔵からの施し物」金貨のこと。

10. wherefore = for what; why

17-19. And whilst ... heard at once 狩りの光景。 **the babbling echo mocks the hounds** 「せせらぐ小川に響く (角笛の) こだまが猟犬たちを揶揄(やゆ)い」

19. a double hunt were heard こだまのイメージ

20. yellowing noise「(猟犬たちの) 吠え立てる響き」 yellow = yell; howl noise 2. 2. 6 注参照

21-24. conflict such as was supposed / The wand'ring prince and Dido once ... cave 狩の途中で驟雨に遭ったアエネーアース (= the wandering prince) とカルターゴーの女王ディードーは洞窟に逃げ込み、そこでおそらく (as was supposed) 契りを結ぶ。以後女王は2人の結婚を公言する (*Aeneis*, 4. 160-172)。 2. 1. 128 注参照。 **23. happy** 「幸せな」に加えて「偶然の」という意味合いも強い。 **were surprised** 「襲われた」 **24. curtained** = concealed, protected **counsel-keeping** 「秘密を守る、口の固い」

25. wreathèd 「絡ませて」

28-29. a nurse's song / Of lullaby to bring her babe asleep 似たイメージとして *Venus and Adonis*, 973-74 'By this, far off she hears some huntsman hallow; / A nurse's song ne'er pleased her babe so well.' (Berthoud) タモラの求愛の言葉は美少年アドーニスに求愛するウェヌスを思わせる。エアロンはアドーニスのように美しい。

30-31. Venus govern your desires, / Saturn is dominator over mine 惑星が人の性格・気質・行動を支配するという占星術風の迷信に引っ掛けたジョーク。シェイクスピア劇の代表的な悪党 (villains) は占星術を信じないのが一般。例えば『リア王』のエドマンド (Edmund) (*King Lear*, 1. 2)。ここでエアロンは、「美と愛欲」の女神ウェヌス (Venus ヴィーナス) に自分の愛人タモラを擬(なぞら)える一方で、彼女がまんまとローマ新皇帝妃の座に収まったことを皇帝サターナイナスの名前に引っ掛けて揶揄っている。Saturninus の語源は Saturn (Lat. Saturnus)「サトゥルヌス、土星」で、土星は占星術的に「冷たさ、不活発、陰気」などと結びつけられる。機敏で行動的な悪漢エアロンにはまず当てはまらない特徴で、愛を激しく求めるタモラへ向けた戯言。

32. deadly-standing eye 「命はないぞとばかりに屹(きっ)と構えた目」

33. melancholy 「憂鬱、不機嫌」中世の医術で四体液の1つである黒胆汁 (black bile) と結びつけられた気質。 **34. fleece of** 「羊毛状の」

No, madam, these are no venereal signs.
Vengeance is in my heart, death in my hand,
Blood and revenge are hammering in my head.
Hark, Tamora, the empress of my soul,   40
Which never hopes more heaven than rests in thee,
This is the day of doom for Bassianus.
His Philomel must lose her tongue today,
Thy sons make pillage of her chastity
And wash their hands in Bassianus' blood.   45
Seest thou this letter? Take it up, I pray thee,
And give the King this fatal-plotted scroll.   [*Gives a letter*]
Now, question me no more. We are espied.
Here comes a parcel of our hopeful booty,
Which dreads not yet their lives' destruction.   50

Enter Bassianus and Lavinia.

TAMORA   Ah, my sweet Moor, sweeter to me than life!
AARON   No more, great empress. Bassianus comes.
  Be cross with him, and I'll go fetch thy sons
  To back thy quarrels, whatsoe'er they be.   [*Exit*]
BASSIANUS   Who have we here? Rome's royal Empress,   55
  Unfurnished of her well-beseeming troop?
  Or is it Dian, habited like her,
  Who hath abandonèd her holy groves
  To see the general hunting in this forest?
TAMORA   Saucy controller of my private steps,   60
  Had I the power that some say Dian had,
  Thy temples should be planted presently
  With horns, as was Actaeon's, and the hounds
  Should drive upon thy new-transformèd limbs,
  Unmannerly intruder as thou art.   65
LAVINIA   Under your patience, gentle empress,
  'Tis thought you have a goodly gift in horning,

37. venereal signs = signs of love「色恋・愛欲の兆候」 venereal = of Venus; of sexual desire　占星術で sign は黄道十二宮の1つを指す。ここでは占星術的イメージを単なる言葉遊びとして軽く用いる。

38. Vengeance is in my heart　エアロンは復讐を専ら個人の心理的問題すなわち残虐な行為への欲望だと見做し、さらに人々の復讐心を巧妙に操る自分の技をも vengeance と呼んで誇る。5. 1. 58 注参照。5幕2場でタモラが派手な変装をして演じることになる復讐の女神（Revenge）は、人々の復讐心を操るとする点で後者の神格化。　⇒解説 22-25 頁。

42. doom = final fate, death（*OED* doom, *n.* 4. b.）

43. Philomel must lose her tongue　ギリシャ神話でピロメーラ（Philomela）は義兄テーレウス（Tereus）にレイプされ、口封じに舌を切り取られる。Ovidius, *Metamorphoses*, 6. 520-62.

47. fatal-plotted = plotted for a fatal purpose

49. parcel = a portion, a small part
hopeful booty「期待できる（promising）獲物」と「（罠に気づかず）おめでたい獲物」両方の含みがある。

50. dreads not「不安にも思っていない」

53. cross = inclined to quarrel or disagree「反抗的な」（*OED* cross, *adj.* 5.a.）

56. Unfurnished of = not accompanied with
well-beseeming「（皇帝の妃に）相応の、きちんとした」

57. Dian, habited like her　ディアーナ女神（Diana）はしばしば狩人の出で立ちで描かれる。

58. her holy groves　アクタイオーンが迷い込んだ森のディアーナの神域。

60. Saucy controller「無礼な監視役」

63. horns, as was Actaeon's　ディアーナの神域の森に迷い込み沐浴する女神の姿を目にした狩人アクタイオーンは、その怒りに触れて鹿に変身させられ自分の猟犬に咬み殺される。*Metamorphoses*, 3. 155-252.　horns はここでは「（ディアーナがアクタイオーンの頭に付けた）鹿の角」

67-71. horning ... they should take him for a stag.　それまでタモラとバシエイナスの2人がディアーナとアクタイオーンの神話を引き合いに出して応酬していたが（55-65）、ここでラヴィニアも寝取られ亭主（cuckold）の額に角（horns）が生えるという俗信・ジョークに言及して口を挟む。

And to be doubted that your Moor and you
Are singled forth to try experiments.
Jove shield your husband from his hounds today! 70
'Tis pity they should take him for a stag.

BASSIANUS   Believe me, queen, your swarthy Cimmerian
Doth make your honour of his body's hue,
Spotted, detested, and abominable.
Why are you sequestered from all your train, 75
Dismounted from your snow-white goodly steed,
And wandered hither to an obscure plot,
Accompanied but with a barbarous Moor,
If foul desire had not conducted you?

LAVINIA   And being intercepted in your sport, 80
Great reason that my noble lord be rated
For sauciness. [*To Bassianus*] I pray you, let us hence,
And let her joy her raven-coloured love.
This valley fits the purpose passing well.

BASSIANUS   The King my brother shall have notice of this. 85

LAVINIA   Ay, for these slips have made him noted long.
Good king to be so mightily abused!

TAMORA   Why, I have patience to endure all this.

Enter Chiron and Demetrius.

DEMETRIUS   How now, dear sovereign and our gracious
        mother,
Why doth your highness look so pale and wan? 90

TAMORA   Have I not reason, think you, to look pale?
These two have ticed me hither to this place,
A barren, detested vale you see it is;
The trees, though summer, yet forlorn and lean,
Overcome with moss and baleful mistletoe. 95
Here never shines the sun, here nothing breeds,
Unless the nightly owl or fatal raven.

68. be doubted = be suspected

69. singled forth to try experiments 「（角を生やす）実験を試みるために選び出された」

70. Jove shield ...! = May Jove protect ...! 祈願文。Jove は Jupiter の英語名。英語形の語源は Jupiter の属格 Jovis または目的格 Jovem から。God と同じく単音節語のためか、後者の代用として頻繁に用いられた。

72. swarthy Cimmerian 「黒い肌のキンメリア人」キンメリア人は紀元前7世紀頃小アジアに住んだ遊牧民。叙事詩では常闇の地に住む民族とされる。*Odysseia*, 11. 13-19; *Metamorphoses*, 11. 592-95. バシエイナスがムーア人のエアロンをこう呼ぶのは、いずれにしてもかなり的外れ。バシエイナスの性格か。

73. make your honour of his body's hue 「あなたの名誉まで自分の肌の色に染めている」（松岡訳） dishonour と言いたいところを honour と皮肉っている。 honour = chastity

74. Spotted 「まだらの、汚れた」

75. sequestered = separated
train = a retinue, suite 「（皇帝お連れの）ご一行」

81. Great reason that ... 「… するのも無理はない」
rated = berated 「叱りつけられた」

82. hence = go hence; depart

83. joy = rejoice at

84. passing = surpassingly; exceedingly

90. wan 「青ざめた」

94. forlorn 「さびれた」

95. Overcome with ... baleful mistletoe 「苔と毒ヤドリギに覆われた」
overcome = spread over; cover (*OED* overcome, *v.* 5.a.)

97. nightly 「夜に活動する、闇夜の世界に住む」(*OED* nightly, *adj.* 2.a.)
fatal raven 「凶兆のワタリガラス」「致命傷を負わせるワタリガラス」の両様にとれる。息子たちを煽る目的でのタモラの演技という文脈では、後者が効果的か。

And when they showed me this abhorrèd pit,
They told me, here at dead time of the night
A thousand fiends, a thousand hissing snakes, 100
Ten thousand swelling toads, as many urchins,
Would make such fearful and confusèd cries
As any mortal body hearing it
Should straight fall mad, or else die suddenly.
No sooner had they told this hellish tale 105
But straight they told me they would bind me here
Unto the body of a dismal yew
And leave me to this miserable death.
And then they called me foul adulteress,
Lascivious Goth, and all the bitterest terms 110
That ever ear did hear to such effect.
And had you not by wondrous fortune come,
This vengeance on me had they executed.
Revenge it as you love your mother's life,
Or be you not henceforth called my children. 115
DEMETRIUS   This is a witness that I am thy son. *Stab [Bassianus]*
CHIRON   And this for me, struck home to show my strength.

[*Stab Bassianus, who dies*]

LAVINIA   Ay, come, Semiramis, nay, barbarous Tamora,
For no name fits thy nature but thy own.
TAMORA   Give me the poniard! You shall know, my boys, 120
Your mother's hand shall right your mother's wrong.
DEMETRIUS   Stay, madam, here is more belongs to her.
First thrash the corn, then after burn the straw.
This minion stood upon her chastity,
Upon her nuptial vow, her loyalty, 125
And with that painted hope braves your mightiness;
And shall she carry this unto her grave?
CHIRON   And if she do, I would I were an eunuch!

98. pit　「穴」この芝居で象徴的な舞台空間の1つ。第1幕で戦死者を埋葬したアンドロニカス家の墓の件と同様に、舞台中央の落とし戸ないし迫（せり）（trap door）を使用したとも推測される。

101. toads　「ヒキガエル」いまわしい物のメタファーとして頻繁に用いられる。
urchins = goblins or elves「小鬼、妖精」原義はハリネズミ（hedgehogs）。小鬼・妖精が時にハリネズミの姿をとるという俗信から。（*OED* urchin, *n.* 1.c.）

103. mortal body = human being who is mortal　mortal は，神々が不死であるのに対し人間が「死すべき存在の」。　body は human being の換喩。

104. straight = immediately

107. dismal yew　「恐ろしいイチイの木」墓地との連想で、イチイの木は果実が有毒で、人がその下に寝ると死ぬという迷信があった（Waith）。

108. to this miserable death　「このように惨めな死に方をするように」

111. ear「聴覚を持つ人間」の換喩。
to such effect　「そのような意味の」

112. And had you not = If you had not

113. vengeance　嫉みによる蛮行。復讐心は狂気の一種。5. 1. 58 注参照。
had they executed = they would have executed

118. Semiramis　2. 1. 22 注参照。

120. poniard　「細身の短剣」

122. more belongs to = more [value] that belongs to her

123. First thrash the corn ...「まず麦を脱穀して」　thrash = thresh「叩く / 脱穀する」は露骨なレイプのイメージ（Rubinstein）。

124. minion = mistress, paramour　もともと「お稚児（ちご）」を連想させる語。
stood upon her chastity ...　「自分の貞潔と … が頼りで / を鼻にかけて」
stand upon = rely on, depend on（*OED* stand, *v.* PV stand upon—, 4.）

128. And if = If

Drag hence her husband to some secret hole,
And make his dead trunk pillow to our lust. 130

TAMORA But when you have the honey you desire,
Let not this wasp outlive, us both to sting.

CHIRON I warrant you, madam, we will make that sure.
Come, mistress, now perforce we will enjoy
That nice-preservèd honesty of yours. 135

LAVINIA O Tamora, thou bearest a woman's face —

TAMORA I will not hear her speak. Away with her.

LAVINIA Sweet lords, entreat her hear me but a word.

DEMETRIUS Listen, fair madam. Let it be your glory
To see her tears, but be your heart to them 140
As unrelenting flint to drops of rain.

LAVINIA When did the tiger's young ones teach the dam?
O, do not learn her wrath; she taught it thee.
The milk thou suck'st from her did turn to marble.
Even at thy teat thou hadst thy tyranny. 145
Yet every mother breeds not sons alike.
[*To Chiron*] Do thou entreat her show a woman's pity.

CHIRON What, wouldst thou have me prove myself a bastard?

LAVINIA 'Tis true; the raven doth not hatch a lark.
Yet have I heard — O, could I find it now — 150
The lion, moved with pity, did endure
To have his princely paws pared all away.
Some say that ravens foster forlorn children,
The whilst their own birds famish in their nests.
O, be to me, though thy hard heart say no, 155
Nothing so kind, but something pitiful.

TAMORA I know not what it means. Away with her.

LAVINIA O, let me teach thee for my father's sake,
That gave thee life when well he might have slain thee,
Be not obdurate; open thy deaf ears. 160

TAMORA Hadst thou in person ne'er offended me,

130. pillow to our lust 「俺たちの楽しみの枕」 lust = pleasure, delight (*OED* lust, *n.* 1.)

135. nice-preservèd「大事に守っておいての」

honesty = chastity

137. Away with her = get away with her; take away her (*OED* away, *adv.* 11.)

138. Sweet = amiable; gracious

entreat her hear = entreat her to hear

140. them は her tears を指す。

141. As unrelenting flint to drops of rain 「固い石が雨粒に情を示さぬように」

142. dam 「(四肢動物の) 母獣」

143. learn = teach (*OED* learn, *v.* 4.c.)

144. marble 「大理石」 *figurative*. As a type of something hard, inflexible, durable, or smooth (*OED* marble, *n.* 1.c.) 石の硬さと表面の滑らかさのイメージ。

145. Even at thy teat 「他でもなくあなたが乳を飲んだその乳首のところで」

146. alike = in the same manner; like one another

149. the raven doth not hatch a lark ヒバリは夜明けあるいは昼間天高くへの飛翔を連想させ、黒いワタリガラスの印象と対照的。近い諺に Tilley E1 'The eagle does not hatch a dove.' (Bate)。

151-52. The lion, moved with pity, did endure / To have his princely paws pared all away 格言的。Tilley L316 'The lion spares the suppliant.' Aesop's fable 'Lion in Love.' (Hughes) 人間の女性に恋したライオンが、娘の父親から結婚の条件として脚の爪を剥がし牙を抜くことを課され、その条件に応じるが結局騙される。

153. ravens foster forlorn children 旧約聖書の列王記に神の送ったカラスが預言者エリヤを救ったという話が記されている。(1 Kings 17. 4-6) (Bate)

154. their own birds「自分の雛鳥たち」 bird = a nestling or fledgling; a chick (*OED* bird, *n.* 1.) 現在は成鳥も含めて一般に「鳥」を指すが、「雛」が元来の意味。

156. Nothing so kind, but something pitiful 「そこまで親切でなくとも、少しは哀れんで」

Even for his sake am I pitiless.
Remember, boys, I poured forth tears in vain
To save your brother from the sacrifice,
But fierce Andronicus would not relent.   165
Therefore away with her, and use her as you will;
The worse to her, the better loved of me.

LAVINIA   O Tamora, be called a gentle queen,
And with thine own hands kill me in this place!
For 'tis not life that I have begged so long;   170
Poor I was slain when Bassianus died.

TAMORA   What begg'st thou then? Fond woman, let me go.

LAVINIA   'Tis present death I beg, and one thing more
That womanhood denies my tongue to tell.
O, keep me from their worse-than-killing lust,   175
And tumble me into some loathsome pit
Where never man's eye may behold my body.
Do this, and be a charitable murderer.

TAMORA   So should I rob my sweet sons of their fee.
No, let them satisfy their lust on thee.   180

DEMETRIUS   [*To Lavinia*]   Away, for thou hast stayed us here
    too long!

LAVINIA   No grace, no womanhood? Ah, beastly creature,
The blot and enemy to our general name,
Confusion fall —

CHIRON   Nay, then, I'll stop your mouth. Bring thou her
    husband;   185
This is the hole where Aaron bid us hide him.
    [*They throw Bassianus' body in the pit, and exeunt with Lavinia*]

TAMORA   Farewell, my sons. See that you make her sure.
Ne'er let my heart know merry cheer indeed
Till all the Andronici be made away.
Now will I hence to seek my lovely Moor,   190
And let my spleenful sons this trull deflower.   *Exit*

165. would not relent 「断固として譲らなかった」 relent = yield; give up a previous resolution, obstinacy, or course of action (*OED* relent, *v.* 4.a.)

166. use = copulate with (Partridge)

167. the better loved of me 「それだけ多く私に愛される」 of = by

172. Fond = foolish

174. womanhood denies my tongue to tell この後口封じのため実際に舌を切られる運命を知らずして語っている劇的アイロニー。ギリシャ悲劇以来の手法。

176. tumble = throw or cast down

180. satisfy their lust on thee 前置詞 on は欲望の対象を示す。(*OED* on, *prep.* 24.b.)

181. thou hast stayed us 「俺たちを待たせやがった」 stay は他動詞。

183. our general name = all of us that have the name of 'woman' name は「そのような名を持つ人」を指す換喩（metonymy）。

184. Confusion fall ── = May confusion fall on thee! 言いかけた途中でラヴィニアは口を塞がれる。 confusion 「破滅」ruin, perdition (*OED* confusion, *n.* 1.a.)

189. made away = killed

190. hence 2. 3. 82 注参照。

Enter Aaron with two of Titus' sons [Quintus and Martius]

AARON   Come on, my lords, the better foot before.
  Straight will I bring you to the loathsome pit
  Where I espied the panther fast asleep.
QUINTUS   My sight is very dull, whate'er it bodes.   195
MARTIUS   And mine, I promise you. Were it not for shame,
  Well could I leave our sport to sleep awhile.   [*Falls into the pit*]
QUINTUS   What, art thou fallen? What subtle hole is this,
  Whose mouth is covered with rude-growing briers
  Upon whose leaves are drops of new-shed blood   200
  As fresh as morning dew distilled on flowers?
  A very fatal place it seems to me.
  Speak, brother! Hast thou hurt thee with the fall?
MARTIUS   O, brother, with the dismal'st object hurt
  That ever eye with sight made heart lament!   205
AARON   [*Aside*]   Now will I fetch the King to find them here,
  That he thereby may have a likely guess
  How these were they that made away his brother.   *Exit*
MARTIUS   Why dost not comfort me and help me out
  From this unhallowed and bloodstainèd hole?   210
QUINTUS   I am surprisèd with an uncouth fear.
  A chilling sweat o'erruns my trembling joints.
  My heart suspects more than mine eye can see.
MARTIUS   To prove thou hast a true-divining heart,
  Aaron and thou look down into this den   215
  And see a fearful sight of blood and death.
QUINTUS   Aaron is gone, and my compassionate heart
  Will not permit mine eyes once to behold
  The thing whereat it trembles by surmise.
  O, tell me who it is, for ne'er till now   220
  Was I a child to fear I know not what.
MARTIUS   Lord Bassianus lies berayed in blood,

192. the better foot before 「お急ぎください」格言風の表現。 Tilley F570 'To set the better foot before / best foot forward.'

195. bodes ＝ predicts; is indicative of

197. sport 「狩り」

198. subtle ＝ cunning in a treacherous way; (of the ground) uneven, 'tricky'

201. distilled 「露のように滴らせた」

203. hurt thee ＝ hurt thyself

204. dismal'st ＝ most dreadful

205. eye with sight made heart lament「目が視覚で心を嘆かせた」感覚器官など身体の部位を擬人化し、理性・意志で制御できない心理的混乱を強調する。

210. unhallowed ＝ unholy, wicked

211. surprisèd with ＝ seized with

uncouth ＝ unfamiliar, strange; uncanny

212. joints 「諸関節、四肢」

213. My heart suspects more than mine eye can see 2. 3. 205 注参照。

215. den ＝ the lair or habitation of a wild beast; a place hollowed out of the ground, a cavern (*OED* den, *n.¹* 1. and 2.)

218. not ... once ＝ never (*OED* once, *adv.* 3.a.)

219. whereat ＝ at which

surmise ＝ suspicion, imagination

221. to fear I know not what 「正体のわからぬものを怖がるような」

222. berayed ＝ disfigured, defiled

All on a heap, like to a slaughtered lamb,
In this detested, dark, blood-drinking pit.

QUINTUS If it be dark, how dost thou know 'tis he? 225

MARTIUS Upon his bloody finger he doth wear
A precious ring that lightens all this hole,
Which like a taper in some monument
Doth shine upon the dead man's earthy cheeks
And shows the ragged entrails of this pit. 230
So pale did shine the moon on Pyramus
When he by night lay bathed in maiden blood.
O, brother, help me with thy fainting hand —
If fear hath made thee faint as me it hath —
Out of this fell devouring receptacle, 235
As hateful as Cocytus' misty mouth.

QUINTUS Reach me thy hand, that I may help thee out,
Or, wanting strength to do thee so much good,
I may be plucked into the swallowing womb
Of this deep pit, poor Bassianus' grave. 240
I have no strength to pluck thee to the brink.

MARTIUS Nor I no strength to climb without thy help.

QUINTUS Thy hand once more. I will not loose again
Till thou art here aloft or I below.
Thou canst not come to me. I come to thee. *Both fall in* 245

Enter the Emperor and Aaron the Moor [with Attendants]

SATURNINUS Along with me. I'll see what hole is here
And what he is that now is leapt into it.
Say, who art thou that lately didst descend
Into this gaping hollow of the earth?

MARTIUS The unhappy sons of old Andronicus, 250
Brought hither in a most unlucky hour
To find thy brother Bassianus dead.

SATURNINUS My brother dead? I know thou dost but jest.

223. like to = like 「のように」の意味で like が後ろに to を伴うのは古風な形。シェイクスピアの英語では、このように to を従える like と現代英語と同様に to を伴わない like の両方が用いられる。

227. A precious ring that lightens 伝説的な宝石 carbuncle は暗闇で光を発するとされていた。(*OED* carbuncle, *n.* 1.a.)

228. taper 「(礼拝や祈禱用の) 蠟燭」

230. entrails of this pit 「この穴の内臓」人を喰う猛獣にこの穴を喩える。

231. Pyramus 『変身物語』第 4 巻で語られる悲恋の主人公。ピュラムスは、恋人ティスベー (Thisbe) がライオンに襲われて死んだものと誤解して自死する。ティスベーも後を追って死ぬ (*Metamorphoses*, 4. 55-166)。『夏の夜の夢』では最終場の劇中劇として機織職人ボトムが演じる。

232. maiden blood 不幸な恋人ピュラムスとティスベーは添い遂げることが叶わぬままに死んだ。

235. fell devouring receptacle 上記 2. 3. 230 注参照。
fell = treacherous; savage

236. Cocytus' misty mouth 「コーキュートスの霧深い河口」Cocytus は冥界を流れる川の 1 つ。ステュクスから枝分かれしてアケローンに注ぐ。(*Aeneis*, 6. 295-416; *Odysseia*, 10. 508-15)

239. the swallowing womb 「人を呑み込む腹」多様な解釈を可能にするこの劇の身体的イメージの 1 つ。古典的なヘカベー伝説とタモラに共通する子を殺された母による復讐のテーマや深層心理で言う「不在の母」の連想などは容易なはず。終局で「復讐への復讐」としてタイタスが計画・実行する残忍な復讐方法の、凄惨なイメージにも繋がる。さらにはピロメーラの姉プロクネーが自分の子を殺してレイプ犯の夫テーレウスに食わせる話が、この劇に通底するオウィディウス的ギリシャ神話として影を落としている。

womb = belly; stomach, bowels　もともと「子宮 (uterus)」に限らず「胃」や「腸」を含めて「腹」一般を指した。またシェイクスピア時代の大衆劇場では舞台中央部に落とし戸 (trapdoor) があったと推測されているが、それが第 1 幕の墓やこの場の落とし穴として使用されるとともに、この芝居のある種のテーマを終始視覚的に象徴し続けるような演出・上演なども想像できる。

241. pluck 「ぐいと引っ張る」

243. loose = let loose; unclasp (*OED* loose, *v.* 2.c.)

He and his lady both are at the lodge
Upon the north side of this pleasant chase.   255
'Tis not an hour since I left them there.
MARTIUS   We know not where you left them all alive,
But, out alas, here have we found him dead.

Enter Tamora, [Titus] Andronicus, and Lucius

TAMORA   Where is my lord the King?
SATURNINUS   Here, Tamora, though grieved with killing grief.   260
TAMORA   Where is thy brother Bassianus?
SATURNINUS   Now to the bottom dost thou search my wound.
Poor Bassianus here lies murderèd.
TAMORA   Then all too late I bring this fatal writ,
The complot of this timeless tragedy,   265
And wonder greatly that man's face can fold
In pleasing smiles such murderous tyranny.
                                        She giveth Saturnine a letter
SATURNINUS   *Reads the letter*
'An if we miss to meet him handsomely,
Sweet huntsman — Bassianus 'tis we mean —
Do thou so much as dig the grave for him;   270
Thou know'st our meaning. Look for thy reward
Among the nettles at the elder tree
Which overshades the mouth of that same pit
Where we decreed to bury Bassianus.
Do this, and purchase us thy lasting friends.'   275
O Tamora, was ever heard the like?
This is the pit, and this the elder tree.
Look, sirs, if you can find the huntsman out
That should have murdered Bassianus here.
AARON   My gracious lord, here is the bag of gold.   280
SATURNINUS   *[To Titus]*   Two of thy whelps, fell curs of bloody
    kind,

255. chase 2.2.21 注参照。

256. 'Tis not an hour 「1時間も経っていない」

258. out 悲しみ、嫌悪、怒りなどを表わす感嘆詞。(*OED* out, *int.* 1.)

260. grieved = vexed

262. search my wound 「(患部を診断するために) 私の傷口を探る」

264. fatal writ 「殺しの企みを書き記したもの」

265. complot = a design of a covert nature planned in concert; a conspiracy「陰謀、謀議」

timeless = untimely「予期せぬ時に起こる、早すぎる」

266. fold 「〜をつつみ隠す」

268. An if = If

handsomely = fittingly, properly (*OED* handsomely, *adv.* 1.)

272. the elder tree 「ニワトコ」ユダがその木で首を吊ったという伝説を連想させる不吉なイメージ (Berthoud)。

273. overshades = casts a shadow over

274. decreed = decided

275. purchase us thy lasting friends 「我らを永遠の友人として手に入れよ」
purchase = acquire, obtain 現在の「贖う、購入する」という意味の他に、古くは支払い・代償に関わりなく一般に「獲得する」の意味で使われた。

276. the like 「それと似たようなこと」

279. should have murdered 「殺したはず」

281. kind = nature, character (*OED* kind, *n.*1.)

Have here bereft my brother of his life.
Sirs, drag them from the pit unto the prison.
There let them bide until we have devised
Some never-heard-of torturing pain for them.   285
TAMORA   What, are they in this pit? O wondrous thing!
How easily murder is discoverèd.

[Attendants pull Quintus, Martius, and Bassianus's
body from the pit]

TITUS   [*Kneels*]   High Emperor, upon my feeble knee
I beg this boon with tears not lightly shed,
That this fell fault of my accursèd sons,   290
Accursèd if the faults be proved in them —
SATURNINUS   If it be proved? You see it is apparent.
Who found this letter? Tamora, was it you?
TAMORA   Andronicus himself did take it up.
TITUS   I did, my lord, yet let me be their bail,   295
For by my father's reverend tomb I vow
They shall be ready at your highness' will
To answer their suspicion with their lives.
SATURNINUS   Thou shalt not bail them. See thou follow me.
Some bring the murdered body, some the murderers.   300
Let them not speak a word. The guilt is plain.
For, by my soul, were there worse end than death,
That end upon them should be executed.
TAMORA   Andronicus, I will entreat the King.
Fear not thy sons; they shall do well enough.   305
TITUS   [*Rising*]   Come, Lucius, come. Stay not to talk with
them.

Exeunt

[ACT II SCENE IV]

Enter the Empress' sons, Demetrius and Chiron, with Lavinia, her

282. bereft = deprived, robbed

284. bide = wait, remain

289. boon = gift, favour

295. bail 「保釈のための保証人」

299. See thou follow me タモラに呼びかけている。

302. end = a mode or manner of death (*OED* end, *n.* 8.b.)

death 「死」で「処刑（death penalty, execution）」を意味する換喩。話し手の粗暴で大雑把な思考様式が現れる例。

305. Fear not thy sons; they shall do well enough サターナイナスと対照的に機知に富むタモラのアイロニー。 Fear not は「心配なさるな」の意味だが曖昧。 they shall do well enough の do にも多様な含みがある。

〔2. 4〕あらすじ……………………………………………………………………………………

　ディミートリアスとカイロンが舌を切られ両手を切断されたラヴィニアを連れて登場し、彼女に嘲笑を浴びせて置き去りにする。そこでタイタスの弟マーカスが無残な姿になった自分の姪を見つけ、連れて帰る。

……………………………………………………………………………………………………

hands cut off, and her tongue cut out, and ravished

DEMETRIUS   So, now go tell, an if thy tongue can speak,
  Who 'twas that cut thy tongue and ravished thee.
CHIRON   Write down thy mind; bewray thy meaning so,
  An if thy stumps will let thee play the scribe.
DEMETRIUS   See how with signs and tokens she can scrowl.   5
CHIRON   Go home. Call for sweet water; wash thy hands.
DEMETRIUS   She hath no tongue to call, nor hands to wash;
  And so let's leave her to her silent walks.
CHIRON   An 'twere my cause, I should go hang myself.
DEMETRIUS   If thou hadst hands to help thee knit the cord.   10

Exeunt

Wind horns. Enter Marcus from hunting

MARCUS   Who is this? My niece, that flies away so fast?
  Cousin, a word. Where is your husband?
  If I do dream, would all my wealth would wake me.
  If I do wake, some planet strike me down
  That I may slumber an eternal sleep.   15
  Speak, gentle niece. What stern ungentle hands
  Hath lopped and hewed and made thy body bare
  Of her two branches, those sweet ornaments
  Whose circling shadows kings have sought to sleep in,
  And might not gain so great a happiness   20
  As half thy love? Why dost not speak to me?
  Alas, a crimson river of warm blood,
  Like to a bubbling fountain stirred with wind,
  Doth rise and fall between thy rosèd lips,
  Coming and going with thy honey breath.   25
  But sure some Tereus hath deflowered thee,
  And lest thou shouldst detect him cut thy tongue.
  Ah, now thou turn'st away thy face for shame,

2. 'twas = it was

3. bewray = reveal, disclose

4. stumps 「手を切り落とされた両腕の残り部分」（*OED* stump, *n.*[1] 1.a.）

　play the scribe 「書記の真似をして遊ぶ、演じる」

6. sweet water = fresh water （*OED* sweet, *adj.* 3.b.）

9. An 'twere = If it were

10 SD. *from hunting* 「狩りの場から来たという出で立ちで」

12. Cousin 現代の従兄弟・従姉妹に限らず、兄弟よりも遠い親戚一般を指す。

13-55. If I do dream ... tears thy father's eyes? 場違いに詩的な台詞だという批判が多かった箇所。上演でまるまる削除あるいは短く切られる場合が多いが、デボラ・ウォーナーの演出（1987/88）では、マーカス役のアラン・ウェッブが原文通りの台詞で舞台を成功させたという（Dessen）。嫌われる真の理由は、「詩的」であるということよりも、性暴力被害者の傷と痛みをその長い台詞の間まともに目撃させられることにあるのかもしれない。『タイタス・アンドロニカス』は、得てして誤解される「流血のエンターテインメント」でなく、観客に残虐行為の被害者たちの苦痛を直視・共感させる悲劇であったと考えるべきか。台詞をカットせずに演じるならば、マーカス役の俳優の技量が試される。台詞にどのようなイデオロギーを読み込むかは、多くの場合において受容の問題。

13. would all my wealth would wake me 「私の全財産を賭けてでも（この悪夢から）目覚めさせてくれ」 would ... = I wish that ...

14. If I do wake 「もし（これが夢でなく）私がいま目覚めているのならば」

　some planets strike me down 「いずれかの惑星が私を打ちのめしてくれ」惑星の運行が人間界に影響を与え、人間界の出来事を支配すると信じられた。

15. That I may = so that I may

16. stern = merciless, cruel

　ungentle = harsh, violent

17. lopped and hewed 「（両手を）乱暴に切り落とした」 lop「（枝などを）切り落とす」 hew「（斧などで木を）切り倒す」

18. her 「お前の身体の」身体を木に喩え、その木を女性と見做す。

19. Whose circling shadows 「丸く包んでくれるようなその（枝の）木陰」

20. might not = could not

24. rosèd = rose-coloured

26. some Tereus 「テーレウスのような暴漢」2. 3. 43 注参照。

　deflowered = ravished

27. detect him = expose him by making known his guilt; accuse him「その男の罪を公にして訴える」

111

And notwithstanding all this loss of blood,
As from a conduit with three issuing spouts,   30
Yet do thy cheeks look red as Titan's face,
Blushing to be encountered with a cloud.
Shall I speak for thee, shall I say 'tis so?
O, that I knew thy heart, and knew the beast,
That I might rail at him to ease my mind.   35
Sorrow concealèd, like an oven stopped,
Doth burn the heart to cinders where it is.
Fair Philomela, why she but lost her tongue,
And in a tedious sampler sewed her mind;
But, lovely niece, that mean is cut from thee.   40
A craftier Tereus, cousin, hast thou met,
And he hath cut those pretty fingers off
That could have better sewed than Philomel.
O, had the monster seen those lily hands
Tremble like aspen leaves upon a lute   45
And make the silken strings delight to kiss them,
He would not then have touched them for his life.
Or had he heard the heavenly harmony
Which that sweet tongue hath made,
He would have dropped his knife and fell asleep,   50
As Cerberus at the Thracian poet's feet.
Come, let us go and make thy father blind,
For such a sight will blind a father's eye.
One hour's storm will drown the fragrant meads;
What will whole months of tears thy father's eyes?   55
Do not draw back, for we will mourn with thee.
O, could our mourning ease thy misery!

Exeunt

30. conduit 「(庭園などに作られる) 噴水」(*OED* conduit, *n*. 2.a.)

spouts = nozzles「噴水の吹き出し口」

31. Titan's face 「太陽面」1. 1. 227 注参照。

32. to be encountered with a cloud 「雲に襲われて」

33. Shall I speak for thee ...? この芝居に通底するテーマの1つ。

35. That I might = so that I might

36-37. Sorrow concealèd, like an oven stopped ... 姪の痛みへの共感と苛立ちを台所の竈という身辺的比喩で表わす。

37. where it is 「動けずに留まったまま」

38. Fair Philomela 「美しいピロメーラ」Philomela は Philomel (2. 4. 43) のラテン語原形。英詩では韻律に合わせて両者を自由に使い分ける。

why 感嘆詞。

but lost = only lost

39. in a tedious sampler sewed her mind 「手間のかかる面倒な刺繍に自分の思いを縫い込んだ」 ⇒後注

40. mean = method; trick, contrivance 監禁されたピロメーラは、テーレウスの目を欺き、問題の織物を姉プロクネーのもとへ届けさせて犯行を暴く。

41. A craftier Tereus 「テーレウスより狡猾な男 (レイプ犯)」

42-46. those pretty fingers ... to kiss them 切り落とされる前のラヴィニアの手の繊細な動きを、視覚的・音楽的に想起させる一節。

44. lily 白、美しさ、純粋さの象徴。

45. like aspen leaves 「ポプラの葉のように」 **lute** 「リュート」16・17世紀の詩や絵画の中にしばしば現れる絃楽器。官能的な、またシェイクスピアのソネット (Sonnet 8) では、結婚の幸福と家族の調和のイメージ。

46. delight = be very pleased (*OED* delight, *v*. 2.a.)

48-49. the heavenly harmony ... sweet tongue hath made 「あの愛らしい舌が奏でた天上のハーモニー」幾重にも重なる天球に天使が座し、それらが回転して妙なる音楽を奏でるというのが、伝統的な宇宙の調和のイメージ。

51. As Cerberus at the Thracian poet's feet 「ケルベロスがトラキアの詩人 (オルペウス) の足元で」ギリシャ神話で、竪琴の名手で詩人のオルフェウスは死んだ妻を取り戻しに冥界 (Erebus) へ下る。ケルベロスは冥界の入り口を見張る番犬で、3つの頭を持つ (Vergilius, *Georgica*, 4. 453-527)。

54. meads = meadows

57. O, could our mourning ...! = O that our mourning could ...! 祈願文。

[ACT III SCENE I]

Enter the Judges and Senators with Titus' two sons [Quintus and
Martius] bound, passing on the stage to the place of execution,
and Titus going before, pleading

TITUS   Hear me, grave fathers; noble tribunes, stay.
 For pity of mine age, whose youth was spent
 In dangerous wars whilst you securely slept;
 For all my blood in Rome's great quarrel shed,
 For all the frosty nights that I have watched,   5
 And for these bitter tears which now you see,
 Filling the agèd wrinkles in my cheeks,
 Be pitiful to my condemnèd sons,
 Whose souls is not corrupted as 'tis thought.
 For two-and-twenty sons I never wept   10
 Because they died in honour's lofty bed.

Andronicus lieth down, and the Judges pass by him

 For these, tribunes, in the dust I write
 My heart's deep languor and my soul's sad tears.
 Let my tears stanch the earth's dry appetite.
 My sons' sweet blood will make it shame and blush.   15
 O Earth, I will befriend thee more with rain

Exeunt [the Judges]

 That shall distil from these two ancient ruins
 Than youthful April shall with all his showers.
 In summer's drought I'll drop upon thee still;
 In winter with warm tears I'll melt the snow   20
 And keep eternal springtime on thy face,
 So thou refuse to drink my dear sons' blood.

Enter Lucius with his weapon drawn

 O reverend tribunes, O gentle agèd men,

〔**3.1**〕あらすじ‥‥‥‥‥‥‥‥‥‥‥‥‥‥‥‥‥‥‥‥‥‥‥‥‥‥‥‥‥‥‥‥‥‥

　タイタスは裁判官と元老院議員たちに息子２人の赦免を嘆願するが聞き入れ
られない。そこへ無惨な姿のラヴィニアがマーカスに連れられて登場し、タイタ
スの悲嘆が極に達する。さらにエアロンが皇帝の使いと称して登場し、タイタス
かその近親者が片腕を切って献上すれば２人の息子を赦免すると告げる。タイ
タスは自分の腕を切って差し出す。実はそれが陰謀で、代わりに２人の生首が
送り返される。アンドロニカス一族は復讐を誓う。一方でタイタスの長男ルーシ
アスは、ゴート族を率いて再起を図るべくローマを離れる。

‥‥

0 SD. *passing on the stage* ＝ *passing over the stage*　舞台奥両脇にある出入
り口の一方から行列が入場して、舞台を行進して回り、もう一方の出入り口か
ら退場する。スペクタクルを強調する舞台技法。

3. securely 「何の心配もなく安心して、安全に」

4. quarrel ＝ cause「大義」（*OED* quarrel, *n.²* 2.）

5. watched ＝ kept vigil

9. souls is ＝ souls are　主語の数と定動詞形が合致しない場合もある。

13. languor ＝ grief, sorrow

14. stanch ＝ quench, extinguish

16. befriend ＝ act as a friend to; favour

17. distil 「滴り落ちる」

　two ancient ruins 「２つの古い廃墟」老いた自分の両目を指すメタファー。
　3. 1. 208 注参照。　ancient ＝ going far back in history; of living beings:
　that have lived many years; aged（*OED* ancient, *adj.* 6.）

22. So ＝ so long as

Unbind my sons, reverse the doom of death,
And let me say, that never wept before, 25
My tears are now prevailing orators.

LUCIUS   O noble father, you lament in vain.
The Tribunes hear you not; no man is by,
And you recount your sorrows to a stone.

TITUS   Ah, Lucius, for thy brothers let me plead. 30
Grave tribunes, once more I entreat of you.

LUCIUS   My gracious lord, no tribune hears you speak.

TITUS   Why, 'tis no matter, man. If they did hear,
They would not mark me; if they did mark,
They would not pity me. Yet plead I must, 35
And bootless unto them.
Therefore I tell my sorrows to the stones,
Who, though they cannot answer my distress,
Yet in some sort they are better than the Tribunes,
For that they will not intercept my tale. 40
When I do weep, they humbly at my feet
Receive my tears and seem to weep with me,
And were they but attirèd in grave weeds,
Rome could afford no tribunes like to these.
A stone is soft as wax, tribunes more hard than stones; 45
A stone is silent and offendeth not,
And tribunes with their tongues doom men to death.
But wherefore stand'st thou with thy weapon drawn?

LUCIUS   To rescue my two brothers from their death,
For which attempt the Judges have pronounced 50
My everlasting doom of banishment.

TITUS   O happy man, they have befriended thee!
Why, foolish Lucius, dost thou not perceive
That Rome is but a wilderness of tigers?
Tigers must prey, and Rome affords no prey 55
But me and mine. How happy art thou then

26. prevailing orators 「優れた弁論家たち」

29. recount ... to a stone 「石にくどくど話すようなもの」続くタイタスとの会話は格言を踏まえている。Tilley S877 'As deaf as a Stone'; S878 'As hard as a Stone.' Cf. *Richard III*, 3. 7 'I am not made of stones, / But penetrable to your kind entreaties'; *King Lear*, 5. 3 'O, you are men of stones.'

31. Grave = respected

33. 'tis no matter = it is of no consequence or importance「それは重要でない、どのみち同じことだ」(*OED* matter, *n*[1]. 14.)

36. bootless = bootlessly; unsuccessfully, uselessly

40. For that = for   **intercept** = interrupt

43. were they but attirèd in grave weeds 「彼らがいかめしい(護民官の)服さえ着ていたら」   weeds = garments

44. afford = supply, offer   **like to** = like   2. 3. 223 注参照。

48. wherefore = for what; why

52. befriended thee 「お前に親切なことをしてくれた」3. 1. 16 注参照。

54. Rome is but a wilderness of tigers 「ローマは虎が跋扈する荒野にすぎない」虎は英詩でも古くから残忍あるいは激しい人物の比喩として諺的に用いられる。Chaucer, *The Squire's Tale*, 419-21 'That ther nys tygre, ne noon so crueel beest / That dwelleth outher in wode or in forest, / That nolde han wept, if that he wepe koude'(虎にせよ、森や林に棲む他の獰猛な獣にせよ、もし泣くことができたなら泣かないものはなかっただろう). 伝統的メタファーの応用でありながら舞台で効果的であるのは、文明都市ローマを荒野であるかのように虎が跋扈するという視覚的イメージが衝撃的であるため。この他には、薔薇戦争を扱ったシェイクスピア初期の歴史劇『ヘンリー六世・第三部』で、捕虜となったヨーク公リチャードが自分をいたぶるマーガレット王妃の残虐さに耐えかねて言った台詞 'O, tiger's heart wrapped in a woman's hide' (*Henry VI, Part 3*, 1. 4) が、若いシェイクスピアが創作した虎のイメージとして有名。

From these devourers to be banishèd.
But who comes with our brother Marcus here?

Enter Marcus with Lavinia

MARCUS   Titus, prepare thy agèd eyes to weep,
  Or, if not so, thy noble heart to break.   60
  I bring consuming sorrow to thine age.
TITUS   Will it consume me? Let me see it, then.
MARCUS   This was thy daughter.
TITUS   Why, Marcus, so she is.
LUCIUS   Ay me, this object kills me.   65
TITUS   Faint-hearted boy, arise and look upon her.
  Speak, Lavinia, what accursèd hand
  Hath made thee handless in thy father's sight?
  What fool hath added water to the sea
  Or brought a faggot to bright-burning Troy?   70
  My grief was at the height before thou cam'st,
  And now like Nilus it disdaineth bounds.
  Give me a sword. I'll chop off my hands too,
  For they have fought for Rome and all in vain;
  And they have nursed this woe in feeding life;   75
  In bootless prayer have they been held up,
  And they have served me to effectless use.
  Now all the service I require of them
  Is that the one will help to cut the other.
  'Tis well, Lavinia, that thou hast no hands,   80
  For hands to do Rome service is but vain.
LUCIUS   Speak, gentle sister. Who hath martyred thee?
MARCUS   O, that delightful engine of her thoughts,
  That blabbed them with such pleasing eloquence,
  Is torn from forth that pretty hollow cage   85
  Where, like a sweet melodious bird, it sung
  Sweet varied notes, enchanting every ear.

59. prepare thy agèd eyes to weep 「兄さんの老いぼれた眼に泣く準備をさせなさい」心が受ける衝撃を身体の一器官のできごとであるかのように語る。眼・心臓など身体の器官を人格化する比喩は、シェイクスピアの詩『ルークリースの陵辱』『ソネット集』などに多く見られる。例えば *The Rape of Lucrece*, 435-36 'His drumming heart cheers up his burning eye; / His eye commends the leading to his hand ...'; Sonnet 47, 3-4 'When that mine eye is famished for a look, / Or heart in love with sighs himself doth smother ...'

61. consuming sorrow to thine age 「燃やし尽くすような悲しみをお前の老齢に」thee の代わりに thine age と言い、老齢の親が子を失う悲哀を強調する。寓意になりがちな抽象的概念を用いて、逆に心理的リアリズムを生み出す。

64. Why ... so she is. 「なんだと、今だってそうだ」

65. object = something placed before the eyes (*OED* object, *n.* 1.)

69. added water to the sea 諺的。Tilley W106 'To cast water into the sea.' the sea は涙に掻き暮れるタイタス自身の眼を指す。

70. bright-burning Troy トロイアー落城の物語は、トロイアー王家最後の王プリアモスと妃へカベーが多くの子を次々と失う話でもある。

72. Nilus = the river Nile
disdaineth bounds 大河が堤防を越えて氾濫する光景に擬えるメタファー。disdaineth「軽蔑する、歯牙にも掛けない」は涙・河川を人格化した言い方。-eth の形については 1. 1. 109 注参照。

75. in feeding life 「生きるためにと食物を口に運んで」

82. martyred = tormented; mutilated martyr *v.* 原義は「殉教させる」で、それを「(身体を)切り刻む」の意味に使用するのは換喩。純潔・貞節を至上と見做すアンドロニカス一族の家風も思わせる。(*OED* martyr, *v.* 1.c. and 2.b.) 1. 1. 168 注参照。

83-84. that delightful engine of her thoughts, / That blabbed them with such pleasing eloquence 「彼女の思いを声にするあの楽しい道具、あんなに心地よい雄弁で自分の思いをお喋りした」雄弁と思想を若い女性ラヴィニアの魅力・美点としている。
engine = implement, tool (*OED* engine, *n.* 4.)
blab = chatter, babble (*OED* blab, *v.* 1)

85. hollow cage 口蓋を鳥籠に喩える。

86. sung sing の過去形。

Lucius O, say thou for her, who hath done this deed?

Marcus O, thus I found her straying in the park,
Seeking to hide herself as doth the deer   90
That hath received some unrecuring wound.

Titus It was my dear, and he that wounded her
Hath hurt me more than had he killed me dead.
For now I stand as one upon a rock,
Environed with a wilderness of sea,   95
Who marks the waxing tide grow wave by wave,
Expecting ever when some envious surge
Will in his brinish bowels swallow him.
This way to death my wretched sons are gone;
Here stands my other son a banished man,   100
And here my brother, weeping at my woes.
But that which gives my soul the greatest spurn
Is dear Lavinia, dearer than my soul.
Had I but seen thy picture in this plight
It would have madded me. What shall I do,   105
Now I behold thy lively body so?
Thou hast no hands to wipe away thy tears,
Nor tongue to tell me who hath martyred thee.
Thy husband he is dead, and for his death
Thy brothers are condemned, and dead by this.   110
Look, Marcus! Ah, son Lucius, look on her!
When I did name her brothers, then fresh tears
Stood on her cheeks as doth the honeydew
Upon a gathered lily almost withered.

Marcus Perchance she weeps because they killed her
husband,   115
Perchance because she knows them innocent.

Titus If they did kill thy husband, then be joyful,
Because the law hath ta'en revenge on them.
No, no, they would not do so foul a deed.

91. unrecuring = incurable「治ることのない」

94-98. For now I stand ... in his brinish bowels swallow him　荒海を前にして岸壁に立つ男のイメージ。次々と自分の家族を襲う難儀と悲惨な現実に打ちのめされるタイタスの心理を映す光景であるとともに、昨日まで美しい盛りであった娘が無残な姿に変貌してしまったことに万物の避けがたい変転を思い知る瞬間のイメージでもある。後者はおそらくオウィディウスから。この種のイメージとしてはシェイクスピアの後年の詩集『ソネット集（*The Sonnets*)』に最も重要な例が見られる。そこでは海の光景を目に浮かべながら万物の無常・変転を嘆く視点において、ソネット詩人シェイクスピアと古代ローマの詩人オウィディウスと古代ギリシャの哲学者ピュータゴラース（Pythagoras）の視線が劇的に重なる。*Metamorphoses*, 15. 177-85; Shakespeare, Sonnets 60 and 64. また『タイタス・アンドロニカス』の海のイメージには、セネカの悲劇『ヒッポリュトゥス（*Hippolytus*)』の影響も指摘されている（Burrow)。

95. Environed = surrounded

　　wilderness of sea　「荒涼と広がる海」（*OED* wilderness, *n.* 2.)

96. Who　関係代名詞。先行詞は 94 行の one。

97. envious surge　「悪意のある高波」（*OED* envious, *adj.* 2.)

98. his　現代英語の its にあたる。

102. spurn = a kick「足蹴」

105. madded = maddened

106. lively = living

108. martyred　3. 1. 82 注参照。

110. by this　「今頃はもう」

113. Stood = were placed; rested

　　honeydew　「蜜」

Witness the sorrow that their sister makes. 120
Gentle Lavinia, let me kiss thy lips,
Or make some sign how I may do thee ease.
Shall thy good uncle and thy brother Lucius
And thou and I sit round about some fountain,
Looking all downwards to behold our cheeks, 125
How they are stained like meadows yet not dry
With miry slime left on them by a flood?
And in the fountain shall we gaze so long
Till the fresh taste be taken from that clearness
And made a brine pit with our bitter tears? 130
Or shall we cut away our hands like thine?
Or shall we bite our tongues and in dumb shows
Pass the remainder of our hateful days?
What shall we do? Let us that have our tongues
Plot some device of further misery 135
To make us wondered at in time to come.

LUCIUS   Sweet father, cease your tears, for at your grief
See how my wretched sister sobs and weeps.

MARCUS   Patience, dear niece. Good Titus, dry thine eyes.

TITUS   Ah, Marcus, Marcus! Brother, well I wot 140
Thy napkin cannot drink a tear of mine,
For thou, poor man, hast drowned it with thine own.

LUCIUS   Ah, my Lavinia, I will wipe thy cheeks.

TITUS   Mark, Marcus, mark. I understand her signs.
Had she a tongue to speak, now would she say 145
That to her brother which I said to thee.
His napkin, with his true tears all bewet,
Can do no service on her sorrowful cheeks.
O, what a sympathy of woe is this,
As far from help as limbo is from bliss. 150

Enter Aaron the Moor alone

126-27. like meadows yet not dry / With miry slime left on them by a flood
　牧草地・降水の比喩は若いシェイクスピアに特徴的なイメージ。例えば小叙事詩（epyllion）と呼ばれる形式で書かれた官能的物語詩『ヴィーナスとアドーニス』(1593) では、アドーニスへの報われぬ想いに女神ヴィーナス（＝ウェヌス）の瞼から水晶のように透き通った涙（crystal tide）が押さえがたく溢れ出る様を、大雨による増水が耕地の用水路の水門（sluices / floodgates ）を押し開けて流れ出す光景に喩える。*Venus and Adonis*, 955-60 'Here, overcome as one full of despair, / She vailed her eyelids, who like sluices stopped / The crystal tide, that from her two cheeks fair / In the sweet channel of her bosom dropped; / But through the floodgates breaks the silver rain, / And his strong course opens them again.'

127. miry slime　「ねば土」

130. brine pit　「塩水だらけの穴」

132. dumb shows　「(芝居の初めに演じられる短い) 黙劇」Cf. *Hamlet*, 3. 2

135-36. Plot some device of further misery / To make us wondered　前項に続き演劇的メタファー。　device 「筋書き」

140-41. well I wot / Thy napkin ...　テクスト内に埋め込まれたト書き（embedded stage direction）。マーカスがハンカチを差し出すアクションがこの台詞に含意されているものと読む。　wot = 2. 1. 48 注参照。

142. drowned = drenched

146. which　先行詞は That。

150. as limbo is from bliss　「冥界から天国まで（の距離）と同じほどに」limbo は地獄との境目にあるとされる領域だが、ここは近接関係にあるものを喩える換喩で「冥界（Hades）」を指す。(*OED* limbo, *n.*¹1.c.)　bliss は「天国（heaven）」の換喩。異教的世界像とキリスト教的世界像との混在は、他のシェイクスピア劇にもしばしば見られるアナクロニズムの例。この劇ではそれが特に頻繁に見られ、その自由奔放な縦横無尽さはたまたまの錯誤とは言えない。意図して非歴史的なものを提示しているのであろうか。4. 2. 72 注参照。
⇒解説 10-15 頁

AARON   Titus Andronicus, my lord the Emperor
  Sends thee this word, that if thou love thy sons,
  Let Marcus, Lucius, or thyself, old Titus,
  Or any one of you, chop off your hand
  And send it to the King; he for the same   155
  Will send thee hither both thy sons alive,
  And that shall be the ransom for their fault.
TITUS   O gracious emperor! O gentle Aaron!
  Did ever raven sing so like a lark,
  That gives sweet tidings of the sun's uprise?   160
  With all my heart I'll send the Emperor my hand.
  Good Aaron, wilt thou help to chop it off?
LUCIUS   Stay, father, for that noble hand of thine,
  That hath thrown down so many enemies,
  Shall not be sent. My hand will serve the turn.   165
  My youth can better spare my blood than you,
  And therefore mine shall save my brothers' lives.
MARCUS   Which of your hands hath not defended Rome
  And reared aloft the bloody battleax,
  Writing destruction on the enemy's castle?   170
  O, none of both but are of high desert.
  My hand hath been but idle; let it serve
  To ransom my two nephews from their death;
  Then have I kept it to a worthy end.
AARON   Nay, come, agree whose hand shall go along, 175
  For fear they die before their pardon come.
MARCUS   My hand shall go.
LUCIUS   By heaven, it shall not go!
TITUS   Sirs, strive no more. Such withered herbs as these
  Are meet for plucking up, and therefore mine.
LUCIUS   Sweet father, if I shall be thought thy son, 180
  Let me redeem my brothers both from death.
MARCUS   And for our father's sake and mother's care,

155. the same ＝ the aforesaid thing; the equivalent of the personal pronoun *it* (*OED* same, *pron.* 4.a.)

157. ransom キリストによる罪の贖いを指す言葉であり、エアロンがそれを悪意のアイロニーを込めて使用するのは冒瀆（Waith）。

159. raven ... like a lark 2. 3. 149 注参照。

166. spare my blood 「血を流しても持ちこたえられる」（松岡訳）

170. Writing destruction on the enemy's castle 「敵の城に破壊の跡を刻んで」

171. none of both but are of high desert ＝ both of them are of high desert

176. For fear they die ＝ lest they should die

178. withered herbs 「枯れて萎んだ草」タイタスの老化した両手を指すメタファー。植物・園芸・耕作の多様なメタファーはシェイクスピアが頻繁に使用する詩的イメージ群。例えば、Sonnet 5. 7-8 'Sap check'd with frost and lusty leaves quite gone, / Beauty o'ersnow'd and bareness every where.'

179. meet ＝ suitable

182. for our father's sake and mother's care 「父の大義と母の慈しみのために」機能的には for our caring parents' sake とほぼ同義のレトリカルな表現。for one's sake の sake には suit, cause, action などの含みがある。（*OED* sake, *n.¹* 1.）mother's care への言及は、逆に『リア王』などの場合と同様に、母の不在とその寂寞とした心象風景を連想させる。

Now let me show a brother's love to thee.

TITUS   Agree between you; I will spare my hand.

LUCIUS   Then I'll go fetch an axe.   185

MARCUS   But I will use the axe.   *Exeunt [Lucius and Marcus]*

TITUS   Come hither, Aaron. I'll deceive them both.

Lend me thy hand, and I will give thee mine.

AARON   [*Aside*]   If that be called deceit, I will be honest

And never whilst I live deceive men so.   190

But I'll deceive you in another sort,

And that you'll say ere half an hour pass.

He cuts off Titus' hand

Enter Lucius and Marcus again

TITUS   Now stay your strife; what shall be is dispatched.

Good Aaron, give his majesty my hand.

Tell him it was a hand that warded him   195

From thousand dangers. Bid him bury it.

More hath it merited; that let it have.

As for my sons, say I account of them

As jewels purchased at an easy price,

And yet dear, too, because I bought mine own.   200

AARON   I go, Andronicus, and for thy hand

Look by and by to have thy sons with thee.

[*Aside*]   Their heads, I mean. O, how this villainy

Doth fat me with the very thoughts of it!

Let fools do good and fair men call for grace;   205

Aaron will have his soul black like his face.   *Exit*

TITUS   [*Kneels*]   O, here I lift this one hand up to heaven,

And bow this feeble ruin to the earth.

If any power pities wretched tears,

To that I call. What, wouldst thou kneel with me?   210

Do, then, dear heart, for heaven shall hear our prayers,

Or with our sighs we'll breathe the welkin dim

190. never whilst I live deceive men so 「俺は断じて、そんな風には人を騙さ<ruby>ない<rt>だま</rt></ruby>」

192. that 「俺に騙されたと」

ere half an hour pass 「半時も経たぬうちに」 ere = before

193. dispatched = accomplished, settled

195-96. warded him / From = defended him from

197. that = burial

198. say = tell the Emperor that

202. Look = expect, hope

by and by = before long; soon

204. fat = make fat, fatten

205. fair = agreeable; honest

208. this feeble ruin 「この弱り果てた廃墟」タイタス自身の老体を指すメタファー。 ruin = the state or condition of collapse or downfall 傷ついた自分の身体を破壊された都市や建造物の光景に擬えると同時に、ローマの凱旋将軍としての栄光から失墜し、無力で惨めな父親となった今の境遇を嘆く。タイタスは先に自分の両目を two ancient ruins と呼んでいる（3. 1. 17）。

209. wretched tears 「哀れな涙」涙の一語で泣く人自身に擬える、よくある換喩。

211. dear heart 娘ラヴィニアへの呼びかけ。 heart = as a term of endearment: a loved one（*OED* heart, *n*. 21.）

212. with our sighs we'll breathe the welkin dim 「俺たちが嘆く息で天空を曇らせる」 welkin = the sky, the firmament

And stain the sun with fog, as sometime clouds
When they do hug him in their melting bosoms.

MARCUS O brother, speak with possibility,   215
And do not break into these deep extremes.

TITUS Is not my sorrow deep, having no bottom?
Then be my passions bottomless with them.

MARCUS But yet let reason govern thy lament.

TITUS If there were reason for these miseries,   220
Then into limits could I bind my woes.
When heaven doth weep, doth not the earth o'erflow?
If the winds rage, doth not the sea wax mad,
Threat'ning the welkin with his big-swoll'n face?
And wilt thou have a reason for this coil?   225
I am the sea. Hark how her sighs doth flow!
She is the weeping welkin, I the earth.
Then must my sea be movèd with her sighs;
Then must my earth with her continual tears
Become a deluge, overflowed and drowned,   230
Forwhy my bowels cannot hide her woes
But like a drunkard must I vomit them.
Then give me leave, for losers will have leave
To ease their stomachs with their bitter tongues.

Enter a Messenger with two heads and a hand

MESSENGER Worthy Andronicus, ill art thou repaid   235
For that good hand thou sent'st the Emperor.
Here are the heads of thy two noble sons,
And here's thy hand in scorn to thee sent back.
Thy grief their sports, thy resolution mocked,
That woe is me to think upon thy woes   240
More than remembrance of my father's death.   *Exit*

MARCUS Now let hot Etna cool in Sicily,
And be my heart an ever-burning hell!

214. hug him in their melting bosoms 「（涙となって）溶ける自分の胸に彼（＝太陽）を抱きしめる」悲嘆する家族を、太陽を覆い隠す雨雲に喩える。

218. them ＝ sorrow 代名詞と名詞で数が一致しない例もたまにある。

221. Then into limits could I bind my woes 「（そんなことがありうるなら）俺の嘆きを節度のうちに縛っておくこともできるだろう」

222. o'erflow ＝ flood「洪水になる」o'er- は over- の v が落ちた形。韻律的に後者よりも1音節少なく数える。

223. wax mad「膨れ上がって狂う」 wax ＝ grow, increase

224. his big-swoll'n face 荒れ狂う海面を涙で膨れ上がる人の顔に喩える。his は中性人称代名詞 it の古い所有格形にも男性人称代名詞の所有格形にもとれる。

225. coil ＝ tumult, confusion

226-27. I am the sea ... She is the weeping welkin, I the earth. 自分とラヴィニアの苦悶を荒れ狂う天地海に喩える壮大なメタファー。天変地異を人間界の出来事と関連づける迷信はこの時代にも多くあったが、この場の一連のメタファーでは、人間が自分の心理を自然界の現象に読み込み投影していることが明らか。

229-30. my earth ... a deluge, overflowed and drowned タイタス自身が大地であり、かつ洪水そのものであり、そしてその水に溺れる存在。

231. Forwhy ＝ because

my bowels cannot hide her woes タイタスは娘の悲嘆を自分の腹の中に抱えきれずにいる。

233. losers will have leave 諺的。Tilley L458 'Give losers leave to speak (talk).' leave 「（激しく嘆くことの）許し、容赦」

236. good hand 「高貴な手」あるいは「誠意で献じられた手」

240. woe is me ＝ I am distressed; alas「ああ悲しい」

242-43. let hot Etna cool in Sicily, / And be my heart an ever-burning hell
「熱いエトナ火山を冷え切らせ、俺の心を永劫灼熱の地獄にしてくれ」エトナ山はシチリア島の活火山。ギリシャ神話では、神々に逆らった巨人テュポーエウス（Typhoeus）の頭の上にシチリア島が被せられてできた山。下に埋められている巨人が怒って吐き出す息が火山の噴火になり、体を揺すると地震が起こる（*Metamorphoses*, 5. 346-58）。またやはり神々に逆らってユーピテルの雷に焼かれた巨人エンケラドスの体もエトナ山の下に埋められ、その巨人が体を動かすたびにシチリア島全域が震え、空に噴煙が立ち込めると伝えられる（*Aeneis*, 3,570-82）。この劇の後段で、父親になったエアロンが同じ神話に言及する。4. 2. 95-96 後注参照。

These miseries are more than may be borne.
To weep with them that weep doth ease some deal,   245
But sorrow flouted at is double death.

LUCIUS   Ah, that this sight should make so deep a wound
And yet detested life not shrink thereat!
That ever death should let life bear his name,
Where life hath no more interest but to breathe.   250

[Lavinia kisses Titus]

MARCUS   Alas, poor heart, that kiss is comfortless
As frozen water to a starvèd snake.

TITUS   When will this fearful slumber have an end?

MARCUS   Now farewell, flatt'ry; die, Andronicus.
Thou dost not slumber. See thy two sons' heads,   255
Thy warlike hand, thy mangled daughter here,
Thy other banished son with this dear sight
Struck pale and bloodless; and thy brother, I,
Even like a stony image cold and numb.
Ah, now no more will I control thy griefs.   260
Rent off thy silver hair, thy other hand,
Gnawing with thy teeth, and be this dismal sight
The closing up of our most wretched eyes.
Now is a time to storm. Why art thou still?

TITUS   Ha, ha, ha!   265

MARCUS   Why dost thou laugh? It fits not with this hour.

TITUS   Why, I have not another tear to shed.
Besides, this sorrow is an enemy
And would usurp upon my wat'ry eyes
And make them blind with tributary tears.   270
Then which way shall I find Revenge's cave?
For these two heads do seem to speak to me
And threat me I shall never come to bliss
Till all these mischiefs be returned again
Even in their throats that hath committed them.   275

244. may = can　2. 1. 83 注参照。

245. them that weep = those who weep　　**deal** = portion

246. flouted at = mocked

247-48. Ah, that ...!　「 … とは何たることか」

248. And yet detested life not shrink thereat　「それにも関わらず、忌み嫌わ
れている命が枯れ果ててしまわないとは」　thereat = at that

249. That ...　247 行の Ah, that ... と同様に嘆きの続き。

　his name = its name「命という名称」3. 1. 224 注参照。

250. no more ... but = no more ... than　　**interest** = concern, advantage

251. poor heart　「かわいそうに」共感を表わす句。

252. starvèd = perished with cold（*OED* starved, *ppl. adj.* 4.）

254. flatt'ry　「都合の好い幻想、妄想」

255. dost not slumber　「お前は寝ている（＝夢を見ている）わけではない」

256. Thy warlike hand　「武勇に優れたお前の手」切り取られたタイタスの手
を指す。

257-58. with this dear sight / Struck pale and bloodless　「この悲惨な光景の
ショックで青ざめ、血の気も失せている」　dear = severe, grievous; fell,
dire（*OED* dear, *adj.*²2.）

259. Even like a stony image　「まるで石像のように」　even = very

262. be this dismal sight ...　三人称命令。

263. closing up　「閉じて終わり」

264. storm = rage　　**still** = silent

265. Ha, ha, ha!　嘆きを絶した不条理な笑い。

269. usurp upon = seize possession of

270. with tributary tears　「（悲しみへの）貢物のように（私の）涙を流させて」

271. Revenge's cave　擬人化された復讐が隠れ住む洞窟。隠れるべき「復讐」と
は何なのか、またなぜ隠れるのか、いずれも曖昧。容易に逆転する復讐者と
仇との関係は劇の重要なプロットの1つ。後段の劇中劇風の場面（5. 2. 30-
63）参照。

273. threat = threaten

　come to bliss　「天上の喜びに至る」

275. in their throats that hath committed them　「この悪行を犯した連中の喉
に」that の先行詞は their。throats は猛獣が人間を貪り食う姿も連想させ
る。3. 1. 54 注参照。後段（5. 2. 180ff.）でタイタスが語り実行する陰惨な復讐
手段の伏線にもなる。

Come, let me see what task I have to do.
You heavy people, circle me about
That I may turn me to each one of you
And swear unto my soul to right your wrongs.
The vow is made. Come, brother, take a head,   280
And in this hand the other will I bear.
And, Lavinia, thou shalt be employed in these arms.
Bear thou my hand, sweet wench, between thy teeth.
As for thee, boy, go get thee from my sight.
Thou art an exile, and thou must not stay.   285
Hie to the Goths and raise an army there.
And if you love me, as I think you do,
Let's kiss and part, for we have much to do.

Exeunt [all but Lucius]

LUCIUS   Farewell, Andronicus, my noble father,
The woefull'st man that ever lived in Rome.   290
Farewell, proud Rome, till Lucius come again.
He loves his pledges dearer than his life.
Farewell, Lavinia, my noble sister.
O, would thou wert as thou tofore hast been!
But now nor Lucius nor Lavinia lives   295
But in oblivion and hateful griefs.
If Lucius live he will requite your wrongs
And make proud Saturnine and his empress
Beg at the gates like Tarquin and his queen.
Now will I to the Goths and raise a power   300
To be revenged on Rome and Saturnine.   *Exit*

[ACT III SCENE II]

*A banquet. Enter Titus Andronicus, Marcus, Lavinia,
and the boy [Young Lucius, with Servants]*

TITUS   So, so. Now sit, and look you eat no more

277. heavy = sorrowful, sad

277-83. circle me ... between thy teeth 台詞に埋め込まれた一連のト書き（embedded stage directions）として機能する。文字通りに演じるならば、復讐を決意した家族の退場シーンが狂気と恐怖のスペクタクルになる。

278. turn me = turn myself

279. right your wrongs 「お前らが被った不当な仕打ちを正す」復讐のこと。

284. As for thee ルーシアスに向かって言う。

get thee from my sight 「わしの目の届かぬ遠くへ行け」 get thee = get thyself　from = away from

286. Hie = hasten, go quickly

291. proud Rome この proud は曖昧。「高慢な」と「誇るべき、立派な」の両方の含みがある。 Shakespeare, Sonnet 25. 2 'Of public honour and proud titles boast'; Sonnet 86. 1 'Was it the proud full sail of his great verse ...'

292. He ルーシアス自身を指す。

294. O, would ... 「〜であってくれたらいいのに」would は願望を表わす。

296. in oblivion and hateful griefs 「人から忘れられ、恨みに満ちた嘆きのうちに」 hateful = full of hate; malevolent (*OED* hateful, *adj.* 2.)

297-99. requite your wrongs ... like Tarquin and his queen 「お前の受けたひどい仕打ちの復讐をしてやる」ルーシアスは、ルクレーティア凌辱への報復としてタルクィニウスをローマから追放し、共和政を樹立して初代執政官（consul）になったブルートゥス（Lucius Junius Brutus）に自分を擬えている。

299. Beg at the gates 伝説の典拠リーウィウス、オウィディウスのいずれにもない。復讐心と政治的野心を秘めたルーシアスの空想か。2. 1. 110 注参照。

300. a power 「軍勢」

〔**3. 2**〕あらすじ……………………………………………………………………

　タイタスの館での会食場面。タイタス、マーカス、ラヴィニア、孫のルーシアスが復讐への思いを胸に秘めながら家族で食事をしている。折しもテーブルに飛んできた蠅をマーカスが殺し、さらにタイタスがその黒い蠅をエアロンに見立ててテーブルナイフで激しく襲いかかる。タイタスの狂気をアクションで強調する。この場はもとの Q1 になく、後年誰かが書き加えたものと推測されている。
⇒解説 9-10 頁および 3. 2. 85 SD 後注参照。
……………………………………………………………………………………

Than will preserve just so much strength in us
As will revenge these bitter woes of ours.
Marcus, unknit that sorrow-wreathen knot.
Thy niece and I, poor creatures, want our hands   5
And cannot passionate our tenfold grief
With folded arms. This poor right hand of mine
Is left to tyrannize upon my breast,
Who, when my heart, all mad with misery,
Beats in this hollow prison of my flesh,   10
Then thus I thump it down.
[*To Lavinia*]   Thou map of woe, that thus dost talk in signs,
When thy poor heart beats with outrageous beating,
Thou canst not strike it thus to make it still.
Wound it with sighing, girl, kill it with groans;   15
Or get some little knife between thy teeth
And just against thy heart make thou a hole,
That all the tears that thy poor eyes let fall
May run into that sink and, soaking in,
Drown the lamenting fool in sea-salt tears.   20
MARCUS Fie, brother, fie! Teach her not thus to lay
Such violent hands upon her tender life.
TITUS How now! Has sorrow made thee dote already?
Why, Marcus, no man should be mad but I.
What violent hands can she lay on her life?   25
Ah, wherefore dost thou urge the name of hands,
To bid Aeneas tell the tale twice o'er
How Troy was burnt and he made miserable?
O, handle not the theme, to talk of hands,
Lest we remember still that we have none.   30
Fie, fie, how franticly I square my talk,
As if we should forget we had no hands
If Marcus did not name the word of hands!
Come, let's fall to, and, gentle girl, eat this.

4. unknit　「(結び目) をほぐす」

　　sorrow-wreathen knot　「悲しみで巻きつけられた結び目」マーカスの腕組み
　　（folded arms）を指す。

5. want = lack

6. passionate = express or perform with passion

8. tyrannize　「暴君のように振る舞う」

12. map of woe「嘆きの地図」　map は傷つき苦悩するラヴィニアの姿を同時代
　　の地図のイメージに喩える視覚的メタファー。

13. outrageous = furious; excessively fierce （*OED* outrageous, *adj.* 2.)

17. against thy heart make thou a hole　「お前の心臓へ向けて、穴を開けろ」

19. sink　「排水溝」

　　soaking in　「染み込んで」

20. the lamenting fool = thy heart that is lamenting

　　sea-salt　「海塩のような」塩分と同時に、流す涙の量をも海に喩えるメタ
　　ファー。

21. Fie, brother, fie!　「兄さん、とんでもない。ダメですよ！」　fie はもともと
　　怒りや嫌悪を表わす間投詞。ここは諫め。

22. her tender life　「優しく傷つきやすい、この娘の命」

23. How now = How is it now　間投詞的に使用。「何だと」（松岡訳）

　　dote　「老齢で頭の働きが悪くなる」

26. urge = bring forward; present

27-28. Aeneas tell ... How Troy was burnt　ウェルギリウスの叙事詩では
　　ディードーの求めに応じてアエネーアスが、落城するトロイアーからの脱出
　　とその後の放浪の旅を物語る （*Aeneis*, 1. 748-3. 718）。シェイクスピア時代の
　　受容例としては、Marlowe, *Dido, Queen of Carthage*, 2. 1; Shakespeare,
　　Hamlet, 2. 2.

29. handle = touch with the hands; deal with in speech　自分と娘に手がな
　　いことを意識して「手」を連想させる言葉に過敏になっている。

30. remember still　「ずっと忘れずにいる」　still = always, constantly

34. fall to = begin eating voraciously or with relish （*OED* fall, *v.* PV fall
　　to, 3.b.)

Here is no drink! Hark, Marcus, what she says.   35
I can interpret all her martyred signs.
She says she drinks no other drink but tears
Brewed with her sorrow, mashed upon her cheeks.
Speechless complainer, I will learn thy thought.
In thy dumb action will I be as perfect   40
As begging hermits in their holy prayers.
Thou shalt not sigh, nor hold thy stumps to heaven,
Nor wink, nor nod, nor kneel, nor make a sign,
But I of these will wrest an alphabet
And by still practice learn to know thy meaning.   45

YOUNG LUCIUS Good grandsire, leave these bitter deep
   laments.
Make my aunt merry with some pleasing tale.

MARCUS Alas, the tender boy, in passion moved,
Doth weep to see his grandsire's heaviness.

TITUS Peace, tender sapling. Thou art made of tears,   50
And tears will quickly melt thy life away.

> *Marcus strikes the dish with a knife*

What dost thou strike at, Marcus, with thy knife?

MARCUS At that that I have killed, my lord, a fly.

TITUS Out on thee, murderer! Thou kill'st my heart.
Mine eyes are cloyed with view of tyranny;   55
A deed of death done on the innocent
Becomes not Titus' brother. Get thee gone.
I see thou art not for my company.

MARCUS Alas, my lord, I have but killed a fly.

TITUS 'But'? How if that fly had a father and mother?   60
How would he hang his slender gilded wings
And buzz lamenting doings in the air!
Poor harmless fly,
That, with his pretty buzzing melody,
Came here to make us merry! And thou hast killed him.   65

36. her martyred signs = her martyred body's signs, or martyred Lavinia's bodily signs　martyred = mutilated　3. 1. 82 注参照。切り刻まれ傷ついているのが、ラヴィニアの発する合図・仕草とも、彼女の身体とも、彼女の心とも取れる曖昧な言い方。見えているのは傷ついた娘の身体とその仕草のみで、そこから彼女の真の苦悩と思いを読み取ることが可能なのかという問題。逆にタイタス自身の動揺・混乱を窺わせる。martyr の原義「殉教させる」も心理的には有効。第1幕でルーシアス達がアラーバスの身体を切り刻んで生贄に捧げたことも、タモラが嘆く irreligious piety（1. 1. 130）であった。この芝居を見る際に、シェイクスピア同時代の宗教対立と迫害・流血を等閑視することはできない。

38. Brewed 「醸造された」涙をビールに喩えるメタファー。

mashed = mingled or dispersed　これもビールの醸造を連想させる。エリザベス朝時代の汚染された都市部では、水の代わりにビールを飲んだ（Berthoud）。

40. perfect = accurately or thoroughly learned

41. begging hermits in their holy prayers 托鉢修道士のイメージで、この芝居中にしばしば見られるアナクロニズムの1つ。5. 1. 21 後注参照。

42-44 Thou shalt not sigh ... But I of these will wrest an alphabet = I will be sure to forcibly read an alphabet from every sigh ... of thine

44. of = from

44-45. wrest an alphabet / And by still practice learn to know thy meaning 学校での文字の手習いのイメージ。　wrest 「捻り出す」　still = constant

46. grandsire = grandfather

50. sapling 「未熟な若者」原義は若木。

54. Out on thee 「こら、この野郎」2. 3. 258 注参照。

55. cloyed = satiated, disgusted with the excess

59. but killed a fly = only killed a fly

62. lamenting doings = lamentations（Waith; Bate）; sad stories（Hughes）さまざまな解釈があり意味は不確か。

MARCUS   Pardon me, sir. It was a black, ill-favoured fly,
   Like to the Empress' Moor. Therefore I killed him.
TITUS   O, O, O!
   Then pardon me for reprehending thee,
   For thou hast done a charitable deed.   70
   Give me thy knife. I will insult on him,
   Flattering myself as if it were the Moor
   Come hither purposely to poison me.
   There's for thyself, and that's for Tamora.
   Ah, sirrah!   75
   Yet I think we are not brought so low
   But that between us we can kill a fly
   That comes in likeness of a coal-black Moor.
MARCUS   Alas, poor man, grief has so wrought on him
   He takes false shadows for true substances.   80
TITUS   Come, take away. Lavinia, go with me.
   I'll to thy closet and go read with thee
   Sad stories chancèd in the times of old.
   Come, boy, and go with me. Thy sight is young,
   And thou shalt read when mine begin to dazzle.   *Exeunt*   85

66. ill-favoured　「人相の悪い」　favour = countenance, face

72. Flattering myself as if it were the Moor　「気休めに、そいつがムーアであるかのように思って」虚しい気休めに過ぎないと自覚している言い方。

75. sirrah　「おい、こら」子供や目下の人に向かい軽蔑・非難などを込めて言う高飛車な呼びかけ。

76. brought ... low = humbled

77. But that ... can ...　「〜できないほどまで」

79. has so wrought on him　「彼の身に応えてしまっている」　wrought　1. 1. 265 注参照。

80. takes false shadows for true substances　タイタスは自分が正気のつもりだが（3. 2. 72）、マーカスは兄の精神状態を狂気と見做している。

81. take away = clear the table

84. Thy sight is young = Thy sight is good because thou art young.「目（視力）が良いこと」は「若さ」の１つの特徴で換喩。

85 SD.　*Exeunt*　⇒後注

[ACT IV SCENE I]

Enter Lucius' son and Lavinia running after him, and
the boy flies from her with his books under his arm.
Enter Titus and Marcus

YOUNG LUCIUS   Help, grandsire, help! My aunt Lavinia
    Follows me everywhere, I know not why.
    Good uncle Marcus, see how swift she comes.
    Alas, sweet aunt, I know not what you mean.
MARCUS   Stand by me, Lucius. Do not fear thine aunt.   5
TITUS   She loves thee, boy, too well to do thee harm.
YOUNG LUCIUS   Ay, when my father was in Rome she did.
MARCUS   What means my niece Lavinia by these signs?
TITUS   Fear her not, Lucius. Somewhat doth she mean.
    See, Lucius, see, how much she makes of thee.   10
    Somewhither would she have thee go with her.
    Ah, boy, Cornelia never with more care
    Read to her sons than she hath read to thee
    Sweet poetry and Tully's *Orator*.
[MARCUS]   Canst thou not guess wherefore she plies thee thus?   15
YOUNG LUCIUS   My lord, I know not, I, nor can I guess,
    Unless some fit or frenzy do possess her;
    For I have heard my grandsire say full oft,
    Extremity of griefs would make men mad,
    And I have read that Hecuba of Troy   20
    Ran mad for sorrow. That made me to fear,
    Although, my lord, I know my noble aunt
    Loves me as dear as e'er my mother did,
    And would not but in fury fright my youth,
    Which made me down to throw my books and fly,   25
    Causeless, perhaps. But pardon me, sweet aunt.
    And, madam, if my uncle Marcus go,
    I will most willingly attend your Ladyship.

〔**4. 1**〕**あらすじ**………………………………………………………………

　タイタスの館での場。ラヴィニアはオウィディウス『変身物語』の本を抱えてフィロメーラがテーレウスにレイプされる件のページを指し示し、自分がフィロメーラと同様にレイプの被害者であることを家族に悟らせる。さらに砂の上に棒で文字を書くことによって、ラヴィニアは自分を襲った犯人がカイロンとディミートリアスの２人であることを伝える。タイタスとその家族はあらためて復讐を決意し、手始めに孫のルーシアスをタモラの２人の息子のもとへ使いにやる。⇒後注

………………………………………………………………………………………

0 SD.　⇒後注

1. grandsire = grandfather

3. swift = swiftly

5. thine aunt　2. 1. 74 注参照。

9. Somewhat = something

10. makes of = thinks well of; values highly（*OED* make, *v.*¹ 29.b.）

11. Somewhither = to some place; somewhere

　would = would like to

12. Cornelia　グラックス兄弟（Tiberius Sempronius Gracchus（163-133 BC）and Gaius Sempronius Gracchus（153-121 BC））の母コルネーリア。賢母として知られる。Cf. Plutarkhos, 'Tiberius Gracchus', 1. 4.

14. Tully's = Marcus Tullius Cicero's（106-43 BC）「キケローの」

　Orator = *Orator ad Brutum* or *De Oratore*『弁論家』

15. plies thee = urges or solicits thee persistently

18. full oft = very often

20-21. Hecuba of Troy / Ran mad　オウィディウスでは、ヘキュバはポリュメーストールに対して復讐を遂げた後に、犬に変身する（*Metamorphoses*, 13. 556-75）。1. 1. 136-38 後注参照。シェイクスピアの同時代の辞書に以下の記述がある。Thomas Cooper, *Thesaurus Linguae Romanae & Britannicae*（London: Henry Wykes, 1567）, sig.I4ʳ 'her youngest son Polydorus killed, she finally waxed mad, and did bite and strike all men that she met, wherefore she was called dog ...'（Burrow 22）

21. made me to fear = made me fear

24. not but in fury = only in madness

　fright = frighten

25. Which　先行詞は fury。

　made me down to throw = made me throw down

MARCUS Lucius, I will.

TITUS How now, Lavinia? Marcus, what means this?   30
Some book there is that she desires to see.
Which is it, girl, of these? Open them, boy.
[*To Lavinia*] But thou art deeper read and better skilled.
Come and take choice of all my library,
And so beguile thy sorrow till the heavens   35
Reveal the damned contriver of this deed.
Why lifts she up her arms in sequence thus?

MARCUS I think she means that there were more than one
Confederate in the fact. Ay, more there was,
Or else to heaven she heaves them for revenge.   40

TITUS Lucius, what book is that she tosseth so?

YOUNG LUCIUS Grandsire, 'tis Ovid's *Metamorphosis*.
My mother gave it me.

MARCUS   For love of her that's gone,
Perhaps, she culled it from among the rest.

TITUS Soft! So busily she turns the leaves.   45
Help her! What would she find? Lavinia, shall I read?
This is the tragic tale of Philomel,
And treats of Tereus' treason and his rape.
And rape, I fear, was root of thy annoy.

MARCUS See, brother, see! Note how she quotes the leaves.   50

TITUS Lavinia, wert thou thus surprised, sweet girl,
Ravished and wronged as Philomela was,
Forced in the ruthless, vast, and gloomy woods?
See, see! Ay, such a place there is where we did hunt —
O, had we never, never hunted there —   55
Patterned by that the poet here describes,
By nature made for murders and for rapes.

MARCUS O, why should nature build so foul a den,
Unless the gods delight in tragedies?

TITUS Give signs, sweet girl, for here are none but friends,   60

33. read = informed by reading; learned　　**skilled** = possessed of skill or knowledge; properly trained or experienced

39. fact = an evil deed, a crime

40. heaves = raises

41. tosseth = turns over and over; turns the leaves of (a book, etc.)

42. Ovid's *Metamorphosis* 　この芝居の重要な種本であるオウィディウスの本そのものが事件の真相を究明する手がかりとして使用され、メタポエティックな場。オウィディウスの読者である観客に、虚構の古代ローマの家族への共感を促す構造になっている。叙事詩の正確な名称は *Metamorphoses*。

43. My mother gave it me. — For love of her that's gone 　『変身物語』が子供の読み物として与えられる。家族の絆を記憶・象徴するものとしての本の存在が特徴的。ルーシアス父子二代にわたって、すでに母は失われているらしい。

44. culled = selected

45. busily = intently, earnestly　　**leaves** = pages

47. the tragic tale of Philomel 　2.3.43 注参照。

48. Tereus' treason 　テーレウスは妻プロクネー、義妹ピロメーラ、さらにその父でアテーナイの王パンディーオーンの好意と信頼を、ピロメーラへの欲望のために裏切る。

49. annoy = vexation, trouble

50. quotes = refers to; tries to draw our attention to　「～を引用する」は「～に人の注意を引こうとする」のメタファー。

51. surprised = attacked suddenly or unexpectedly

52. Ravished = dragged off or carried away by force or with violence, with occasional implication of subsequent rape (*OED* ravish, *v.* 1.a.)
wronged = done wrong or injury to

53. Forced = used violence to; ravished, raped
ruthless ... woods 「無慈悲な森」擬人化。

55. O, had we never ... hunted = How I wish we had never ... hunted

56. the poet here describes 　オウィディウスのどの詩行を指すかは曖昧。*Metamorphoses*, 6.521 'in stabula alta trahit, silvis obscura vestustis' (太古の森の奥深く、暗く人目につかぬ小屋へと引きずって行き) などか。

58. so foul a den 　マーカスの脳裏にあるのはオウィディウスの描写にある小屋ではなく、バシエイナスの遺体が投げ込まれ、その付近を傷ついた姪が彷徨していた穴であろう。引用におけるぶれが、じつは台詞の話し手の意識や心理を表わす一例。　den = a place hollowed out of the ground; a secret lurking-place of thieves or the like (*OED* den, *n.*¹ 2. and 3.) 2.3.215 注参照。

59. gods delight in tragedies 　古くからある「世界劇場 (theatrum mundi)」のイメージ。

What Roman lord it was durst do the deed.
Or slunk not Saturnine, as Tarquin erst,
That left the camp to sin in Lucrece' bed?
MARCUS   Sit down, sweet niece; Brother, sit down by me.
Apollo, Pallas, Jove, or Mercury   65
Inspire me, that I may this treason find.
My lord, look here. Look here, Lavinia.

He writes his name with his staff and
guides it with feet and mouth

This sandy plot is plain; guide, if thou canst,
This after me. I have writ my name
Without the help of any hand at all.   70
Cursed be that heart that forced us to this shift!
Write thou, good niece, and here display at last
What God will have discovered for revenge.
Heaven guide thy pen to print thy sorrows plain,
That we may know the traitors and the truth.   75

She takes the staff in her mouth, and guides it with her stumps and
writes

O, do you read, my lord, what she hath writ?
TITUS   '*Stuprum.* Chiron, Demetrius.'
MARCUS   What, what! The lustful sons of Tamora
Performers of this heinous, bloody deed?
TITUS   *Magni Dominator poli,*   80
Tam lentus audis scelera, tam lentus vides?
MARCUS   O, calm thee, gentle lord, although I know
There is enough written upon this earth
To stir a mutiny in the mildest thoughts
And arm the minds of infants to exclaims.   85
My lord, kneel down with me; Lavinia, kneel.
And kneel, sweet boy, the Roman Hector's hope,

61. it was durst do = it was who durst do　durst は dare の過去形。

62-63. slunk not Saturnine, as Tarquin erst, / That left the camp to sin in ...
2. 1. 110 注参照。忍び足で近寄るタルクィニウスの姿はタイタスの想像。Cf.
The Rape of Lucrece, 295-301.　slunk = walked in a quiet, stealthy, or
sneaking manner　erst = once upon a time; of old

68. This sandy plot is plain 「この砂場は（表面が）滑らかだ」

68-69. guide ... This after me. 「私に倣ってこの棒を動かしなさい」
guide = direct the course of (a tool)（*OED* guide, *v.* 1.b.）

71. shift = available means of effecting an end（*OED* shift, *n.* 3.b.）

72. display = make manifest

73. God will have discovered「（いずれは）神が暴いてくれたはずの」

75. That = so that

77. *Stuprum* = dishonour, debauchery「淫乱、恥知らず」⇒後注

78-79. The lustful sons of Tamora / Performers ... deed ! 前行でタイタスが
読み上げたラヴィニアのラテン語メッセージを観客向けに言い換えたもの。

79. heinous = odious; highly criminal or wicked

80-81. *Magni Dominator poli ... tam lentus vides?* ⇒後注

87. the Roman Hector's hope ルーシアス父子をトロイアーの英雄ヘクトール
とその子スカマンドリオス（Skamandrios）に擬える。『イーリアス』ヘク
トールとその妻アンドロマケー別れの場ではまだ嬰児。（*Ilias*, 6. 466-81）

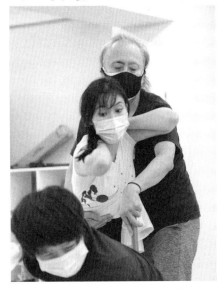

図 6　砂に文字を書くラヴィニ
ア（春名風花）とマーカス（貴
島豪）　木村龍之介演出『シン・
タイタス』稽古場の風景（2022）
© KAKUSHINHAN

And swear with me as with the woeful fere
And father of that chaste dishonoured dame,
Lord Junius Brutus swore for Lucrece' rape   90
That we will prosecute by good advice
Mortal revenge upon these traitorous Goths,
And see their blood or die with this reproach.
TITUS   'Tis sure enough, an you knew how.
But if you hunt these bearwhelps, then beware;   95
The dam will wake an if she wind you once.
She's with the lion deeply still in league,
And lulls him whilst she playeth on her back;
And when he sleeps will she do what she list.
You are a young huntsman, Marcus; let alone.   100
And come, I will go get a leaf of brass,
And with a gad of steel will write these words,
And lay it by. The angry northern wind
Will blow these sands like Sibyl's leaves abroad,
And where's our lesson then? Boy, what say you?   105
YOUNG LUCIUS   I say, my lord, that if I were a man,
Their mother's bedchamber should not be safe
For these base bondmen to the yoke of Rome.
MARCUS   Ay, that's my boy! Thy father hath full oft
For his ungrateful country done the like.   110
YOUNG LUCIUS   And uncle, so will I, an if I live.
TITUS   Come, go with me into mine armory.
Lucius, I'll fit thee, and withal my boy
Shall carry from me to the Empress' sons
Presents that I intend to send them both.   115
Come, come. Thou'lt do my message, wilt thou not?
YOUNG LUCIUS   Ay, with my dagger in their bosoms, grandsire.
TITUS   No, boy, not so. I'll teach thee another course.
Lavinia, come. Marcus, look to my house.
Lucius and I'll go brave it at the court;   120

88. fere = partner　ルクレーティア (Lucretia) の夫コラーティーヌス (Lucius Tarquinius Collatinus) を指す。共和政ローマ初代執政官 (consul) の一人。

89. father of that chaste dishonoured dame　「名誉を傷つけられたあの貞節な婦人の父」ルクレーティアの父ルクレーティウス (Lucretius)。

90. Junius Brutus　ルクレーティアの凌辱と自死を機に第7代ローマ王タルクィニウス (Tarquinius Superbus) を追放し、紀元前509年共和政ローマを樹立してコラーティーヌスとともに初代執政官となったユーニウス・ブルートゥス (Lucius Junius Brutus)。タイタスの長男ルーシアスは自らをこのブルートゥスに擬える。3. 1. 297-99 注参照。

93. with this reproach　「このような屈辱を受けたまま」　reproach = shame, disgrace (*OED* reproach, *n.* 2.a.)　　**94. an** = if

95. bearwhelps　「子熊たち」　**96. dam**　2. 3. 142 注参照。　**an if** = if

97. still = always

98. lulls = soothes with sounds or caresses「あやして寝かしつける」
on her back = in bed　**99. list** = wish, desire

100. young = immature　**let alone** = abstain from interfering with

101. a leaf of brass「真鍮の板」格言的イメージ。Tilley I 71 'Injuries are written in brass.' (Bate)　leaf = metal in the form of a thin sheet, used for engraving (Waith)

102. gad of steel「鉄筆の先」　gad = a sharp-pointed stick

103. lay it by = lay it aside「しまっておけ」

104. blow ... abroad「ばらばらに吹き飛ばす」　abroad = widely asunder
Sibyl's leaves　*Aeneis*, 6. 73-75 'foliis tantum ne carmina manda, / Ne turbata volent rapidis ludibria ventis; / ipsa canas oro'（ただ、速い風に吹かれて遊具のように飛んで行ってしまうといけないから、お告げの歌を木の葉に記さないように。ご自身の口で歌うようお願いする）　アエネーアースが予言を求めてクーマエのシビュラに言う言葉。

105. our lesson　「俺たちの（家族がこの災難に遭って得た）教訓」

107. Their mother's bedchamber should not be safe　「母親の寝室に隠れても容赦しないぞ」とも「仕返しに奴らの母親をレイプしてやる」とも、どちらにも取れる。ただし bedchamber は明らかにセクシャルな含みを持つ語で、アンドロニカス家のミソジニックな家風を思わせる。　**108. bondmen** = slaves

109-10. Thy father ... done the like　父ルーシアスの冷酷な性格を示す台詞。タモラの長男アラーバスを犠牲にしたいと言い出し、タイタスを促したのもルーシアス。(1. 1. 96-101)　**113. fit**　「相応しい身支度をさせる」
withal = with that　**116. Thou'lt** = thou willt (= you will)

120. brave it = boast, swagger (*OED* brave, *v.* 7.)

Ay, marry, will we, sir, and we'll be waited on.

Exeunt [all but Marcus]

MARCUS O heavens, can you hear a good man groan
And not relent, or not compassion him?
Marcus, attend him in his ecstasy,
That hath more scars of sorrow in his heart   125
Than foemen's marks upon his battered shield,
But yet so just that he will not revenge.
Revenge the heavens for old Andronicus!   *Exit*

[**ACT IV SCENE II**]

*Enter Aaron, Chiron, and Demetrius at one door, and at
the other door young Lucius and another, with a bundle
of weapons and verses writ upon them*

CHIRON Demetrius, here's the son of Lucius.
He hath some message to deliver us.
AARON Ay, some mad message from his mad grandfather.
YOUNG LUCIUS My lords, with all the humbleness I may,
I greet your Honours from Andronicus   5
[*Aside*] And pray the Roman gods confound you both.
DEMETRIUS Gramercy, lovely Lucius. What's the news?
YOUNG LUCIUS [*Aside*]
That you both deciphered, that's the news,
For villains marked with rape. —May it please you,
My grandsire, well advised, hath sent by me   10
The goodliest weapons of his armory
To gratify your honourable youth,
The hope of Rome; for so he bid me say,
And so I do, and with his gifts present
Your Lordships, that, whenever you have need,   15
You may be armèd and appointed well,
And so I leave you both —[*aside*] like bloody villains.   *Exit*

121. marry　強調の意味の間投詞。

124. ecstasy = the state of being 'beside oneself', thrown into a frenzy or stupor, with anxiety, astonishment, fear, or passion（*OED* ecstasy, *n*. 1)

126. foemen's marks upon his battered shield　「敵が彼のボコボコの盾につけた（刀傷の）跡」

127. so just ... will not revenge　3. 1. 271-88 でタイタスが復讐の決意を述べたこ
とと矛盾するようだが、マーカスから見ると精神的に参っているタイタスに
はもはや復讐の意志も気力もないと判断される。「あまりにも公正な人（so just）
だから」と言うのは、兄への気遣いと労り故の言い訳であろう。

128. Revenge the heavens = May the heavens take revenge「神々が復讐を
遂げられんことを」　復讐については⇒解説 22-25 頁。

　　for　「～に代わって」

〔**4. 2**〕あらすじ……………………………………………………………………………

　カイロンとディミートリアスのもとにタイタスの孫ルーシアスが使者となって
使いの品を届ける。ついで皇后タモラが出産したとして、肌の黒い新生児がカイ
ロン、ディミートリアスとエアロンのもとに連れてこられる。兄弟はその嬰児を
殺そうとするが、エアロンが自分の子を助け、連れてゴート族のもとへと逃げる。

……………………………………………………………………………………………………

6. confound = overthrow, destroy

7. Gramercy = Thanks ＜ 古フランス語の grant merci から。

8. deciphered = detected, discovered

9. marked with ...「～の烙印を押された」

10. advised「慎重に考えた上で」

12. gratify = show gratitude to

16. appointed ＝ provided with requisites, fitted out（*OED* appointed, *adj*. 2.)

DEMETRIUS   What's here? A scroll, and written round about.
Let's see:

> 'Integer vitae, scelerisque purus,   20
> Non eget Mauri iaculis, nec arcu.'

CHIRON   O, 'tis a verse in Horace; I know it well.
I read it in the grammar long ago.

AARON   Ay, just; a verse in Horace; right, you have it.
[Aside]   Now, what a thing it is to be an ass!   25
Here's no sound jest. The old man hath found their guilt
And sends them weapons wrapped about with lines
That wound, beyond their feeling, to the quick.
But were our witty Empress well afoot,
She would applaud Andronicus' conceit.   30
But let her rest in her unrest awhile. —
And now, young lords, was't not a happy star
Led us to Rome, strangers, and, more than so,
Captives, to be advancèd to this height?
It did me good before the palace gate   35
To brave the tribune in his brother's hearing.

DEMETRIUS   But me more good to see so great a lord
Basely insinuate and send us gifts.

AARON   Had he not reason, Lord Demetrius?
Did you not use his daughter very friendly?   40

DEMETRIUS   I would we had a thousand Roman dames
At such a bay, by turn to serve our lust.

CHIRON   A charitable wish, and full of love!

AARON   Here lacks but your mother for to say amen.

CHIRON   And that would she, for twenty thousand more.   45

DEMETRIUS   Come, let us go and pray to all the gods
For our belovèd mother in her pains.

AARON   Pray to the devils; the gods have given us over. *Flourish*

DEMETRIUS   Why do the Emperor's trumpets flourish thus?

CHIRON   Belike for joy the Emperor hath a son.   50

20-21. *Integer vitae, scelerisque purus, / Non eget Mauri iaculis, nec arcu*
「生き方が純粋で罪に汚れない者は、ムーアの槍も弓も必要なく」 ⇒後注

23. I read it in the grammar long ago　シェイクスピアの同時代英国グラマー・
スクールの教科書を連想させる。例えば William Lily, *Brevissima Institutio*。
4. 2. 20-21 後注参照。劇中人物にシェイクスピア同時代のラテン語教育につい
て言及させるアナクロニズムだが、大衆劇場の観客層の古典受容の状況を彷彿
とさせるユーモア。⇒解説 10-15 頁。

25. what a thing it is to be an ass!　ムーア人のエアロンがゴート族王子の無教
養ぶりに呆れている。なおゴート族は北ヨーロッパの住民だったので、ムーア
人やローマの人々よりも位置的に英国に近い。　ass　「驢馬、ばか」

26. sound = honest, sincere (*OED* sound *adj.* 10.a. and b.)

27. lines = verse

28. beyond their feeling　「奴らは毫も気づいていないが」
to the quick　「急所に」

29. were our witty Empress well afoot = if our clever empress were up and
about　現在タモラは出産の床についている。4. 2. 47 注参照。

30. conceit = idea, thought, mental capacity

31. unrest = disturbance, distress　ここでは「出産の苦しみ、陣痛」。

32. was't not a happy star / Led us = was it not lucky that a certain star
led us　星・天体の動きが人間の世界に影響を与え、そこでの出来事を支配す
るという思想・迷信が古くからあった。ただしここは頭の弱い 2 人に向けて
言っている台詞で、エアロン自身がどれほど信じていたかは不明。happy に
は現在の fortunate, joyous「幸せな」の意味の他に、that happens by
chance; fortuitous「偶然の」(*OED* happy, *adj.* 3.) の意味があった。アイ
ロニーとして「単に運が良かっただけ」という含みがあり得る。

35. did me good = was beneficial to me

36. brave = treat with bravado; defy
the tribune　「護民官」マーカスを指す。

38. insinuate = work or wheedle himself into; ingratiate himself with (*OED*
insinuate, *v.* 2.b.「おもねる」

40. use　2. 3. 166 注参照。　**friendly**　「親切に」アイロニー。

42. bay　狩りで獲物が猟犬に追い詰められた状態を言う。
by turn　「次々と」「性交によって」(Williams) 2. 1. 96, 131 参照。

44. for to say = to say to　不定詞の前に for が付くのは古い形。

45. that would she = she would like to say amen (for a thousand, and
twenty thousand more, Roman dames)

47. pains = labour pains　「陣痛」

50. Belike = in all likelihood, probably

DEMETRIUS   Soft, who comes here?

Enter Nurse, with a blackamoor child

NURSE   Good morrow, lords.
O, tell me, did you see Aaron the Moor?
AARON   Well, more or less, or ne'er a whit at all,
Here Aaron is. And what with Aaron now?   55
NURSE   O, gentle Aaron, we are all undone!
Now help, or woe betide thee evermore.
AARON   Why, what a caterwauling dost thou keep!
What dost thou wrap and fumble in thy arms?
NURSE   O, that which I would hide from heaven's eye,   60
Our Empress' shame and stately Rome's disgrace.
She is delivered, lords, she is delivered.
AARON   To whom?
NURSE   I mean, she is brought abed.
AARON   Well, God give her good rest. What hath he sent her?   65
NURSE   A devil.
AARON   Why, then she is the devil's dam. A joyful issue!
NURSE   A joyless, dismal, black, and sorrowful issue!
Here is the babe, as loathsome as a toad
Amongst the fair-faced breeders of our clime.   70
The Empress sends it thee, thy stamp, thy seal,
And bids thee christen it with thy dagger's point.
AARON   Zounds, you whore, is black so base a hue?
Sweet blowse, you are a beauteous blossom, sure.
DEMETRIUS   Villain, what hast thou done?   75
AARON   That which thou canst not undo.
CHIRON   Thou hast undone our mother.
AARON   Villain, I have done thy mother.
DEMETRIUS   And therein, hellish dog, thou hast undone her.
Woe to her chance, and damned her loathèd choice!   80
Accursed the offspring of so foul a fiend!

51. Soft 「静かに」命令。

54. more or less = in a greater or lesser degree; virtually more は同音の Moor に引っ掛けた駄洒落 (pun)。

　ne'er a whit = not at all, not in the least

55. what with Aaron now? = what do you want with Aaron (= me) now?

56. undone = ruined, destroyed「破滅だ、おしまいだ」

57. or 「助けてくれないなら」　　**betide** = fall, happen　　**thee** = to thee 与格 (the dative case)。　　**evermore** = for all future time

58. caterwauling = the cry of cats at rutting time「発情期の猫の鳴き声」

59. fumble = wrap up clumsily, huddle together (*OED* fumble, *v.* 3.)

60. heaven's eye = the sun　　**62. is delivered**　⇒後注

63. To whom? 「誰のところへだい」エアロンは乳母の意図をはぐらかす。is delivered をわざと「運び届けられる」の意味にとって、このように質問する。

64. I mean ... brought abed 「(出産で) ベッドに運ばれたと言っているのです」エアロンに揶揄われ、単純な乳母が混乱気味に言う台詞。

65. What hath he sent her? 「神様が彼女に何をくださったかい」異教の神なので He ではなく he と書く。

66. A devil 「悪魔を (お産みになった)」黒い肌を持って生まれ、母タモラの立場を危うくする不都合な存在なので「悪魔」。

67. devil's dam 「悪魔の母さん」女性への蔑称。(*OED* dam, *n.*^{2} 2.b.)

68. dismal = unlucky, sinister (*OED* dismal, *adj.* 2.) Cf. the dismal = the devil (*OED* dismal, *n.* 2.a.)

70. fair-faced 「白く美しい顔をした」　fair = beautiful; light, bright (of hair or complexion) (*OED* fair, *adj.* 1. and 17.)

　breeders 「子を作る動物あるいは人間」

71. thy stamp, thy seal 「お前の印鑑、お前の判」　seal 蠟などに押した印影。

72. christen = baptize　⇒後注

73. Zounds [zaʊndz/zuːndz] = God's wounds　間投詞。断言する時の強めとして用いるのは冒瀆的。(*OED* zounds, *int.*) 劇場での神聖冒瀆を取り締まる法令 The Act to Restrain Abuses of Players (1604) を受けて F1 では削除される (Bate)。　　**whore** 「淫売」激しい罵りの言葉。

74. blowse = ruddy fat-faced wench「赤ら顔のかわいい子」

76. undo 「取り消す、もとの状態に戻す」

77. hast undone この場合の undo は「破滅させる」。4. 2. 56 注参照。

78. have done = have made love with

79. therein = in that affair　　**80. chance** = fortune

81. fiend = the devil　母の愛人であることが暴かれそうになったエアロンを、自身レイプ犯であるディミートリアスが「悪魔」と呼んで罵っている。

CHIRON It shall not live.

AARON It shall not die.

NURSE Aaron, it must. The mother wills it so.

AARON What, must it, nurse? Then let no man but I   85
Do execution on my flesh and blood.

DEMETRIUS I'll broach the tadpole on my rapier's point.
Nurse, give it me. My sword shall soon dispatch it.

AARON Sooner this sword shall plow thy bowels up!
Stay, murderous villains, will you kill your brother?   90
Now, by the burning tapers of the sky
That shone so brightly when this boy was got,
He dies upon my scimitar's sharp point
That touches this my firstborn son and heir.
I tell you, younglings, not Enceladus   95
With all his threat'ning band of Typhon's brood,
Nor great Alcides, nor the god of war
Shall seize this prey out of his father's hands.
What, what, you sanguine, shallow-hearted boys,
Ye white-limed walls, ye alehouse painted signs!   100
Coal-black is better than another hue
In that it scorns to bear another hue;
For all the water in the ocean
Can never turn the swan's black legs to white,
Although she lave them hourly in the flood.   105
Tell the Empress from me, I am of age
To keep mine own, excuse it how she can.

DEMETRIUS Wilt thou betray thy noble mistress thus?

AARON My mistress is my mistress, this myself,
The vigour and the picture of my youth.   110
This before all the world do I prefer;
This maugre all the world will I keep safe,
Or some of you shall smoke for it in Rome.

DEMETRIUS By this our mother is forever shamed.

82. shall not live 「生かしてはおかない」

84. wills = wants

87. broach the tadpole 「そのオタマジャクシを串刺しにしてやる」残忍で淫乱なメタファー。レイプと舌・両手切断の犯行を連想させる。

88. dispatch = make away with, kill

89. plow thy bowels up 「お前の腑を掘り起こす」

91. by the burning tapers of the sky 「空の燃えさかる蠟燭にかけて」4. 2. 32 注参照。

92. was got 「身籠られた」

93. scimitar 「シミタール刀」トルコや中東で使用された新月形の刀。

94. my firstborn son and heir 2. 3. 2-3 後注参照。子を儲けたエアロンが悪党から子煩悩な父親に変身する瞬間はこの芝居の有名な見せ場。タイタスとは対照的な父親像がこの先提示される。

95-96. Enceladus ... band of Typhon's brood ⇒後注

97. Alcides 「ヘーラクレース」(Hercules / Gk. Herakles)

the god of war 「軍神マルス」(Mars / Gk. Ares)

98. this prey エアロンは我が子を手強い捕食者に狙われる獲物に喩える。

99. sanguine 「多血質の」古代生理学で言う四体液の中でも血液が多い体質。赤ら顔、勇敢・好色などの性格がその特徴のうちに数えられるが、続くshallow-hearted と矛盾するので「勇敢」は該当しない。

shallow-hearted 「臆病な」

100. Ye 古い形の二人称複数主格形。

white-limed = whitewashed「偽善者の」

alehouse painted signs 「酒場の色を塗りたくって（隠している）看板」

101. Coal-black = as black as coal

102. scorns to bear another hue 格言的。Tilley B436 'Black will take no other hue.'

103-04. all the water in the ocean / Can never turn the swan's black legs to white 「たとえ白鳥が毎時間かけて自分の脚を波に浸けて洗おうとも、黒い脚を白く変えることはできない」

105. lave = wash

107. excuse it how she can 「あいつにはなんとでも言い訳をさせておけ」

how = in the way that

112. maugre = in spite of

113. smoke = smart, suffer severely (*OED* smoke, *v.* 4.)

CHIRON   Rome will despise her for this foul escape.   115

NURSE   The Emperor in his rage will doom her death.

CHIRON   I blush to think upon this ignomy.

AARON   Why, there's the privilege your beauty bears.

Fie, treacherous hue, that will betray with blushing

The close enacts and counsels of thy heart.   120

Here's a young lad framed of another leer.

Look how the black slave smiles upon the father,

As who should say 'Old lad, I am thine own.'

He is your brother, lords, sensibly fed

Of that self blood that first gave life to you,   125

And from that womb where you imprisoned were

He is enfranchisèd and come to light.

Nay, he is your brother by the surer side,

Although my seal be stampèd in his face.

NURSE   Aaron, what shall I say unto the Empress?   130

DEMETRIUS   Advise thee, Aaron, what is to be done,

And we will all subscribe to thy advice.

Save thou the child, so we may all be safe.

AARON   Then sit we down, and let us all consult.

My son and I will have the wind of you.   135

Keep there. Now talk at pleasure of your safety.

DEMETRIUS   [*To Nurse*]   How many women saw this child of
  his?

AARON   Why, so, brave lords! When we join in league,

I am a lamb; but if you brave the Moor,

The chafèd boar, the mountain lioness,   140

The ocean swells not so as Aaron storms.

But say again, how many saw the child?

NURSE   Cornelia the midwife and myself,

And no one else but the delivered Empress.

AARON   The Empress, the midwife, and yourself.   145

Two may keep counsel when the third's away.

115. escape = an outrageous transgression, applied especially to breaches of chastity (*OED* escape, *n.*[1] 7)

118. privilege アイロニー。

120. close enacts and counsels 「秘密にすべき目的や計画」 close = concealed, secret   enact = *fig.* purpose, resolution (*OED* enact, *n.*)
counsel = plan, design; matter of confidence

121. leer = cheek, face; look or appearance

122. slave = rascal, fellow (OED slave, *n.*[1] 1.c.)

123. As who should = like one who would

124. sensibly = in a manner perceptible to the senses; so far as can be perceived (*OED* sensibly, *adv.* 1.a.)

125. self = same, identical, selfsame

127. enfranchisèd = released from confinement

128. by the surer side = by your mother's side

129. my seal be stampèd 4. 2. 71 注参照。

131. Advise thee = deliberate, consider   thee = thyself

132. subscribe to = declare or consider oneself to be in agreement with (a statement, opinion, proposal, theory, or the like) (*OED* subscribe, *v.* 2.a.)

133. so = so long as

135. have the wind of = scent or detect by or as by the wind; keep under observation   狩猟の用語。

136. at pleasure = with pleasure; at will 「喜んで」、「お好きなように」

139. brave 4. 2. 36 注参照。

140. chafèd = angered, vexed

144. delivered 「出産を終えた」

146. keep counsel = observe secrecy

Go to the Empress; tell her this I said.   *He kills her*

'Wheak, wheak!' So cries a pig preparèd to the spit.

DEMETRIUS   What mean'st thou, Aaron? Wherefore didst thou
    this?

AARON   O Lord, sir, 'tis a deed of policy.   150

Shall she live to betray this guilt of ours,

A long-tongued babbling gossip? No, lords, no.

And now be it known to you my full intent:

Not far one Muliteus my countryman

His wife but yesternight was brought to bed.   155

His child is like to her, fair as you are.

Go pack with him, and give the mother gold,

And tell them both the circumstance of all,

And how by this their child shall be advanced

And be receivèd for the Emperor's heir,   160

And substituted in the place of mine,

To calm this tempest whirling in the court;

And let the Emperor dandle him for his own.

Hark you, lords, you see I have given her physic,

And you must needs bestow her funeral.   165

The fields are near, and you are gallant grooms.

This done, see that you take no longer days,

But send the midwife presently to me.

The midwife and the nurse well made away,

Then let the ladies tattle what they please.   170

CHIRON   Aaron, I see thou wilt not trust the air

With secrets.

DEMETRIUS   For this care of Tamora,

Herself and hers are highly bound to thee.

                    Exeunt [Demetrius and Chiron]

AARON   Now to the Goths, as swift as swallow flies,   175

There to dispose this treasure in mine arms

And secretly to greet the Empress' friends. —

148. Wheak = squeak, whine

　spit 「焼き串」

150. policy = a device, an expedient, a stratagem, a trick (*OED* policy, *n.*[1] 2.b.)

152. long-tongued = talkative, chattering; prone to speaking out of turn or revealing secrets 「余計なことを喋りがちな」

155. was brought to bed = was put to bed to be delivered of a child

156. like to = like　2. 3. 223 参照。

157. pack = enter into a private arrangement; conspire

163. for his own 「自分の子だと思って」

164. given her physic 「治療してやった」アイロニー。

　physic = cathartic, purgative; medical treatment

165. must needs = of necessity; necessarily　needs は副詞。

166. grooms = fellows; (in pastoral poetry) shepherds (*OED* groom, *n.*[1] 2.)

168. presently = immediately

169. made away　2. 3. 189 注参照。

170. tattle = talk idly, chatter, gossip

　please = desire, like

171. wilt not trust the air = will not trust even the air 「風にさえバラさないんだな」（松岡訳）　wilt は主語 thou に対する will の定動詞形。

173. this care of Tamora 「母のタモラをこのように気遣ってくれること」

176. dispose = put into the proper or suitable place (*OED* dispose, *v.* 1.b.)

Come on, you thick-lipped slave, I'll bear you hence,
For it is you that puts us to our shifts.
I'll make you feed on berries and on roots,   180
And feed on curds and whey, and suck the goat,
And cabin in a cave, and bring you up
To be a warrior and command a camp.   *Exit [with the baby]*

[ACT IV SCENE III]

Enter Titus, old Marcus, young Lucius, and other gentlemen
[Publius, Caius and Sempronius] with bows, and Titus bears the
arrows with letters on the ends of them

TITUS   Come, Marcus, come. Kinsmen, this is the way.
Sir boy, let me see your archery.
Look you draw home enough and 'tis there straight.
Terras Astraea reliquit.
Be you remembered, Marcus, she's gone, she's fled.   5
Sirs, take you to your tools. You, cousins, shall
Go sound the ocean and cast your nets;
Happily you may catch her in the sea;
Yet there's as little justice as at land.
No; Publius and Sempronius, you must do it.   10
'Tis you must dig with mattock and with spade,
And pierce the inmost center of the Earth.
Then, when you come to Pluto's region,
I pray you, deliver him this petition.
Tell him it is for justice and for aid,   15
And that it comes from old Andronicus,
Shaken with sorrows in ungrateful Rome.
Ah, Rome! Well, well, I made thee miserable
What time I threw the people's suffrages
On him that thus doth tyrannize o'er me.   20
Go, get you gone, and pray be careful all,

178. thick-lipped　Cf. *Othello*, 1. 1. 'What a full fortune does the thicklips owe / If he can carry't thus!'（こんな風にまんまと彼女を手に入れられるなら、あの唇の太い野郎たいした果報者だ）『オセロー』では横恋慕のロダリーゴーがオセローに嫉妬して言う台詞。それとは対照的に、ここではエアロンがアフリカ系の血統とその身体的特長を自負する。　　**slave** = rascal; fellow 親しみを込めて「おまえ、こいつ」、あるいは我が子のこの先の苦労を憐れんで「奴隷」の意味に。　　**hence** = away from this place

179. shifts = evasive devices, stratagems

181. curds　「凝乳」　**whey**　「乳漿」　**suck the goat**　「山羊の乳を吸う」

182. cabin = dwell, take shelter, as in a cabin

183. camp = combat, battle（*OED* camp, *n.¹* 1.）

〔4. 3〕あらすじ……………………………………………………………………………

　タイタスが一族を連れて現れ、神々へ宛てた手紙を結わえつけた矢をサターナイナスのいる宮廷へ向けて射掛けさせる。場の後半では、訴訟ごとで鳩を携えて護民官へ嘆願に向かう途中の道化が通りかかる。道化は、道化特有のナンセンスな言葉の遣り取りの末、何も知らぬままタイタスから悪意の挑戦状らしきものを渡され、それで小刀を包み皇帝サターナイナスへ届けるよう託される。道化は褒美を期待して皇帝のもとへ向かう。　⇒後注

………………………………………………………………………………………………

3. Look = take care, make sure (with clause as object)　**draw home**　「(弓を)目一杯に引け」　home = to the ultimate position（*OED* home, *adv.* 4.b.）

4. *Terras Astraea reliquit* = Astraea has quit the earth（Lat.）　⇒後注

5. Be you remembered = remember

6. take you = take yourselves　　**cousins**　2. 4. 12 注参照。

7. sound = investigate (water, etc.) by the use of the line and lead or other means, in order to ascertain the depth or quality of the bottom（*OED* sound, *v.²* 4.a.）.「(女神アストライアが海中に隠れているだろうから)海底まで探れ」の意。　　**nets**　「(魚を獲る)網」

8. Happily = by chance; perhaps, possibly

11. mattock and ... spade　「つるはしと鋤」

13. Pluto's region = Hades 「冥界」ギリシャ神話で神プルートーンが支配する。

19. What time = when

19-20. threw people's suffrages / On him　「(俺への)民衆の支持をあの男にくれてやった」1. 1. 20-24, 179-86, 224-30（特に 184, 229 各注）参照。

21. get you gone = go, be off（*OED* get *v.* P3.b.）　　**careful** = circumspect, watchful「油断なく偵察・監視して」（*OED* careful, *adj.* 4.）

And leave you not a man-of-war unsearched.
This wicked emperor may have shipped her hence,
And, kinsmen, then we may go pipe for justice.

MARCUS   O Publius, is not this a heavy case   25
To see thy noble uncle thus distract?

PUBLIUS   Therefore, my lords, it highly us concerns
By day and night t' attend him carefully,
And feed his humor kindly as we may,
Till time beget some careful remedy.   30

MARCUS   Kinsmen, his sorrows are past remedy
But [   ]
Join with the Goths, and with revengeful war
Take wreak on Rome for this ingratitude,
And vengeance on the traitor Saturnine.   35

TITUS   Publius, how now? How now, my masters?
What, have you met with her?

PUBLIUS   No, my good lord, but Pluto sends you word,
If you will have Revenge from hell, you shall.
Marry, for Justice, she is so employed,   40
He thinks, with Jove in heaven, or somewhere else,
So that perforce you must needs stay a time.

TITUS   He doth me wrong to feed me with delays.
I'll dive into the burning lake below
And pull her out of Acheron by the heels.   45
Marcus, we are but shrubs, no cedars we,
No big-boned men framed of the Cyclops' size,
But metal, Marcus, steel to the very back,
Yet wrung with wrongs more than our backs can bear;
And sith there's no justice in earth nor hell,   50
We will solicit heaven and move the gods
To send down Justice for to wreak our wrongs.
Come, to this gear. You are a good archer, Marcus.

He gives them the arrows

22. man-of-war 「軍艦」

23. shipped her hence = sent her off by ship her 「正義」の人格化すなわち 女神アストライア（Astraea）。 4. 3. 4 注参照。

24. pipe = blow a pipe; whistle (*OED* pipe, *v.*¹ 5.b.)

for justice 「正義を求めて」

26. distract = deranged in mind; mad 少なくともマーカス他一族の者には タイタスの狂気は真性のものと思われている。『ハムレット』でも主人公の狂 態に最も怯え傷つくのは恋人オフィーリアと母ガートルードで、家族。

29. feed = gratify, minister to the demands of **kindly** = in a suitable or appropriate manner, fittingly 「（病状等に）適切に」; with natural and familial affection 「優しく情愛を込めて」(*OED* kindly, *adv.* 1. c. and 3.) **may** = can

30. beget = furnish, provide; (of a father or of both parents) to procreate 時を人の親に喩えるメタファーともとれる。 **careful** = full of care or concern for; taking good care of (*OED* careful, *adj.* 3.)

32. But [　] But で始まる 1 行分の本文が Q1 で欠落している。

33. revengeful war「復讐心を燃やした戦い、報復戦」 revengeful = characterized by a desire for revenge; vindictive

34. wreak = pain or punishment inflicted in return for an injury, wrong, offence; hurt or harm done from vindictive motives; vengeance, revenge 「仕返し、復讐」(*OED* wreak, *n.* 1.)

38. Pluto sends you word ... タイタスの甥パブリアスは伯父の狂気を信じて、 そのファンタジーに迎合する作り話をする。

39. will have = want to have **Revenge** ⇒後注

40. Marry 4. 1. 121 注参照。

41. He = Pluto

42. perforce = of necessity, inevitably **must needs stay** 「待たなければ ならない」4. 2. 165 注参照。

43. feed 4. 3. 29 注参照。

44-45. the burning lake below ... Acheron ⇒後注

47. big-boned = of large build **the Cyclops' size** ⇒後注

48. to the very back 「まさに背中に至るまで」

49. wrung 「打ちひしがれた」wring の過去分詞形。 **backs** 「背中、体」

50. sith = since

51. solicit = entreat, ask earnestly **heaven** = the power or majesty of heaven

52. for to = in order to **wreak** = revenge

53. gear = armour, arms ここでは矢を指す。

'*Ad Jovem,*' that's for you; here, '*Ad Apollinem*';

'*Ad Martem,*' that's for myself;   55

Here, boy, 'to Pallas'; here, 'to Mercury';

'To Saturn,' Caius — not to Saturnine;

You were as good to shoot against the wind.

To it, boy; Marcus, loose when I bid.

Of my word, I have written to effect;   60

There's not a god left unsolicited.

MARCUS   Kinsmen, shoot all your shafts into the court.

We will afflict the Emperor in his pride.

TITUS   Now, masters, draw. [*They shoot*]

                      O, well said, Lucius!

Good boy, in Virgo's lap! Give it Pallas.   65

MARCUS   My lord, I aim a mile beyond the moon.

Your letter is with Jupiter by this.

TITUS   Ha, ha! Publius, Publius, what hast thou done?

See, see, thou hast shot off one of Taurus' horns!

MARCUS   This was the sport, my lord; when Publius shot,   70

The Bull, being galled, gave Aries such a knock

That down fell both the Ram's horns in the court,

And who should find them but the Empress' villain?

She laughed and told the Moor he should not choose

But give them to his master for a present.   75

TITUS   Why, there it goes. God give his Lordship joy!

Enter the Clown with a basket and two pigeons in it

News, news from heaven! Marcus, the post is come.

Sirrah, what tidings? Have you any letters?

Shall I have Justice? What says Jupiter?

CLOWN   Ho, the gibbet-maker? He says that he hath taken   80
them down again, for the man must not be hanged till the
next week.

TITUS   But what says Jupiter, I ask thee?

54-55. Ad Jovem ... Ad Apollinem ... Ad Martem　⇒後注

57. Saturn ... not to Saturnine　⇒後注

58. were as good to shoot against the wind　「(サターナイナスに嘆願などしたら) 風に向かって矢を放つようなものだろう」

59. loose = let loose, release　動詞。

60. Of my word = on my word「誓って言うが」　**to effect** = to accomplish my purpose (*OED* effect, *v.* 2.)

64. well said = well done (Waith)

65. in Virgo's lap　⇒後注　　**Pallas** = Pallas Athena アテーナーも処女神。

66. aim ... beyond the moon　諺風。Tilley M1114 'He casts beyond the Moon (= He indulges in wild conjecture).' (Waith) シェイクスピアの悲劇で諺を多く使うのは、主人公の補佐役的地位にある人物の台詞の特徴の1つ。

67. is with Jupiter by this　「いまごろはもうユーピテル神に届いている」

69. shot off one of Taurus' horns　「牡牛座の角の1つを射落とした」角は寝取られ亭主 (cuckold) の頭に生えるとされる角を連想させ、次行以下のマーカスの戯言に繋がる。

70-75. This was the sport ... for a present　⇒後注

71. The Bull　上述69行のラテン語 Taurus を英語に言い換えている。観客への配慮。　　**being galled** = being harassed with arrows　**Aries**「牡羊座」これもすぐに次行で英訳 Ram に言い換えられる。

73. villain = servant (with a play on wickedness) (Waith)

76. there it goes = common exclamation when a thing falls, disappears, goes off, breaks, bursts, or the like　「あらまあ、おやおや」(*OED* there, *adv.* 16.)

76 SD.　Clown = countryman, rustic, or peasant (*OED* clown, *n.* 1.); a fool or jester, as a stage-character (*OED* clown, *n.* 3.)

77. the post is come　「手紙の配達人が来た」 post = a person who travels express with letters, dispatches, etc.; a courier　実際にはただの田舎者の請願者であることが明白ながら、手紙を持たせるつもりで勝手にこう呼んでいる。

78. Sirrah　身分の低い者に対して、軽蔑しあるいは自分の権威をかさに着て言う呼びかけの言葉。「やい、おい、こら」　**what tidings?**　先ほどそれぞれの矢につけて放った神々へ宛てた手紙への反応を訊いている。

80. gibbet-maker　「絞首台作りの職人」道化は Jupiter という語を聞き取れず、英語で発音の近い gibbet-maker ととる。古代の神様の名前も知らない田舎者として、道化はシェイクスピアの劇場の観客であった大衆に近い感覚の役柄。　　**80-81. hath taken them down**　「絞首台を取り外した」

Clown   Alas, sir, I know not Jubiter; I never drank with him
in all my life.   85

Titus   Why, villain, art not thou the carrier?

Clown   Ay, of my pigeons, sir; nothing else.

Titus   Why, didst thou not come from heaven?

Clown   From heaven? Alas, sir, I never came there. God forbid
I should be so bold to press to heaven in my young days. Why,   90
I am going with my pigeons to the tribunal plebs, to take up
a matter of brawl betwixt my uncle and one of the Emperal's
men.

Marcus   Why, sir, that is as fit as can be to serve for your
oration; and let him deliver the pigeons to the Emperor from   95
you.

Titus   Tell me, can you deliver an oration to the Emperor with
a grace?

Clown   Nay, truly, sir, I could never say grace in all my life.

Titus   Sirrah, come hither. Make no more ado,   100
But give your pigeons to the Emperor.
By me thou shalt have justice at his hands.
Hold, hold; meanwhile here's money for thy charges.
Give me pen and ink.   [*Writes*]
Sirrah, can you with a grace deliver up a supplication?   105

Clown   Ay, sir.

Titus   Then here is a supplication for you, and when you
come to him, at the first approach you must kneel, then kiss
his foot, then deliver up your pigeons, and then look for your
reward. I'll be at hand, sir. See you do it bravely. [*Gives him a*   110
paper]

Clown   I warrant you, sir. Let me alone.

Titus   Sirrah, hast thou a knife? Come, let me see it.
Here, Marcus, fold it in the oration;
For thou must make it like an humble suppliant,
And when thou hast given it to the Emperor,   115

84. Jubiter ⇒後注

86. carrier 一般に「（委託されて）物を運ぶ人」を指すが、タイタスはa person (or animal) that carries or conveys a message or other communication (*OED* carrier, *n.*¹ 3.b.) という特殊な意味で用いている。田舎者の道化は伝書鳩並みの扱い。後者の意味ではシェイクスピアのこの場面が *OED* で初出の例。

88-89. from heaven? / From heaven? タイタスが意図するのはユーピテル他の神々が住む天。一方で道化にとって heaven は「（キリスト教における）天国」。タイタスが悪意の佯狂か真性の狂気か問題のところだが、道化の無垢との対比が明白なやり取り。

90. press = advance with force or eagerness; hasten

91. pigeons 4. 3. 86 注参照。鳩はたぶん道化から護民官への土産あるいは賄賂。道化としては伝書鳩として携行しているつもりはない。 **tribunal plebs** 道化による「平民の護民官（Lat. tribunus plebis）」の言い損ないだが、その英訳 tribune of the people よりもラテン語の元の名称に近い発音。

take up = arrange a friendly settlement of (Waith)

92. brawl = a noisy turbulent quarrel「騒々しい喧嘩」これも道化による言い間違え。「揉めごと（trouble, dispute）」あるいは「裁判沙汰（lawsuit）」とでも言うべきところ。Emperal's「皇帝の（Emperor's）」の言い間違え。

94-99. ⇒後注

95. oration = A formal discourse delivered in elevated and dignified language, esp. one given on a ceremonial occasion「式辞」

95-96. let him deliver the pigeons to the Emperor from you 「（道化の持っている）鳩をあなたからの贈り物として皇帝に届けさせなさい」タイタスに道化の鳩を横領させる提案だが、マーカスが両者をそれぞれ狂気および無知と見做してのことか。無防備な道化の善意が復讐者の狂気（vengeance）の中で孤立する。 **97-98. with a grace** = appropriately, gracefully

99. say grace 「（食前または食後に）感謝の祈りを捧げる」ごく短い祈りですら憶えられず、唱えることができなかったという意味で言っている。

100-01. Make no more ado, / But = without further fuss or ceremony

102. have justice at his hands 「皇帝から正当な裁きを下してもらう」観客には後でアイロニーとわかる台詞。

103. charges = tasks laid upon one (*OED* charge, *n.* 12.)

105-11. Sirrah, can you ... Let me alone. ⇒後注

110. bravely = finely, handsomely

113-14. oration; / For thou must make it like an humble suppliant, T. W. Craik による修正（Bate）。Q1 の Oration, / For thou hast made it like an humble Suppliant. では文意が通じない。

Knock at my door and tell me what he says.

CLOWN   God be with you, sir. I will.   *Exit*

TITUS   Come, Marcus, let us go. — Publius, follow me. *Exeunt*

[ACT IV SCENE IV]

Enter Emperor and Empress and her two sons [Chiron and Demetrius, with Attendants]; the Emperor brings the arrows in his hand that Titus shot at him

SATURNINUS   Why, lords, what wrongs are these! Was ever seen
An emperor in Rome thus overborne,
Troubled, confronted thus, and for the extent
Of equal justice, used in such contempt?
My lords, you know, as know the mightful gods,   5
However these disturbers of our peace
Buzz in the people's ears, there naught hath passed
But even with law against the wilful sons
Of old Andronicus. And what an if
His sorrows have so overwhelmed his wits?   10
Shall we be thus afflicted in his wreaks,
His fits, his frenzy, and his bitterness?
And now he writes to heaven for his redress!
See, here's 'to Jove,' and this 'to Mercury,'
This 'to Apollo,' this to the god of war.   15
Sweet scrolls to fly about the streets of Rome!
What's this but libeling against the Senate
And blazoning our unjustice everywhere?
A goodly humour is it not, my lords?
As who would say, in Rome no justice were.   20
But if I live, his feignèd ecstasies
Shall be no shelter to these outrages,
But he and his shall know that justice lives
In Saturninus' health, whom, if he sleep,

〔**4. 4**〕あらすじ・・

　タイタスから射掛けられた矢を手にした皇帝サターナイナスが、タイタスの大胆な挑発に怒りをぶちまける。そこへタイタスから手紙を託された道化が登場し、ナイフを包んだ手紙を鳩とともにサターナイナスに差し出す。手紙を読んだ皇帝によって、道化は即座に縛り首を宣告される。次いで伝令が到着し、追放されていたタイタスの長男ルーシアスがゴート族を率いてローマへ向かって進軍しているという知らせをもたらす。それを聞いたサターナイナスは、ローマの民衆から支持の厚いルーシアスが相手では勝ち目がないと思って怯える。タモラが夫サターナイナスを説得し、策略でタイタスを騙してルーシアスとの講和交渉に持ち込もうと提案する。交渉の場をタイタスの居宅に指定し、使者をルーシアスのもとへ送る。

・・

2. overborne = oppressed, overcome

3. confronted < confront = face in hostility or defiance

3-4. for the extent / Of equal justice 「公平な裁きをしてやった報いに」
extent ＝ the showing or exercising (justice, kindness, etc.) (*OED*
extent, *n.* 6.a.)　　**4. used** ＝ treated in a specified manner (*OED* use, *v.*
17.a.)　　**6. However** ＝ No matter how

7-8. there naught ... with law 「合法でない裁定はいっさいなされなかった」

8. even = in accord (Waith)　　**wilful** = perverse, obstinate

9. And what an if ... ＝ And what if ...「仮に…だとして、それがなんだ」

10. wits ＝ The understanding or mental faculties in respect of their
condition; chiefly 'right mind', 'reason', 'senses', sanity (*OED* wit, *n.* 4.)

11. wreaks = vengeance「復讐心」4. 3. 34 注参照。

12. fits ... frenzy ... bitterness　⇒後注

13. redress ＝ remedy for trouble; amendment of a grievance (*OED*
redress, *n.* 1.c. and 2.)　　**16. Sweet** ＝ pleasant　アイロニー。

17. but ＝ nothing but; neither more nor less than, actually (*OED* but, *adv.*
2.a. and b.)　　**libeling** 「誹謗」

18. blazoning < blazon = proclaim, make public, 'trumpet' ＝ blaze「大袈裟に吹聴して広める」

19. goodly 「結構な」アイロニー。(*OED* goodly, *adj.* 3.b.)
humour ＝ behaviour regarded as whimsical, odd, or quaint

20. As who would say ＝ as if he would say

21. ecstasies ＝ the state of being 'beside oneself', thrown into a frenzy or
a stupor, with anxiety, fear or passion (*OED* ecstasy, *n.* 1.)「忘我、恍惚」

23. he and his ＝ Titus and his family

24. whom　サターナイナスを指す。　　**he sleep** ＝ Saturninus sleep

He'll so awake as he in fury shall 25
Cut off the proud'st conspirator that lives.
TAMORA My gracious lord, my lovely Saturnine,
Lord of my life, commander of my thoughts,
Calm thee, and bear the faults of Titus' age,
Th' effects of sorrow for his valiant sons, 30
Whose loss hath pierced him deep and scarred his heart,
And rather comfort his distressèd plight
Than prosecute the meanest or the best
For these contempts. [*Aside*] Why, thus it shall become
High-witted Tamora to gloze with all. 35
But, Titus, I have touched thee to the quick.
Thy lifeblood out, if Aaron now be wise,
Then is all safe, the anchor in the port.

Enter Clown

How now, good fellow, wouldst thou speak with us?
CLOWN Yea, forsooth, an your Mistresship be Emperial. 40
TAMORA Empress I am, but yonder sits the Emperor.
CLOWN 'Tis he! God and Saint Stephen give you good e'en. I
have brought you a letter and a couple of pigeons here.
                              [*Saturninus*] *reads the letter.*
SATURNINUS Go, take him away, and hang him presently.
CLOWN How much money must I have? 45
TAMORA Come, sirrah, you must be hanged.
CLOWN Hanged! By 'r Lady, then I have brought up a neck to
      a fair end.   *Exit* [*with Attendants*]
SATURNINUS Despiteful and intolerable wrongs!
Shall I endure this monstrous villainy?
I know from whence this same device proceeds. 50
May this be borne? — as if his traitorous sons,
That died by law for murder of our brother,
Have by my means been butchered wrongfully!

25. He'll = Titus will

as he = as Saturninus　21 行からの一文で人称代名詞 he が過剰に繰り返され文意が取りにくくなっている。文の乱れは話し手サターナイナスの心の動揺・不安・興奮を映し出すもの。

29. Calm thee = calm thyself　　**faults** = misdeeds, transgressions

33. prosecute the meanest or the best = institute legal proceedings, whether the meanest or the best punishment; seek the worst or the best revenge

34. contempts = cases of disobedience to or open disrespect for the lawful commands of the monarch (*OED* contempt, *n.* 2.a.)

35. High-witted < wit = mental faculties, intellectual powers (*OED* wit, *n.* 3.c.)

gloze = veil with specious comments; palliate「へつらう、言い繕う」

36. touched thee to the quick「おまえの急所を捕まえた」　quick = any part of a wound, an ulcer, the body, etc., that is sensitive or painful

37. lifeblood = the blood necessary for life

38. the anchor in the port「港に錨をおろして」危険が回避されたというメタファー。

39. How now = elliptical for 'How is it now?' Often used interjectionally.

40. an = if　　**Emperial**　Empress の言い間違え。

42. God and Saint Stephen　この異教的設定の芝居で明確にキリスト教（カトリック）信仰のイメージと関連づけられるのは、田舎者であるこの道化のみ。他には、曖昧で解釈が難しいが、乳飲み児を連れたエアロンが修道院の廃墟に隠れるシーン（5. 1. 20-26）。　Saint Stephen　聖ステファヌス（?-AD 36）はキリスト教最初の殉教者として知られる。　　**good e'en** = good evening

45. must I have?　ここで could などの代わりに must と言うのは道化らしいおとぼけか。古英語・中英語では must は現代英語の might, could, should に相当する意味で使われたが現代は廃語。*OED* 最後の用例は 15 世紀（must, *v*[1] 1.a. and b.）。

46. sirrah　4. 3. 78 注参照。

47. By 'r Lady = by Our Lady「聖母様にかけて、おやまあ」4. 4. 42 注参照。

47-48. have brought up a neck to a fair end「これまで育ててやった首も結構な最期だ」さらに「裁判に訴えて、とんだ決着だ」　neck = punning on 'laying of a charge in law'（Bate, Taylor）

Go, drag the villain hither by the hair.
Nor age nor honour shall shape privilege. 55
For this proud mock, I'll be thy slaughterman,
Sly, frantic wretch, that holp'st to make me great
In hope thyself should govern Rome and me.

Enter nuntius, Aemilius.

Saturninus   What news with thee, Aemilius?
Aemilius   Arm, my lords! Rome never had more cause. 60
  The Goths have gathered head, and with a power
  Of high-resolvèd men bent to the spoil,
  They hither march amain under conduct
  Of Lucius, son to old Andronicus,
  Who threats, in course of this revenge, to do 65
  As much as ever Coriolanus did.
Saturninus   Is warlike Lucius general of the Goths?
  These tidings nip me, and I hang the head
  As flowers with frost or grass beat down with storms.
  Ay, now begins our sorrows to approach. 70
  'Tis he the common people love so much.
  Myself hath often heard them say,
  When I have walkèd like a private man,
  That Lucius' banishment was wrongfully,
  And they have wished that Lucius were their emperor. 75
Tamora   Why should you fear? Is not your city strong?
Saturninus   Ay, but the citizens favour Lucius
  And will revolt from me to succor him.
Tamora   King, be thy thoughts imperious like thy name.
  Is the sun dimmed that gnats do fly in it? 80
  The eagle suffers little birds to sing
  And is not careful what they mean thereby,
  Knowing that with the shadow of his wings
  He can at pleasure stint their melody.

54. hither　「こっちへ」　**55. shape** = create, form, produce

57. wretch = a vile, sorry, or despicable person; a mean or contemptible creature (*OED* wretch, *n.* 3.a.)　**holp'st** = helped　二人称単数過去の古い形

58. In hope = in hope that

58 SD.　*nuntius* = messenger（Lat.）もとはギリシャ悲劇の「使者（アンゲロス）」。使者の報告が決定的に重要な演劇的機能を担ったが、初期近代の演劇では一般に形骸化して単なる「使者」を指す。　**60. cause** = 1. 1. 2 注参照。

61. head = a body of people gathered; a force raised, esp. in insurrection or revolt (*OED* head, *n.¹* 55.)

62. bent = determined, resolute, inclined　the spoil「（占領軍による）略奪」

63. amain = at full speed　**conduct** = leading, command

65. threats = threatens　動詞。

66. Coriolanus = Gnaeus（or Gaeus）Marcius Coriolanus　紀元前 5 世紀頃のローマの伝説的英雄。民衆に反感を持たれてローマを追われ、ウォルスキー（Volsci）の軍勢を率いてローマに進軍したとされる。Livius, *Ab Urbe Condita*, 2. 33-54; Plutarchus（Plutarkhos）, 'Coriolanus'. 後にシェイクスピア自身も彼を主人公とする悲劇『コリオレイナス（*Coriolanus*）』を書く。

67. warlike = skilled in war, valiant

68-69. These tidings nip me ... with storms.　ホメーロス叙事詩に由来する比喩（Homeric simile）に現れた花のイメージを連想させる。

　nip = pinch, bite;（of frost）injure or affect painfully; distress

　beat = beaten　過去分詞として flowers と grass の両方に掛かる。

71. 'Tis he the common people love = It is Lucius that the common people love

73. have walkèd like a private man　「（皇帝の身分を隠して）私人として歩いた」世相を探り庶民の声を聞くために、王や公爵が正体を隠してして巷を歩くという筋は、シェイクスピアの時代に流行した変装プロットの 1 つ。例えば Shakespeare, *Henry V*, 4. 1; *Measure for Measure*, 1. 3.

74. wrongfully = wrongfully done

79. imperious = of the nature or rank of an emperor; dominant「皇帝に相応しい、強権を振るう」

80. the sun ... gnats　君主を太陽に民衆を羽虫に喩えるメタファーの類例としては、*Henry VI, Part 3*, 2. 6 'The common people swarm like flies, / And whither fly the gnats but to the sun?'（Bate）

81. suffers = tolerates, allows

82. careful = troubled, anxious, heedful　**thereby** = by that

84. at pleasure = at will, at discretion　**stint** = cut short, stop

Even so mayst thou the giddy men of Rome.   85
Then cheer thy spirit, for know, thou Emperor,
I will enchant the old Andronicus
With words more sweet and yet more dangerous
Than baits to fish or honey-stalks to sheep,
Whenas the one is wounded with the bait,   90
The other rotted with delicious feed.

SATURNINUS   But he will not entreat his son for us.

TAMORA   If Tamora entreat him, then he will,
For I can smooth and fill his agèd ears
With golden promises, that were his heart   95
Almost impregnable, his old ears deaf,
Yet should both ear and heart obey my tongue.
[*To Aemilius*]   Go thou before to be our ambassador.
Say that the Emperor requests a parley
Of warlike Lucius, and appoint the meeting   100
Even at his father's house, the old Andronicus.

SATURNINUS   Aemilius, do this message honourably,
And if he stand in hostage for his safety,
Bid him demand what pledge will please him best.

AEMILIUS   Your bidding shall I do effectually.   *Exit* 105

TAMORA   Now will I to that old Andronicus
And temper him with all the art I have
To pluck proud Lucius from the warlike Goths.
And now, sweet emperor, be blithe again,
And bury all thy fear in my devices.   110

SATURNINUS   Then go successantly, and plead to him.

Exeunt

85. Even so 「まさにそのように」 even = exactly, precisely

mayst thou = mayst thou stint

giddy = mad, stupid; mentally intoxicated

89. honey-stalks＝clover S. Johnson, Plays of Shakespeare VI. 345/1: 'Honey-stalks clover flowers, which contains a sweet juice. It is common for cattle to overcharge themselves with clover, and die.' (*OED* honey, *n*, C1.b. (c) honey-stalks, *n*.)

90. Whenas = at the time at which; when

the one = fish

91. The other = sheep

feed = eating, grazing

rotted = destroyed ＜ rot「腐敗病（＝羊の肝臓病）」

93. If Tamora entreat 三人称単数で動詞が原形なのは、一種の仮定法現在。意味は If Tamora entreats とほとんど変わらない。

95. were his heart = if his heart were

96. impregnable = invincible, unconquerable

101. Even 4. 4. 85 注参照。

105. effectually = so as adequately to answer the purpose「首尾良くご命令どおりに

109. blithe = joyous, cheerful

110. devices 「計略、筋書き」実際にタモラは芝居がかったことをすることになる。

111. successantly = in succession？（*OED* successantly, *adv*.）*OED* の挙げる唯一の用例で、他に使用例がなく意味が不明。

⌈Act V Scene I⌉

Flourish. Enter Lucius with an army of Goths, with drum and soldiers.

LUCIUS   Approvèd warriors and my faithful friends,
    I have receivèd letters from great Rome
    Which signifies what hate they bear their emperor
    And how desirous of our sight they are.
    Therefore, great lords, be as your titles witness,   5
    Imperious, and impatient of your wrongs,
    And wherein Rome hath done you any scath,
    Let him make treble satisfaction.
FIRST GOTH   Brave slip sprung from the great Andronicus,
    Whose name was once our terror, now our comfort,   10
    Whose high exploits and honourable deeds
    Ingrateful Rome requites with foul contempt,
    Be bold in us. We'll follow where thou lead'st,
    Like stinging bees in hottest summer's day
    Led by their master to the flowered fields,   15
    And be avenged on cursèd Tamora.
GOTHS   And as he saith, so say we all with him.
LUCIUS   I humbly thank him, and I thank you all.
    But who comes here, led by a lusty Goth?

    Enter a Goth, leading of Aaron with his child in his arms.

SECOND GOTH   Renownèd Lucius, from our troops I strayed   20
    To gaze upon a ruinous monastery,
    And as I earnestly did fix mine eye
    Upon the wasted building, suddenly
    I heard a child cry underneath a wall.
    I made unto the noise, when soon I heard   25
    The crying babe controlled with this discourse:
    'Peace, tawny slave, half me and half thy dame!

〔**5. 1**〕あらすじ···

　ローマから追放されてゴート族のもとに身を寄せていたルーシアスが、ゴート人の軍勢を率いてローマへ進軍しようとする。そこへ乳飲み子とともに捕らえられたエアロンが連行される。見せしめにまず乳児からその父親エアロンの目の前で処刑しようとするルーシアスに対して、エアロンは自分の悪事をすべて告白することと引き換えに我が子を助けるよう要求する。ルーシアスはエアロンの告白を聴いた後、ひとまず親子の処刑を取りやめ、悪党に相応しいさらに過酷で効果的な処罰の機会を待つ。そこへさらに皇帝からの使者が到着し、ルーシアスの軍に講和交渉の申し入れを伝える。

■■

1. **Approvèd warriors** 「歴戦の勇士」 approvèd = proved or established by experience, tried, tested (*OED* approved, *adj.* 1.)

3. **signifies** 主語 letters の数と定動詞形が一致しない。この時代の英語ではしばしばあった。　　**they** ローマ市民たちを指す。

4. **how desirous of our sight they are** = how desirous they are to see us「彼らがいかに我が軍勢の到着を待ち望んでいるか」

5. **as your titles witness** 「(歴戦の勇士という)諸君の名が証人(証拠)であるように」動詞 witness の原義は「証言する」で、titles を擬人化している。

6. **Imperious** = dominant; stately
   your wrongs = the evil or damage that has been inflicted on you

7. **wherein** = in that respect in which (*OED* wherein, *adv.* 3.b.)
   Rome ローマの国家と同時に皇帝を指す。国家と国王／皇帝は同一という了解。ルーシアスはその曖昧さをゴート人の軍勢を動かすためのレトリックとして使う。　　**scath** = harm, damage

8. **him** 前行 Rome の注参照。　　**treble** = three times as much; triple
   satisfaction = the action or fact of paying compensation, or undergoing punishment in restitution for an injury or offence (*OED* satisfaction, *n.* 2.a.)

9. **slip** = a small shoot or scion; descendant

12. **requites** = repays; rewards　　**13. bold in** = confident in, sure of

14-15. **Like stinging bees ... flowered fields** 叙事詩的明喩 (Homeric simile)。

16. **be avenged on** = avenge yourself on; take vengeance on
   cursèd Tamora ⇒後注

19. **lusty** = healthy, strong, vigorous

21. **a ruinous monastery** ⇒後注および解説 10-15 頁。

25. **made unto** = proceeded towards, approached

26. **controlled** = checked, pacified「あやされて」

27. **dame** = a female parent of animals, dam ; mother (*OED* dame, *n.* 8. = dam *n²*.) 2. 3. 142 注参照。

Did not thy hue bewray whose brat thou art,
Had nature lent thee but thy mother's look,
Villain, thou mightst have been an emperor.   30
But where the bull and cow are both milk white,
They never do beget a coal-black calf.
Peace, villain, peace!' — even thus he rates the babe —
'For I must bear thee to a trusty Goth
Who, when he knows thou art the Empress' babe,   35
Will hold thee dearly for thy mother's sake.'
With this, my weapon drawn, I rushed upon him,
Surprised him suddenly, and brought him hither
To use as you think needful of the man.

LUCIUS   O worthy Goth, this is the incarnate devil   40
That robbed Andronicus of his good hand;
This is the pearl that pleased your empress' eye;
And here's the base fruit of her burning lust.
Say, wall-eyed slave, whither wouldst thou convey
This growing image of thy fiendlike face?   45
Why dost not speak? What, deaf? Not a word?
A halter, soldiers! Hang him on this tree,
And by his side his fruit of bastardy.

AARON   Touch not the boy. He is of royal blood.

LUCIUS   Too like the sire for ever being good.   50
First hang the child, that he may see it sprawl,
A sight to vex the father's soul withal.
Get me a ladder.

    [*Goths bring a ladder, and force Aaron to climb it*]

AARON   Lucius, save the child
And bear it from me to the Empress.
If thou do this, I'll show thee wondrous things   55
That highly may advantage thee to hear.
If thou wilt not, befall what may befall,

28. Did not thy hue bewray = If your hue did not bewray　bewray = expose, reveal

29. Had nature lent thee but = if nature had lent you only

30. Villain brat (5. 1. 28) と同様に、戯ぎれてあるいは親しみを込めて言う。

32. beget 「子をもうける」父親あるいは両親に関して言う。

33. even thus = just like this　　**rates** = scolds, berates

36. for thy mother's sake マーカスの 'for our father's sake and mother's care' (3. 1. 182) とジェンダーが対照的。

37. With this = hereupon

38. Surprised = attacked and captured suddenly and without warning

39. use = deal with; make use of 「処分する」と「利用する」両様の意味にとれる。　　**needful of the man** = as you think he deserves (Hughes)

40. incarnate devil = devil in flesh or in a human bodily form

42. pearl 真珠の白い色とエアロンの肌の黒い色に引っ掛けたアイロニー。

43. fruit = issue, product

44. wall-eyed = having eyes of an excessively light colour so that the iris is hardly distinguishable from the white　ルーシアスはこの劇の登場人物の中でも際立って人種的偏見の強い人物。

45. growing image of thy fiendlike face 「悪魔のようなお前の顔にどんどんそっくりになる似姿」エアロンの子を指す。

48. bastardy = the begetting of an illegitimate children; fornication (*OED* bastardy, *n.* 2.)

50. sire = male parent　　**ever** = in any degree　　**good** = having the qualities or characteristics (of royal blood)

51-52. First hang the child ... father's soul withal この芝居の初めで母親タモラの目の前でアラーバスを切り刻んで生贄にしようと言い出したのもルーシアス (1. 1. 96-99)。親の前で平然と子殺しをする点で、ルーシアスは悪党のエアロン、タモラ、カイロン、ディミートリアス以上に冷酷な軍人・政治家として造形されている。　　**sprawl** = move the limbs in a convulsive effort or struggle

56. advantage = profit, benefit

57. befall what may befall = let whatever can befall befall (on you)

I'll speak no more but 'Vengeance rot you all!'

LUCIUS   Say on, and if it please me which thou speak'st,
Thy child shall live, and I will see it nourished.   60

AARON   And if it please thee? Why, assure thee, Lucius,
'Twill vex thy soul to hear what I shall speak;
For I must talk of murders, rapes, and massacres,
Acts of black night, abominable deeds,
Complots of mischief, treason, villainies,   65
Ruthful to hear, yet piteously performed.
And this shall all be buried in my death,
Unless thou swear to me my child shall live.

LUCIUS   Tell on thy mind. I say thy child shall live.

AARON   Swear that he shall, and then I will begin.   70

LUCIUS   Who should I swear by? Thou believest no god.
That granted, how canst thou believe an oath?

AARON   What if I do not? As indeed I do not.
Yet, for I know thou art religious
And hast a thing within thee callèd conscience,   75
With twenty popish tricks and ceremonies
Which I have seen thee careful to observe,
Therefore I urge thy oath; for that I know
An idiot holds his bauble for a god
And keeps the oath which by that god he swears,   80
To that I'll urge him. Therefore thou shalt vow
By that same god, what god soe'er it be
That thou adorest and hast in reverence,
To save my boy, to nourish and bring him up,
Or else I will discover naught to thee.   85

LUCIUS   Even by my god I swear to thee I will.

AARON   First know thou, I begot him on the Empress.

LUCIUS   O, most insatiate and luxurious woman!

AARON   Tut, Lucius, this was but a deed of charity
To that which thou shalt hear of me anon.   90

58. Vengeance rot you all! 「復讐で、皆くたばれ！」子供を助けなかった場合の「復讐」という呪い。人間が陥りがちな「復讐心」を致命的な狂気としてアイロニックに述べている。合理主義者エアロンが放つ道化的な逆説（paradox）。⇒解説 22-25 頁。リチャード三世やイアーゴーなどシェイクスピア劇の代表的悪党と同様に、悪党エアロンは道化的機能を持つ人物。2. 3. 38 注参照。エアロンは悪事を純粋に悪事として、離れ業の遊戯のようにその実行に興じた。rot = cause to decay or decline　　**59. which**　先行詞は it。

61. And if = If　　**assure thee** = assure thyself; have confidence, trust

63. massacres　⇒後注

65. Complots = designs of a covert nature planned in concert（*OED* complot, *n.*)

66. Ruthful = dreadful, calamitous（*OED* ruthful, *adj.* 2.a.)
piteously = in a way that arouses pity

69. Tell on = speak　　**72. That granted** = If that is agreed

74. thou art religious 1. 1. 130 後注参照。嘆願を聞き入れず無抵抗のアラーバスを死者への犠牲として惨殺したルーシアスらの行為を、前者の母タモラは irreligious piety と呼んで非難した。religious と pious はこの芝居で終始問題含みの概念だが、ここでエアロンがあらためてそれを問う。

76. popish tricks and ceremonies　「カトリック風のインチキ臭い儀式」この芝居で多いアナクロニズムの 1 つ。新教国英国の通俗的感覚を映す。

78. Therefore = for that「それ故に、それにかけて」　　**urge** = demand for
that = for, because

79. idiot「道化」の意味もあった。　　**bauble** = a showy trinket or ornament such as would please a child; a baton or stick, surmounted by a fantastically carved head with asses' ears, carried by the Court Fool or jester of former days（*OED* bauble, *n.* 3. and 4.)

82. that same = that　same は指示詞 this, these, that, those などの後に過剰に添えられた形容詞で、現在では稀な古い用法。（*OED* same, *adj.* 5.)

82-83. what god soe'er it be / That thou adorest ...　シェイクスピア同時代の宗教対立を想起させるアイロニー。soe'er は what などで始まる句を強調する副詞。　　**85. naught** = nothing

86. Even「まさしく、他ならぬ」4. 4. 85 注参照。

87. begot him on the Empress「（父親として）皇后にその子を産ませた」

88. insatiate = never satisfied　　**luxurious** = lascivious, lecherous, unchaste　ルーシアスの女性蔑視については 5. 1. 16 後注参照。

89. but = only

90. To = compared with　　**anon** = straightway, at once

'Twas her two sons that murdered Bassianus.

They cut thy sister's tongue, and ravished her,

And cut her hands, and trimmed her as thou sawest.

Lucius   O detestable villain, call'st thou that trimming?

Aaron   Why, she was washed, and cut, and trimmed; and 'twas   95

Trim sport for them which had the doing of it.

Lucius   O, barbarous beastly villains, like thyself!

Aaron   Indeed, I was their tutor to instruct them.

That codding spirit had they from their mother,

As sure a card as ever won the set;   100

That bloody mind I think they learned of me,

As true a dog as ever fought at head.

Well, let my deeds be witness of my worth.

I trained thy brethren to that guileful hole

Where the dead corpse of Bassianus lay.   105

I wrote the letter that thy father found,

And hid the gold within that letter mentioned,

Confederate with the Queen and her two sons.

And what not done that thou hast cause to rue,

Wherein I had no stroke of mischief in it?   110

I played the cheater for thy father's hand,

And, when I had it, drew myself apart

And almost broke my heart with extreme laughter.

I pried me through the crevice of a wall

When, for his hand, he had his two sons' heads,   115

Beheld his tears, and laughed so heartily

That both mine eyes were rainy like to his.

And when I told the Empress of this sport,

She sounded almost at my pleasing tale,

And for my tidings gave me twenty kisses.   120

Goth   What, canst thou say all this and never blush?

Aaron   Ay, like a black dog, as the saying is.

91. 'Twas　2. 4. 2 注参照。

93. trimmed = cut level, dressed「きれいに刈りそろえた」

96. Trim =（in ironical use）fine, nice, pretty

99. codding = lecherous, lustful　シェイクスピアだけの稀な表現。（*OED* codding, *adj.*）　cod には the scrotum; a testicle の意味もある。（*OED* cod, *n.¹* 3.a.）

100. As sure a card ...　格言的。Tilley C74 'He has a sure card.'

　set = game

101. learned of = learned from

102. As true a dog ... fought at head　「獲物の頭から襲いかかる最強の犬のように」　The best bulldogs attacked the bull's head.（Waith）

103. witness of = witness to

　my worth　「（悪事の教師としての）私の価値・能力」

104. trained = enticed, led astray

　brethren = brothers

　guileful = treacherous

107. the gold within that letter mentioned = the gold within, which that letter mentioned　within　実際には「木の下の地中に」2. 3. 2-3 後注参照。

108. Confederate「共謀犯として」

109-10. what not done ... of mischief in it?　「あんたが悔しがるようなことで、実際そこにこの俺がタチの悪い一撃を加えていないようなことなどあっただろうか。」what not done = what was left undone　否定辞の繰り返し not ... no は二重否定でなく、修辞疑問を強調する。

　rue = regret, feel sorrow

　stroke = an act of striking; a blow

114. pried me = looked closely and curiously; spied

　crevice = crack, chink

117. like to = like　2. 3. 223 参照。

119. sounded = swooned, fainted（*OED* sound, *v.* 4）

120. tidings = reports, news

122. a black dog, as the saying is　Tilley D507 'To blush like a black dog.'

LUCIUS Art thou not sorry for these heinous deeds?

AARON Ay, that I had not done a thousand more.
 Even now I curse the day — and yet, I think,   125
 Few come within the compass of my curse —
 Wherein I did not some notorious ill,
 As kill a man, or else devise his death;
 Ravish a maid or plot the way to do it;
 Accuse some innocent and forswear myself;   130
 Set deadly enmity between two friends;
 Make poor men's cattle break their necks;
 Set fire on barns and haystalks in the night,
 And bid the owners quench them with their tears.
 Oft have I digged up dead men from their graves   135
 And set them upright at their dear friends' door,
 Even when their sorrows almost was forgot,
 And on their skins, as on the bark of trees,
 Have with my knife carvèd in Roman letters
 'Let not your sorrow die, though I am dead.'   140
 But I have done a thousand dreadful things
 As willingly as one would kill a fly,
 And nothing grieves me heartily indeed
 But that I cannot do ten thousand more.

LUCIUS Bring down the devil, for he must not die   145
 So sweet a death as hanging presently.

                    [*Aaron is brought down from the ladder*]

AARON If there be devils, would I were a devil,
 To live and burn in everlasting fire,
 So I might have your company in hell
 But to torment you with my bitter tongue.   150

LUCIUS Sirs, stop his mouth, and let him speak no more.

                    Enter Aemilius.

GOTH My lord, there is a messenger from Rome

123. heinous [ˈheinəs] = hateful, highly criminal

124. Ay [ʌɪ] = aye, yes 　2. 1. 90 注参照。

126. Few come within the compass of my curse 「自分が呪いたいような日は
僅かしかない」ほとんど毎日のように悪事を働いていたということ。
compass = bounds, limits; range within limits

127. Wherein = in which, when

**128-40. As kill a man, or else ... 'Let not your sorrow die, though I am
dead.'** マーロウの悲劇『マルタ島のユダヤ人』で主人公バラバス（Barabas）
が、買い取った奴隷イサモアに向かって言う台詞との類似がしばしば指摘され
ている（Waith）。バラバスは自分の残忍な所業の数々を語る。Marlowe,
The Jew of Malta, 2. 3 'As for myself, I walk abroad a-nights / And kill
sick people groaning under walls: / Sometimes I go about and poison
wells; / ...' 2. 1. 1-11 後注参照。

142. as one would kill a fly タイタス家の食卓でマーカスが蠅を殺しタイタス
がそれを咎め立てする場面（3. 2. 52-80）を参照。3 幕 2 場は Q1（1594）、Q2
（1600）、Q3（1600）にはなく、F1（1623）で初めて現れ、17 世紀になって
から加筆された一場だと推測されている。加筆された 3 幕 2 場の作者は、前
後の文脈に合わせるとともに、既存テクスト全般からイメージを拾った形跡が
窺われる。そのような可能性が指摘される行の一例。

146. sweet = agreeable, favourable, gracious

147-50. If there be devils ... with my bitter tongue エアロンが想像する滑稽
な地獄絵。

Desires to be admitted to your presence.

LUCIUS   Let him come near.
Welcome, Aemilius. What's the news from Rome?   155

AEMILIUS   Lord Lucius, and you princes of the Goths,
  The Roman Emperor greets you all by me;
  And, for he understands you are in arms,
  He craves a parley at your father's house,
  Willing you to demand your hostages,   160
  And they shall be immediately delivered.

GOTH   What says our general?

LUCIUS   Aemilius, let the Emperor give his pledges
  Unto my father and my uncle Marcus,
  And we will come. March away.   165

                              Flourish. Exeunt

[ACT V SCENE II]

Enter Tamora and her two sons, disguised

TAMORA   Thus, in this strange and sad habiliment
  I will encounter with Andronicus
  And say I am Revenge, sent from below
  To join with him and right his heinous wrongs.
  Knock at his study, where they say he keeps   5
  To ruminate strange plots of dire revenge.
  Tell him Revenge is come to join with him
  And work confusion on his enemies.

        They knock, and Titus [above] opens his study door

TITUS   Who doth molest my contemplation?
  Is it your trick to make me ope the door,   10
  That so my sad decrees may fly away
  And all my study be to no effect?
  You are deceived, for what I mean to do,

153. Desires = Who desires

  to your presence 「御前に」特に王侯や高貴な人物の場合に使う表現。ルーシアスはゴート族の将軍あるいは司令官（general）。

159. parley 「（休戦した状態で行う）敵軍との交渉」

160. Willing = desiring

163. pledges = hostages

〔**5. 2**〕あらすじ・・・

  タモラはルーシアスの率いるゴート軍との和平交渉のためタイタスにルーシアスを自分の館へ招くよう説得することを使命として、2人の息子を引き連れてタイタスの館を訪れる。タイタスが正気を失ったものと信じるタモラ母子は、復讐の女神とそのツレの姿に変装し、タイタスを騙して復讐の意図を玩ぼうと企む。しかしタイタスは狂気の幻想を逆手に取ってタモラのみ返し、2人の息子を捕縛する。佯狂を解いて正体を現したタイタスは、お前らの肉をパイにして母親に食べさせると告げてその場で斬殺する。

・・・

0 SD. *Enter Tamora and her two sons, disguised* 「タモラが復讐（の女神／寓意）に変装して登場」 ⇒後注

1. sad habiliment = dismal costume

3. Revenge, sent from below 「冥界から送られて来た復讐」芝居の登場人物としての復讐（Revenge）は、近いところではトーマス・キッドの『スペインの悲劇』（Thomas Kyd, *The Spanish Tragedy*）が有名。

4. right = correct, amend, rectify（*OED* right, *v.* 10 and 11.）

  his heinous wrongs 「彼の受けた酷い仕打ち」

5. keeps = stays（*OED* keep, *v.* 38.a.）

6. ruminate = turn over repeatedly in the mind

  dire = dreadful, terrible

8. confusion = destruction, perdition（*OED* confusion, *n.* 1.）

9. molest = cause trouble; meddle with

10. ope = open

11. sad decrees = solemn decisions　復讐の決意か。

  fly away 「吹き飛ぶ」 4. 1. 104 注参照。そこではタイタスが、復讐の決意がシビュラの予言さながら風で吹き飛ばされてしまわないようにしっかり刻んでおこうと言っている。

See here, in bloody lines I have set down,

And what is written shall be executed. 15

TAMROA   Titus, I am come to talk with thee.

TITUS   No, not a word. How can I grace my talk,

Wanting a hand to give it action?

Thou hast the odds of me; therefore, no more.

TAMORA   If thou didst know me, thou wouldst talk with me. 20

TITUS   I am not mad. I know thee well enough.

Witness this wretched stump; witness these crimson lines;

Witness these trenches made by grief and care;

Witness the tiring day and heavy night;

Witness all sorrow that I know thee well 25

For our proud Empress, mighty Tamora.

Is not thy coming for my other hand?

TAMORA   Know, thou sad man, I am not Tamora.

She is thy enemy, and I thy friend.

I am Revenge, sent from th'infernal kingdom 30

To ease the gnawing vulture of thy mind

By working wreakful vengeance on thy foes.

Come down and welcome me to this world's light.

Confer with me of murder and of death.

There's not a hollow cave or lurking-place, 35

No vast obscurity or misty vale

Where bloody murder or detested rape

Can couch for fear but I will find them out,

And in their ears tell them my dreadful name,

Revenge, which makes the foul offender quake. 40

TITUS   Art thou Revenge? And art thou sent to me

To be a torment to mine enemies?

TAMORA   I am. Therefore come down and welcome me.

TITUS   Do me some service ere I come to thee.

Lo, by thy side, where Rape and Murder stands, 45

Now give some surance that thou art Revenge:

14. in bloody lines 「血で文字を認めて」

17. grace my talk 「俺の話を飾る」 grace = adorn, embellish

18. Wanting ... action 「それに身振りでの演技を添える手がないのに」タモラの態度が芝居がかっているのを見抜いてか、タイタスは芝居・演技の比喩で応じる。

19. Thou hast the odds of me 「お前の方が俺より有利だ」

20. wouldst talk = would like to talk

22. stump 2. 4. 4 注参照。　　**crimson lines** = bloody lines（5. 2. 14）

23. trenches = long, narrow ditches or furrows cut out of the ground; deep wrinkles in the face

26. mighty 「絶大な権力を振るう」

30. I am Revenge 「私は復讐を促す女神」「私は復讐心に燃える者」の両様にとれる。前者は寓意（allegory）・人格化（personification）、後者は性格・性質でその所有者を示す換喩（metonymy）。タモラは前者を演じているつもりだが、聞く者には両様に響くという曖昧さがこの奇妙な劇中劇のトリックの1つ。　　**th'infernal kingdom** 「地下の王国、地獄」そこに悪魔・悪霊が住むとするのはユダヤ教・キリスト教的イメージ。

31. gnawing vulture 「(内臓を)啄むハゲワシ」岩山に鎖で縛られたプロメーテウス（Prometheus）の内臓を啄む鷲のイメージ。2. 1. 17 注参照。

32. wreakful vengeance 「復讐（心）に満ちた復讐」wreak も vengeance も復讐を意味し同意反復的な表現。復讐劇において際限なく繰り返される狂乱的復讐とその過剰さを想起させる劇的アイロニー（dramatic irony）。5. 1. 58 注参照。

33. Come down 「降りて来て」タイタスの役が上部舞台（*above*）あるいはバルコニーで演技されたものと推測されている。

34. Confer = talk together　　**36. obscurity** = a dark place

37-38. murder ... rape / Can couch for fear 「殺人と…レイプが恐怖に慄のき身を潜めることができるような」murder と rape はそれぞれ murderer と rapist の換喩で、タモラの企む筋書きの破綻に繋がる比喩を不用意に使っている。

45. Lo = Look, Behold　間投詞。

Rape and Murder stands = the rapist and the murderer stand　タモラの2人の息子カイロンとディミートリアスをそれぞれ「レイプ」および「殺人」と最初に名付けているのは、タモラでなくタイタス。タイタスはここで巧妙に寓意を換喩にすり替える。タモラの計画した寓意劇の筋書きは破綻し、2人の息子は「レイプ」すなわち「レイプ犯」、「殺人」すなわち「殺人犯」として正体を暴かれたままタイタスの新しい筋書きに引き込まれることになる。

46. surance = assurance, guarantee

Stab them, or tear them on thy chariot wheels,
And then I'll come and be thy wagoner,
And whirl along with thee about the globe,
Provide thee two proper palfreys, black as jet,   50
To hale thy vengeful wagon swift away,
And find out murderers in their guilty caves.
And when thy car is loaden with their heads,
I will dismount and by thy wagon wheel
Trot like a servile footman all day long,   55
Even from Hyperion's rising in the east
Until his very downfall in the sea.
And day by day I'll do this heavy task,
So thou destroy Rapine and Murder there.

TAMORA   These are my ministers and come with me.   60

TITUS   Are they thy ministers? What are they called?

TAMORA   Rape and Murder; therefore callèd so
  'Cause they take vengeance of such kind of men.

TITUS   Good Lord, how like the Empress' sons they are,
  And you the Empress! But we worldly men   65
  Have miserable, mad, mistaking eyes.
  O sweet Revenge, now do I come to thee,
  And if one arm's embracement will content thee,
  I will embrace thee in it by and by.   [*Exits above*]

TAMROA   This closing with him fits his lunacy.   70
  Whate'er I forge to feed his brainsick humors,
  Do you uphold and maintain in your speeches,
  For now he firmly takes me for Revenge;
  And, being credulous in this mad thought,
  I'll make him send for Lucius his son;   75
  And whilst I at a banquet hold him sure,
  I'll find some cunning practice out of hand
  To scatter and disperse the giddy Goths,
  Or, at the least, make them his enemies.

47. on thy chariot wheels 「お前の戦車の車輪に懸けて」シェイクスピアの台本では、実際に大道具の戦車を舞台上に乗せることも、言葉の上での空想として演じることも、どちらの演出も可能。ここでタイタスが狂気を演じているという状況と、この後続く chariot / wagon / car のイメージが曖昧で荒唐無稽に展開することを考慮すると、後者が自然であろうか。5. 2. 0 SD 後注参照。

48. thy wagoner 「お前の（戦車の）御者」(*OED* wagon, *n.* 2.b.)

49. whirl = move in a circle or similar curve; fly about

50. proper palfreys 「立派な馬」　　**black as jet** 「黒玉のように真っ黒な」格言的。Tilley J49 'As black as jet.'

51. hale = haul; pull, tug

52. their guilty caves 「彼らの潜む罪深い洞穴」5. 2. 183 参照。the cave of the guilty murderers と言うべきところ。

53. when thy car is ... heads 「お前の車に奴らの首を積んだら」ここはタイタスが、後部に荷台付きの戦車か、あるいは単純に荷馬車のようなものか、どちらを思い描いているのか曖昧。

55. Trot 「小走りする」馬のみでなく人間の走りについても言う。

　　servile footman = an attendant or foot servant; *esp.* one employed to run ahead of or alongside a coach, carriage or a rider of rank (*OED* footman, *n.* 3.a.)

56. Hyperion's ギリシャ神話「太陽神ヒュペリーオーンの」*Odysseia*, 1. 8.

59. So = so long as　　**Rapine** = the act or practice of seizing and taking away by force the property of others; plunder, pillage, robbery　　レイプはもともと「強要性交」よりも「強奪」という意味合いが強い。タイタスは「自分の娘を奪われた」という古いレイプ観にとらわれている。1. 1. 409 注参照。ここの Rapine を Rape と同義にとる注釈も多い。

60-63. These are my ministers ... of such kind of men　⇒後注

61. What are they called?　⇒後注

62-63. therefore callèd so / 'Cause they take = called so because they take

65. worldly = earthly, mortal

66. miserable = unworthy, inadequate, despicable, mean

69. by and by = presently, straightway, immediately

70. closing = a coming to terms, agreement or union

71. forge = make, fashion　　**humours** = fancies, whims

72. uphold = support

76. whilst [wʌɪlst / (h)waɪlst] = while　　**sure** = firmly　副詞。

77. practice = a scheme, a stratagem, a trick (*OED* practice, *n.* 5.b.)

　　out of hand = at once, immediately

See, here he comes, and I must ply my theme. 80

Enter Titus

Titus Long have I been forlorn, and all for thee.
Welcome, dread Fury, to my woeful house.
Rapine and Murder, you are welcome too.
How like the Empress and her sons you are!
Well are you fitted, had you but a Moor. 85
Could not all hell afford you such a devil?
For well I wot the Empress never wags
But in her company there is a Moor;
And, would you represent our queen aright,
It were convenient you had such a devil. 90
But welcome as you are. What shall we do?
Tamora What wouldst thou have us do, Andronicus?
Demetrius Show me a murderer; I'll deal with him.
Chiron Show me a villain that hath done a rape,
And I am sent to be revenged on him. 95
Tamora Show me a thousand that hath done thee wrong,
And I will be revengèd on them all.
Titus [*To Demetrius*] Look round about the wicked streets
  of Rome,
And when thou findst a man that's like thyself,
Good Murder, stab him; he's a murderer. 100
[*To Chiron*] Go thou with him, and when it is thy hap
To find another that is like to thee,
Good Rapine, stab him; he is a ravisher.
[*To Tamora*] Go thou with them; and in the Emperor's court
There is a queen attended by a Moor. 105
Well shalt thou know her by thine own proportion,
For up and down she doth resemble thee.
I pray thee, do on them some violent death.
They have been violent to me and mine.

80. ply = apply oneself to, practise, work at

81. forlorn = forsaken; in pitiful condition

82. Fury = one of the avenging deities (Lat. Furiae, Dirae, Gk. Ἐρινύες, Εὐμενίδες); frenzied rage 古典悲劇における「復讐の女神の一人」を指すが、同時に劇的アイロニーとして人間の「狂乱」をも指す。

85. Well are you fitted = you are well furnished to resemble the Empress (Waith)

had you but = if only you had

86. afford = supply, provide

87. wot 2. 1. 48 注参照。　　**wags** = stirs, moves, moves one's limbs

88. But = unless

89. would you represent = if you would (like to) represent

aright = rightly, correctly

90. It were convenient ... = it would be convenient that ...

91. welcome as you are = you are welcome indeed

92. wouldst thou have us do = would you like to make us do

93. a murderer ディミートリアスは Murder（殺人の擬人化＝神）と murder（殺人という行為）と murderer（殺人者）はそれぞれ別物と思っているが、タイタスは Murder も murder も murderer の換喩（metonymy）と見做している。すなわち Murder ＝ murderer。前者は後者の換喩的な連想・論理に気づかない。5. 2. 60-63 後注参照。

94. a villain that hath done a rape = a rapist Rape と rape と rapist の関係については前行の Murder と murder と murderer の関係と同様。

95. be revenged on 「～に復讐する」

98. wicked streets = streets that harbour wicked people

101-02. when it is thy hap / To find = when you happen to find

hap = chance

103. Rapine 5. 2. 59 注参照。

ravisher ＜ ravish = drag off or carry away (a woman) by force or with violence (occasionally also implying subsequent rape); rape, violate (a woman) (*OED* ravish, *v.* 1.a. and b.)

106. proportion = form, shape, configuration (of the limbs of the body, etc.), likeness, figure

108. them 皇后タモラとムーア人エアロンを指す。

109. mine = my sons and daughter

TAMORA   Well hast thou lessoned us; this shall we do.   110
   But would it please thee, good Andronicus,
   To send for Lucius, thy thrice-valiant son,
   Who leads towards Rome a band of warlike Goths,
   And bid him come and banquet at thy house?
   When he is here, even at thy solemn feast,   115
   I will bring in the Empress and her sons,
   The Emperor himself, and all thy foes,
   And at thy mercy shall they stoop and kneel,
   And on them shalt thou ease thy angry heart.
   What says Andronicus to this device?   120
TITUS   Marcus, my brother, 'tis sad Titus calls.

Enter Marcus.

   Go, gentle Marcus, to thy nephew Lucius.
   Thou shalt inquire him out among the Goths.
   Bid him repair to me and bring with him
   Some of the chiefest princes of the Goths.   125
   Bid him encamp his soldiers where they are.
   Tell him the Emperor and the Empress too
   Feast at my house, and he shall feast with them.
   This do thou for my love, and so let him,
   As he regards his agèd father's life.   130
MARCUS   This will I do, and soon return again.   [*Exit*]
TAMORA   Now will I hence about thy business
   And take my ministers along with me.
TITUS   Nay, nay, let Rape and Murder stay with me,
   Or else I'll call my brother back again   135
   And cleave to no revenge but Lucius.
TAMROA   [*Aside to Chiron and Demetrius*]
   What say you, boys? Will you abide with him
   Whiles I go tell my lord the Emperor
   How I have governed our determined jest?

110. lessoned = instructed or schooled (a person) in a particular subject or activity　寓意劇を演じているかのようなタモラの台詞遣い。

114. banquet = take part in a banquet; feast「食事、宴会」は伝統的に復讐劇のプロットでしばしば用いられる仕掛け。

115. even「他でもなく、まさに」　　**solemn** = grand, sumptuous

118. stoop = bow to superior power or authority; humble oneself

119. on them shalt thou ease thy angry heart「お前の憤懣を奴らにぶつけて晴らす」　on = indicating the person who is affected or exploited by an action or feeling (*OED* on, *prep.* 24.b.)

120. device = plot, stratagem「(芝居や企みの) 筋書き」4. 4. 110 注参照。

121. 'tis sad Titus calls = it is sad Titus who calls　　sad　5. 2. 11 注参照。

124. repair = come, return

125. chiefest = chief

130. regards = takes care or is mindful of (*OED* regard, *v.* 2.q.)

132. will I hence about thy business「お前の用で私はこれから出かける」古い用法として hence は法助動詞を伴って、あるいは命令文で、go や depart などの移動を表わす動詞を含意した。(*OED* hence, *adv.* 3.a.) 2. 3. 82 注参照。

133. ministers「従者・子分たち」

134. Nay　1. 1. 483 注参照。

136. cleave to = adhere or cling to; to remain devoted to

revenge「復讐」復讐者 (revenger) の換喩 (metonymy)。タモラのRevenge「復讐 (の神)」は寓意 (allegory) あるいは抽象的概念の人格化 (personification) / 神格化 (deification) であり、タイタスが換喩を用いるのと対照的。

139. governed = directed and controlled the actions and affairs of

determined = decided, fixed; planned (Waith)

jest = prank, a practical joke; pageant, masque (*OED* jest, *n.* 7. and 8.)

Yield to his humour, smooth and speak him fair,   140
And tarry with him till I turn again.
TITUS   [*Aside*]   I knew them all, though they supposed me
    mad,
And will o'erreach them in their own devices,
A pair of cursèd hellhounds and their dam.
DEMETRIUS   Madam, depart at pleasure. Leave us here.   145
TAMORA   Farewell, Andronicus. Revenge now goes
To lay a complot to betray thy foes.
TITUS   I know thou dost; and, sweet Revenge, farewell.
                            [*Exit Tamora*]
CHIRON   Tell us, old man, how shall we be employed?
TITUS   Tut, I have work enough for you to do.   150
Publius, come hither, Caius, and Valentine.

        [*Enter Publius, Caius, and Valentine*]

PUBLIUS   What is your will?
TITUS   Know you these two?
PUBLIUS   The Empress' sons, I take them, Chiron, Demetrius.
TITUS   Fie, Publius, fie, thou art too much deceived.   155
The one is Murder, and Rape is the other's name;
And therefore bind them, gentle Publius.
Caius and Valentine, lay hands on them.
Oft have you heard me wish for such an hour,
And now I find it. Therefore bind them sure,   160
And stop their mouths if they begin to cry.   [*Exit*]
CHIRON   Villains, forbear! We are the Empress' sons.
PUBLIUS   And therefore do we what we are commanded.
Stop close their mouths; let them not speak a word.
Is he sure bound? Look that you bind them fast.   165

   Enter Titus Andronicus with a knife, and Lavinia with a basin

TITUS   Come, come, Lavinia. Look, thy foes are bound.

140. humour = a temporary state of mind or feeling; a mood

   smooth = use smooth, flattering or complimentary language to

   fair = carefully, gently　副詞。

141. tarry = stay, remain

143. o'erreach = overpower; outdo

   devices　4. 4. 110 注参照。

144. hellhounds = hounds or dogs of hell; demons in the form of dogs　ここでは悪党を指すメタファー。

147. complot　2. 3. 265 注参照。

150. for you　「お前らのために」

154. take = apprehend, understand, consider

156. Murder ... Rape　それぞれ murderer ... rapist の換喩。5. 2. 60-63 後注参照。

162. forbear = abstain, refrain

164. Stop close = stop and close tightly　close = tightly, fast, so as to leave no interstices, outlets, or openings (*OED* close, *adv.* 4.)

Sirs, stop their mouths. Let them not speak to me,
But let them hear what fearful words I utter.
O villains, Chiron and Demetrius!
Here stands the spring whom you have stained with mud,   170
This goodly summer with your winter mixed.
You killed her husband, and for that vile fault
Two of her brothers were condemned to death,
My hand cut off and made a merry jest,
Both her sweet hands, her tongue, and that more dear   175
Than hands or tongue, her spotless chastity,
Inhuman traitors, you constrained and forced.
What would you say if I should let you speak?
Villains, for shame you could not beg for grace.
Hark, wretches, how I mean to martyr you.   180
This one hand yet is left to cut your throats,
Whiles that Lavinia 'tween her stumps doth hold
The basin that receives your guilty blood.
You know your mother means to feast with me,
And calls herself Revenge, and thinks me mad.   185
Hark, villains, I will grind your bones to dust,
And with your blood and it I'll make a paste,
And of the paste a coffin I will rear,
And make two pasties of your shameful heads,
And bid that strumpet, your unhallowed dam,   190
Like to the earth swallow her own increase.
This is the feast that I have bid her to,
And this the banquet she shall surfeit on;
For worse than Philomel you used my daughter,
And worse than Progne I will be revenged.   195
And now prepare your throats. Lavinia, come.
Receive the blood, and when that they are dead,
Let me go grind their bones to powder small,
And with this hateful liquor temper it,

168. what fearful words I utter 残酷と恐怖が言葉の効果であることを印象付ける台詞。

170. spring 「泉」

171. goodly summer 「美しい夏」英国では夏が最も美しい季節とされる。Cf. Shakespeare, Sonnet 18. 1.

172. fault = misdeed, offence

176. chastity = purity from unlawful sexual intercourse; virginity

177. constrained = violated, forced

179. for shame = shame on you!; you should be ashamed 「恥を知れ」

　grace = favour, mercy

180. martyr = kill, slay esp. by a cruel death; torment　原義は「殉教させる」

181. yet = still

182. Whiles that = while

183. guilty blood タイタスに特徴的な言い方。5. 2. 52 注参照。

185. calls herself Revenge 「復讐（Revenge）」はタモラ自身が自分の役としてそのように称したが、一方で 2 人の「レイプ（Rape）」と「殺人（Murder）」はタイタスが先に名付けている。5. 2. 45 注参照。

186-95. 最も残酷なシーンをアクションよりもむしろ言葉による描写で想像させる。凄惨な人肉パイの調理手順の詳述は、エリザベス朝の観客に同時代の料理法を彷彿とさせたと思われる。'There were many recipes for baking calves' heads in pastry "coffins".'（Waith）

186. Hark = listen

188. coffin = a mould of paste for a pie; the crust of a pie (*OED* coffin, *n.* 4.)　　**rear** = set up the crust of a pie; raise (*OED* rear, *v.¹*, 1.b.)

189. pasties = meat-pies

190. strumpet = unchaste woman, prostitute

　unhallowed = impious, wicked

　dam 2. 3. 142 注参照。

191. Like to = like　2. 3. 223 注参照。　　**increase** = offspring, breed

192. bid = asked, invited

194. worse than Philomel ピロメーラ神話については 2. 3. 43 注参照。

195. worse than Progne 「プログネーがした以上に残酷に」プロクネーはピロメーラの姉で、ピロメーラをレイプした犯人テーレウスの妻。夫の犯行の事実を知ったプロクネーは、復讐として自分たちの子イテュス（Itys）を殺し、その肉を夫に食べさせる。（*Metamorphoses*, 6.601-701; Seneca, *Thyestes*, 272-78）2. 1. 135 注参照。Progne は正しくは Procne。

199. this hateful liquor カイロンとディミートリアスから取った血のこと。

　temper 「（液体などと）ほどよく混ぜて料理する」

And in that paste let their vile heads be baked.   200
Come, come, be everyone officious
To make this banquet, which I wish may prove
More stern and bloody than the Centaurs' feast.

He cuts their throats

So. Now bring them in, for I'll play the cook
And see them ready against their mother comes.   205

Exeunt [with the dead bodies]

[ACT V SCENE III]

Enter Lucius, Marcus, and the Goths [with Aaron prisoner, and one carrying his child]

LUCIUS   Uncle Marcus, since 'tis my father's mind
That I repair to Rome, I am content.
FIRST GOTH   And ours with thine, befall what fortune will.
LUCIUS   Good uncle, take you in this barbarous Moor,
This ravenous tiger, this accursèd devil.   5
Let him receive no sust'nance. Fetter him
Till he be brought unto the Empress' face
For testimony of her foul proceedings.
And see the ambush of our friends be strong.
I fear the Emperor means no good to us.   10
AARON   Some devil whisper curses in my ear
And prompt me that my tongue may utter forth
The venomous malice of my swelling heart.
LUCIUS   Away, inhuman dog, unhallowed slave!
Sirs, help our uncle to convey him in.   15

[Exit Aaron, guarded by Goths]

Flourish

The trumpets show the Emperor is at hand.

Sound trumpets. Enter Emperor and Empress with

201. officious = dutiful

203. Centaurs' feast ⇒後注

205. against = by the time that, before

〔**5. 3**〕あらすじ……………………………………………………………………

　ゴート人の軍勢を率いてローマに迫ったルーシアスがローマ軍と講和交渉のためタイタスの館へ来る。皇帝・皇后他も到着した後、タイタスが料理人の姿で料理を配膳する。タイタスはウィルギーニウスの故事を引いて、皆の面前でラヴィニアを殺す。タモラの２人の息子の肉で作ったパイをそれと知らぬタモラ他の一行が食べた後、タイタスがタモラを、そのタイタスを皇帝サターナイナスが、さらにその皇帝をルーシアスが次々と殺す。次いで、大事を聞いて集まったローマ市民たちを前にルーシアス一行は自己弁護の演説を行う。ルーシアスはローマ市民たちに推挙されて皇帝となり、死んだ皇帝、タイタス、タモラ他の埋葬あるいは死体処分、さらにエアロンの処刑を指示する。

……………………………………………………………………………………………

2. repair 5. 2. 124 注参照。

3. ours = our minds　　**befall what fortune will** = no matter what fortune will befall

4. take you in this barbarous Moor = take this barbarous Moor into the house

5. accursèd = damnable; detestable　5. 1. 16 後注参照。

6. sust'nance = food, victuals　　**Fetter** 「足枷・鎖などで拘束する」

8. proceedings = course of action; conduct, behaviour

9. ambush 「(森などに隠れさせた) 伏兵」

11. whisper 「囁け」 命令法。

12. prompt = assist (a speaker when at a loss) by suggesting something to be said

[Aemilius,] Tribunes, Attendants, and others

SATURNINUS   What, hath the firmament more suns than one?

LUCIUS   What boots it thee to call thyself a sun?

MARCUS   Rome's emperor, and nephew, break the parle.
These quarrels must be quietly debated.   20
The feast is ready which the careful Titus
Hath ordained to an honourable end,
For peace, for love, for league and good to Rome.
Please you therefore draw nigh and take your places.

SATURNINUS   Marcus, we will.   25

*Hoboyes. A table brought in. Enter Titus like a cook, placing
the meat on the table, dishes, and Lavinia with a veil over her
face [,Young Lucius and others]*

TITUS   Welcome, my lord; welcome, dread Queen;
Welcome, you warlike Goths; welcome, Lucius;
And welcome, all. Although the cheer be poor,
'Twill fill your stomachs. Please you eat of it.

SATURNINUS   Why art thou thus attired, Andronicus?   30

TITUS   Because I would be sure to have all well
To entertain your highness and your Empress.

TAMORA   We are beholding to you, good Andronicus.

TITUS   An if your highness knew my heart, you were.
My lord the Emperor, resolve me this: 35
Was it well done of rash Virginius
To slay his daughter with his own right hand
Because she was enforced, stained, and deflowered?

SATURNINUS   It was, Andronicus.

TITUS   Your reason, mighty lord?

SATURNINUS   Because the girl should not survive her shame,   40
And by her presence still renew his sorrows.

TITUS   A reason mighty, strong, and effectual;

17. firmament = the arch or vault of heaven overhead; the sky or heavens
more suns than one 「1つ以上の太陽」太陽は国王・皇帝の象徴として1つ
であるべきところ。*Henry VI, Part 3* 'Three glorious suns, each one a
perfect sun; / Not separated with the racking clouds / But severed in a
pale clear-shining sky.' グロスター公リチャード（後のリチャード3世）
は太陽が3つ現れた奇跡をアイロニックに語る。この場面でサターナイナス
は、ルーシアスが帝位を狙って挙兵しローマへ進軍して来たものと疑ってい
る。ルーシアスはそもそも皇帝候補として推挙されていたタイタス（1. 1. 20-
24）の長男。

18. What boots it thee to ...? = Of what use, or value, is it for you to ...?
（*OED* boot, *v.*[1] 3.a.）

19. break the parle 「会談を始めてください」 break = open, commence,
begin（*OED* break, *v.* 24.）

22. ordained = arranged, prepared

24. draw nigh = come near, approach（*OED* draw, *v.* 68.b.）

25 SD. *Hoboyes* = oboes F1 のト書き。Q1 では *Trumpets sounding*「ファ
ンファーレ」。王・皇帝の登場の場面では後者が普通。F1 のオーボエを使用し
た場合、流血の宴（bloody banquet）というこの場の独特な雰囲気を効果と
して出せる。

26. dread = held in awe; revered 動詞 dread の過去分詞形による形容詞。
（*OED* dread, *adj.*[2] 2.）

28. cheer = what is provided by way of entertainment; viands, food（*OED*
cheer, *n.*[1] 6.a.）

30. attired = dressed

33. beholding to 1. 1. 400 注参照。

34. An if = And if = If 5. 1. 61 注参照。 **you were** = you would be

35. resolve = answer (a question or argument); solve (a problem)

36-38. Was it well done of rash Virginius ... deflowered? ウィルギーニウス
とその娘の件はもとはリウィウスの『ローマ建国史』が伝えるもの。アッピウ
ス・クラウディウス（Appius Claudius）が彼女に欲情を抱きレイプを計画
するが、娘の父ウィルギーニウスがそれを阻むために自分の娘を殺す。
Livius, *Ab Urbe Condita*, 3. 44-49. ここでタイタスが言及する「（実際に）
娘がレイプされたから」という例は、フロールス（Lucius Annaeus
Florus）の『ローマ史梗概（*Epitome de Tito Livio*）』が伝える話などに近い
（Hughes）。
deflowered 2. 4. 26 注参照。

42. effectual = 'to the point', pertinent, conclusive

A pattern, precedent, and lively warrant
For me, most wretched, to perform the like.
Die, die, Lavinia, and thy shame with thee,   45
And with thy shame thy father's sorrow die.   *He kills her*
SATURNINUS   What hast thou done, unnatural and unkind?
TITUS   Killed her for whom my tears have made me blind.
  I am as woeful as Virginius was,
  And have a thousand times more cause than he   50
  To do this outrage, and it now is done.
SATURNINUS   What, was she ravished? Tell who did the deed.
TITUS   Will 't please you eat? Will 't please your highness feed?
TAMORA   Why hast thou slain thine only daughter thus?
TITUS   Not I; 'twas Chiron and Demetrius.   55
  They ravished her and cut away her tongue,
  And they, 'twas they, that did her all this wrong.
SATURNINUS   Go fetch them hither to us presently.
TITUS   Why, there they are, both bakèd in this pie,
  Whereof their mother daintily hath fed,   60
  Eating the flesh that she herself hath bred.
  'Tis true, 'tis true! Witness my knife's sharp point.
                           He stabs the Empress
SATURNINUS   Die, frantic wretch, for this accursèd deed.
                                [*He kills Titus*]
LUCIUS   Can the son's eye behold his father bleed?
                            [*He kills Saturninus*]
  There's meed for meed, death for a deadly deed.   65

    [*A great tumult. Lucius, Marcus, and others go aloft*]

MARCUS   You sad-faced men, people and sons of Rome,
  By uproars severed as a flight of fowl
  Scattered by winds and high tempestuous gusts,
  O, let me teach you how to knit again
  This scattered corn into one mutual sheaf,   70

43. pattern ＝ a precedent, an instance appealed to（*OED* pattern, *n.* 7.）

lively ＝（of evidence）convincing, telling

warrant ＝ authorization; justifying reason or ground for an action

44. wretched ＝ living in a state of misery; sunk in distress or dejection

46. with thy shame thy father's sorrow　「お前の恥とともにお前の父の悲しみが」恥は娘ラヴィニアの、悲しみは父タイタスのもの。その逆ではない。娘の純潔を絶対視するタイタスの価値観は、悲劇的体験の後も第１幕の頃と変わっていない。1. 1. 168 注参照。

47. unnatural and unkind　unnatural と unkind は同義。　unkind ＝ degenerate; unnaturally bad; wicked 「それでも人間か」

48. my tears have made me blind　タイタスが自分で自分を盲目と呼ぶのは一種の劇的アイロニー（dramatic irony）。

51. outrage ＝ extravagant, violent action

53. feed ＝ take food, eat　自動詞。

60. whereof ＝ of which

daintily hath fed　「旨そうに食べた」Cf. *Metamorphoses*, 6. 650-51 'Tereus ... / vescitur inque suam sua viscera congerit alvum.'（テーレウスは…自分の肉を食べ、自分の腹を満たした。）

61. bred ＜ breed ＝ cherish in the womb or egg

63. wretch ＝ a vile or despicable person

65. meed ... for meed ＝ measure for measure　格言的。

meed ＝ wages, recompense

64-66. behold ... bleed / ... meed ... meed, death ... deadly deed　頭韻（alliteration）で復讐・流血の連鎖を強調する。

65 SD. *go aloft*　「上部舞台（balcony）へ移動」第１幕における上部舞台の使用と対称的なアクション。ただしこのト書きは後代の補充。

67. as a flight of ... ＝ like a flight of ...

70. mutual ＝ entertained or performed by each towards or with regard to the other「互いに結束した」（*OED* mutual, *adj.* 1.a.）

These broken limbs again into one body.

ROMAN LORD   Let Rome herself be bane unto herself,
   And she whom mighty kingdoms curtsy to,
   Like a forlorn and desperate castaway,
   Do shameful execution on herself.   75
   But if my frosty signs and chaps of age,
   Grave witnesses of true experience,
   Cannot induce you to attend my words,
   Speak, Rome's dear friend, as erst our ancestor,
   When with his solemn tongue he did discourse   80
   To lovesick Dido's sad-attending ear
   The story of that baleful burning night
   When subtle Greeks surprised King Priam's Troy.
   Tell us what Sinon hath bewitched our ears,
   Or who hath brought the fatal engine in   85
   That gives our Troy, our Rome, the civil wound.
   My heart is not compact of flint nor steel,
   Nor can I utter all our bitter grief,
   But floods of tears will drown my oratory
   And break my utterance even in the time   90
   When it should move you to attend me most
   And force you to commiseration.
   Here's Rome's young captain. Let him tell the tale,
   While I stand by and weep to hear him speak.

LUCIUS   Then, gracious auditory, be it known to you   95
   That Chiron and the damned Demetrius
   Were they that murderèd our emperor's brother,
   And they it were that ravishèd our sister.
   For their fell faults our brothers were beheaded,
   Our father's tears despised, and basely cozened   100
   Of that true hand that fought Rome's quarrel out
   And sent her enemies unto the grave;
   Lastly, myself unkindly banishèd,

72. ROMAN LORD ⇒後注

   bane = death, destruction; that which causes ruin

73. curtsy to = do reverence to

76. But if = Unless

   frosty signs = white hairs

   chaps of age = cracked skin

77. Grave = weighty, authoritative

78. induce = lead by persuasion or some influence

79. erst = earliest   **our ancestor** アエネーアース（Aeneas）を指す。

81. lovesick Dido's sad-attending ear 2. 3. 21-24 および 3. 2. 27-28 注参照。

82-83. The story of that baleful ... King Priam's Troy トロイアー落城の夜
   の話。(*Aeneis*, 2. 1-804)

83. surprised 巨大な木馬に兵士を潜ませてトロイアーを急襲した件を指す。

84. Sinon トロイアー戦争におけるギリシャ方のスパイ。ギリシャ軍が撤退し
   たと見せかけて兵士を中に隠した巨大な木馬を城壁に残した時、シノーンはト
   ロイアー方を騙して木馬を城壁の中に入れるよう説得した。その晩木馬の中か
   ら多数の兵士が現れ、トロイアーを落城させた (*Aeneis*, 2. 57-198)。この文
   脈ではシノーンのようにローマを騙した人物を指す。

85. fatal engine トロイアー戦争伝説の文脈ではトロイアーを落城に導いた攻
   城兵器すなわち「トロイアーの木馬」の名で知られることになる策略を指す。
   だがこの劇の文脈で実際にローマにどのような策略・陰謀が持ち込まれたのか
   は判然としない。あるいは皇帝を操った異国の女王タモラをファム・ファター
   ル（femme fatale）に見立てたものか。

86. the civil wound ローマ市民どうしが争う内乱によって国家が受ける傷。

87-94. My heart is ... hear him speak ⇒後注

87. compact of = framed, composed of（*OED* compact, *ppl.a.*[1] 2.）

89. But = unless（*OED* but, *conj.* 10.）

95. auditory = audience

98. they it were = it was they

99. fell = cruel, ruthless   **faults** = culpability; the wrongdoing to which
   a specified evil is attributable

100. cozened = cheated

101. quarrel 3. 1. 4 注参照。

103. unkindly = with unnatural enmity or harshness

The gates shut on me, and turned weeping out
To beg relief among Rome's enemies, 105
Who drowned their enmity in my true tears
And oped their arms to embrace me as a friend.
I am the turned-forth, be it known to you,
That have preserved her welfare in my blood
And from her bosom took the enemy's point, 110
Sheathing the steel in my advent'rous body.
Alas, you know I am no vaunter, I;
My scars can witness, dumb although they are,
That my report is just and full of truth.
But soft, methinks I do digress too much, 115
Citing my worthless praise. O, pardon me,
For when no friends are by, men praise themselves.
MARCUS Now is my turn to speak. Behold the child.
Of this was Tamora deliverèd,
The issue of an irreligious Moor, 120
Chief architect and plotter of these woes.
The villain is alive in Titus' house,
And as he is to witness, this is true.
Now judge what cause had Titus to revenge
These wrongs unspeakable, past patience, 125
Or more than any living man could bear.
Now have you heard the truth. What say you, Romans?
Have we done aught amiss? Show us wherein,
And from the place where you behold us pleading,
The poor remainder of Andronici 130
Will, hand in hand, all headlong hurl ourselves,
And on the ragged stones beat forth our souls,
And make a mutual closure of our house.
Speak, Romans, speak, and if you say we shall,
Lo, hand in hand, Lucius and I will fall. 135
AEMILIUS Come, come, thou reverend man of Rome,

104. The gates shut on me, and turned weeping out = with the gates being shut on me, and I was turned out weeping

107. oped = opened

108. the turned-forth 「追放の身」（松岡訳）< turn forth = drive or send away

109. That 関係代名詞。the turned-forth (= I) が先行詞。

her = Rome's

welfare = happiness, prosperity

110. point 「切先」

111. Sheathing the steel in my advent'rous body 「向こう見ずな私の体に鋼（の刀）を納めさせ」2. 1. 53-54 注参照。

112. vaunter = boaster, braggart

I 発音上は間投詞の aye, ay (= yes) と同じ。

113. witness = bear witness to; testify to

115. soft「静かに」

digress = depart from the course

116. Citing < cite = make mention of or reference to

119. Of this was Tamora deliverèd = Tamora was delivered of this (child)

128-31. Show us wherein, / And ... all headlong hurl ourselves = If you show us in what we have done amiss ... we will all headlong hurl ourselves このように言う一方でマーカスは、ルーシアスが自分の率いて来たゴート族の軍勢を伏兵として近辺に待機させていることも承知している (5. 3. 9)。マーカスとルーシアス両人の政治家としての演説・演技が微妙な場面。特にルーシアスの性格がどのように描かれているのかは曖昧で、上演の際には多様な解釈と性格づけがあり得る。彼がエアロンの幼児を助けるという約束・誓いを守るかどうかも不明。特に終局の解釈は受容者に任されている。

128. aught = anything whatever

amiss = not in accord with the recognized good order of morality or society

wherein = in what

133. mutual 5. 3. 70 注参照。

closure = a bringing to a conclusion; end

And bring our emperor gently in thy hand,
Lucius our emperor, for well I know
The common voice do cry it shall be so.

MARCUS Lucius, all hail, Rome's royal emperor!   140
[*To Attendants*]   Go, go into old Titus' sorrowful house,
And hither hale that misbelieving Moor
To be adjudged some direful slaught'ring death
As punishment for his most wicked life.

      [*Exeunt Attendants. Lucius and Marcus come down*]

Lucius, all hail, Rome's gracious governor!   145

LUCIUS Thanks, gentle Romans. May I govern so
To heal Rome's harms and wipe away her woe!
But, gentle people, give me aim awhile,
For nature puts me to a heavy task.
Stand all aloof, but, uncle, draw you near   150
To shed obsequious tears upon this trunk.   [*Kisses Titus*]
O, take this warm kiss on thy pale cold lips,
These sorrowful drops upon thy bloodstained face,
The last true duties of thy noble son.

MARCUS Tear for tear, and loving kiss for kiss,   155
Thy brother Marcus tenders on thy lips.   [*Kisses Titus*]
O, were the sum of these that I should pay
Countless and infinite, yet would I pay them.

LUCIUS Come hither, boy. Come, come, and learn of us
To melt in showers. Thy grandsire loved thee well.   160
Many a time he danced thee on his knee,
Sung thee asleep, his loving breast thy pillow;
Many a story hath he told to thee,
And bid thee bear his pretty tales in mind
And talk of them when he was dead and gone.   165

MARCUS How many thousand times hath these poor lips,
When they were living, warmed themselves on thine!
O, now, sweet boy, give them their latest kiss.

140. 145. Q1、F1 ともに Marcus の台詞とするが、Edward Capell（1783）の読みに従い現代版の多くが Romans に修正。その場合マーカスが甥の皇帝擁立を先導する印象が弱まる。

142. hale = draw or pull along

143. adjudged = settled judicially

slaught'ring death = capital punishment that kills in a bloody or brutal manner

151. obsequious = dutiful in performing funeral obsequies or manifesting regard for the dead

trunk = a dead body, a corpse　一部分で体の全体を指す換喩（metonymy）。

156. tenders = offers formally for acceptance

157. were the sum of these = if the sum of these were

159. learn of = learn from

163-65. Many a story hath he told to thee ... when he was dead and gone
物語の伝承への拘りは、死に際のハムレットがホレイショーへ言う台詞に顕著。*Hamlet*, 5. 2 'So tell him with th'occurents more and less / Which have solicited.'

166. these poor lips　タイタスの唇を指す。叙事詩の伝承と「唇」については、『変身物語』最後の一節が連想される。タイタスの一族も叙事詩の読者である。*Metamorphoses*, 15. 871-79 'Iamque opus exegi, quod nec Iovis ira nec ignis / nec poterit ferrum nec edax abolere vetustas. / cum volet, illa dies, quae nil nisi corporis huius / ius habet, incerti spatium mihi finiat aevi: / parte tamen meliore mei super alta perennis / astra ferar, nomenque erit indelebile nostrum, / quaque patet domitis Romana potentia terries, / ore legar populi, perque omnia saecula fama, / siquid habent veri vatum praesagia, vivam.'（さあこれで私は、ユービテルの怒りも炎も、鋼鉄も、全てを食い尽くす歳月も、滅ぼすことのできない作品を完成させた。もし望むならば、この肉体のみにしか力を振るうことのない歳月が、私のおぼつかない命の時間を終わらせるがよい。だが私は、はるかに優れた部分によって高空の星々を超えてとこしえに運ばれ、私たちの名は決して消えることがない。征服した領土の上にローマの勢力がどれほど広がろうと、私は人々の唇で吟じられる。そして神憑りの詩人たちの予言が正しいならば、私は幾世にもわたり名声のうちに生きる。[下線は編注者による強調]）

168. latest = last

211

Bid him farewell; commit him to the grave.
Do them that kindness, and take leave of them.   170
YOUNG LUCIUS   O grandsire, grandsire, ev'n with all my heart
Would I were dead so you did live again!   [*Kisses Titus*]
O Lord, I cannot speak to him for weeping.
My tears will choke me if I ope my mouth.

[*Enter Aaron with Guards*]

ROMANS   You sad Andronici, have done with woes.   175
Give sentence on this execrable wretch
That hath been breeder of these dire events.
LUCIUS   Set him breast-deep in earth and famish him.
There let him stand and rave and cry for food.
If anyone relieves or pities him,   180
For the offense he dies. This is our doom.
Some stay to see him fastened in the earth.
AARON   Ah, why should wrath be mute and fury dumb?
I am no baby, I, that with base prayers
I should repent the evils I have done.   185
Ten thousand worse than ever yet I did
Would I perform, if I might have my will.
If one good deed in all my life I did,
I do repent it from my very soul.
LUCIUS   Some loving friends convey the Emperor hence,   190
And give him burial in his fathers' grave.
My father and Lavinia shall forthwith
Be closèd in our household's monument.
As for that ravenous tiger, Tamora,
No funeral rite, nor man in mourning weed;   195
No mournful bell shall ring her burial;
But throw her forth to beasts and birds to prey.
Her life was beastly and devoid of pity,
And being dead, let birds on her take pity.

170. them = Titus' lips　them は Q1 の読み。F1 では Do him ... take leave of him と本文を改めている。Q1 の唇への拘<ruby>拘<rt>こだわ</rt></ruby>りが不自然だが、言葉のぎごちなさを突然の兄の死に直面したマーカスの心の動揺の表れととることも可能。

171. ev'n　4. 4. 85 注参照。

172. Would I were ...　1. 1. 207 注参照。　　**so** = provided that, if only

176. execrable = abominable, accursed　　**wretch**　4. 4. 57 注参照。

177. dire = dreadful, horrible

181. doom = judgement, sentence

182. Some stay ...　「何人かここに留まって…せよ」　命令文。

183. wrath be mute and fury dumb　自分の感情を客観化する言い方。寓意 (allegory) ではない。

184-85. that with base prayers / I ...　構文的には関係詞節内の余分な I。ここでエアロンは強く自我を主張する。強烈な自我はリチャード三世、イアーゴー、エドマンドなどシェイクスピア劇の代表的な悪党 (villains) に共通する特徴。

186. Ten thousand worse than = ten thousand times worse than

187. if I might = if I could「もしできるものなら」

188-89. If one good deed in all my life I did, / I do repent it　エアロンは直接法 (did, do) で言っているので、「生涯に一度だけ」実際に何か「良い行い」をしたことになる。この劇に登場する以前のエアロンの経歴に想像を逞<ruby>逞<rt>たくま</rt></ruby>しくさせる台詞。

190. Some loving friends convey ...　5. 3. 182 注参照。
convey ... hence　4. 2. 178 注参照。

191. fathers'　Q1 の読みは fathers で father's「父の」と fathers'「父祖の」のどちらにもとれる。ただし劇場で台詞として発声する場合にはどちらに綴っても音は同じ。

192. forthwith = immediately, without delay

193. closèd = enclosed; kept close

194. ravenous = extremely rapacious; voracious
tiger　3. 1. 54 注参照。

195. weed　2. 1. 18 注参照。

197. to prey = to prey on (her)

Exeunt omnes

Finis the Tragedy of Titus Andronicus.

199. SD *Finis* = the end（Lat.）

図7　流血の宴のあとに立つルーシアス（マイクル・ドブスン）とマーカス（ア
ラン・ウェッブ）　ピーター・ブルック演出（1955）© RSC

後　注

1. 1.　この場は共作者ジョージ・ピールの執筆部分ととる解釈が有力で、現在で
はほぼ定説となっている（Vickers, Bate）。演劇は色々な面において共同作業
が当然な芸術であるから、台本作成の段階から複数の詩人が関わったとしても
まったく不思議ではない。問題はシェイクスピア以外の詩人の手になる可能性
が高い部分をどう評価するかにあるが、近年ではシェイクスピアの手が何らか
の形で関わっていれば広義のシェイクスピア作と見做す傾向にある。このエデ
ィションではこの場のテクストが本来ピールが書いたものである可能性が高い
ことを踏まえた上で、シェイクスピアがそれを吸収し全体として統一のとれた
悲劇作品として纏（まと）めていることを重視する。従って以下の注釈においては、両
者を殊更に区別せず、「ピールとシェイクスピア」という意味で一般に「シェ
イクスピア」と呼んで進めている。『タイタス・アンドロニカス』第1幕第1
場のテクストは、まだ若い詩人シェイクスピアが、学識と経験に長じた先輩劇
作家からその技術を学び自家薬籠中のものとしていった過程を想像させる
（Burrow）貴重な資料であるとも言える。

1. 1. 0 SD. _Flourish_　トランペットのファンファーレ。国王など重要人物の登場
を示す。　　　　　**_Tribunes_** = officers appointed to protect the interests and rights
of the plebeians from the patricians「護民官」（Lat. tribuni plebis）。

aloft　舞台上部のギャラリー。　　　　　**_Drum & Colours_**　（F1）「太鼓奏者と旗手」
Q1 では _Drums, and Trumpets_「太鼓奏者とラッパ奏者」

1. 1. 8. Nor = and do not　肯定の節の後に否定の節を繋げる接続詞。（_OED_
nor, _conj._[1] 5.）現代英語 The day was bright, nor were there any clouds above.
（『ランダムハウス英和大辞典』, nor）

1. 1. 10. Caesar = the emperor　もとはユーリウス・カエサル（Gaius Julius
Caesar, 100-44 BC）の第三名（cognomen）だったが、初代皇帝となったアウ
グストゥス（Octavianus / Imperator Caesar Augustus, 63 BC-AD 14）以降は
皇帝の呼び名。

1. 1. 23.　surnamèd Pius　ラテン語 pius は、ウェルギリウスの文脈で「国家・
父親・子孫・さらには神々に対する責務の感が強く、しかもそれらを義務とし
てではなく進んで愛する」（逸身）を意味する形容詞で、英語 pious の語源。
その名詞形 pietas も英語 piety（1. 1. 130）の語源。ローマ建国の伝説的英雄ア
エネーアースが、母である女神ウェヌス（Venus）を前に「私は敬虔なアエネ
ーアース（sum pius Aeneas）」（_Aeneis_, 1. 378）と自称する。すなわち凱旋将
軍タイタスはローマ建国の英雄に擬えられて登場するわけだが、ウェルギリウ
スの pius/pietas への連想はアイロニックでもある。アエネーアースは、父の

窮地を救うため戦いに挑んだ心優しい親思いの少年ラウスス<ruby>斃<rt>たお</rt></ruby>すが、次のように言う。*Aeneis*, 10. 811-12 'quo moriture ruis maioraque viris audes? / fallit te incautum pietas tua.'（死すべき者よ、なぜおまえはかかってくる、自分の力に勝ることに逸るのか、おまえの親孝行（pietas）が不注意なおまえを騙している）（逸身訳）。『タイタス』ではこの後まもなくタイタスが無抵抗の捕虜タモラの長男アラーバスを<ruby>生贄<rt>いけにえ</rt></ruby>に供し、さらには家族を<ruby>庇<rt>かば</rt></ruby>い父の横暴を制止しようとする自分の息子ミューシアスを斬り殺すことになる。古代の英雄叙事詩を連想させながらも、シェイクスピア悲劇では不合理な「<ruby>敬虔<rt>けいけん</rt></ruby>さ」が示す残忍さを強調している。1. 1. 130 後注参照。

1. 1. 35-38. Q1 では the field の後に以下の 3 行半が入る。この場の後段のアクション（1. 1. 96ff.）と矛盾するために、台本原稿の推敲過程における消し忘れ（false start）と考えて本文から削除する現代の版が多い。

> and at this day,
>
> To the Monument of that *Andronicy*
>
> Done sacrifice of expiation,
>
> And slaine the Nobleste prisoner of the *Gothes*

だが Q1 の読みでも「これまでゴート族との戦の度ごとに捕虜のうち最も高貴な者を犠牲に捧げて来た」のように解釈できる（Bate）。その場合、この悲劇で際限のない復讐・流血の発端となる人身御供という儀式的<ruby>殺戮<rt>さつりく</rt></ruby>は、以前から幾度も繰り返されて来たことになり、タイタス一族の冷酷さ因習的残忍さがより強く印象付けられる。この劇はシェイクスピアの同時代に長期間にわたって上演された。Q1 の 3 行半が初期の上演台本を反映したものであり、その後なんらかの演劇状況の変化を受けて削除されたのが F1 であったと推測することもできる。Q1 と F1 どちらの読みを取るにしても悲劇の発端として重要なのは、

犠牲に供される我が子アラーバスの助命をタモラが嘆願し、タイタスがそれを退けるところ。女王タモラの嘆願が拒絶されるシーンは同時代の観客に強い印象を残したらしく、「シェイクスピアの時代の舞台上演の場面を伝える唯一の絵」（Chambers）とされるヘンリー・ピーチャム（Henry Peacham）によるスケッチも、タモラがタイタスの前で<ruby>跪<rt>ひざまず</rt></ruby>く姿が中心に描かれている。

図 8 『タイタス・アンドロニカス』の同時代舞台上演のスケッチ　ヘンリー・ピーチャム絵　ロングリート・ハウス蔵、ウィルトシャー

1. 1. 69 SD ***After them Titus Andronicus*** オックスフォード版全集（Taylor et al.）などでは、*After them Titus Andronicus*［*in a chariot*］と補い、タイ

タスは戦車に乗って登場するものとする。マーロウの『タンバレン大王』での
タンバレン入場のシーンを真似た可能性もあるが、シェイクスピアの同時代に
『タイタス』が繰り返し再演されたことを考慮すると、常時同じ手を繰り返す
ことが果たして有効だろうか。演出は現場の創意工夫に委ねるという自由度の
方が、シェイクスピア劇の台本の長所であるように思われる。ちなみに現代の
例でデボラ・ウォーナー演出（RSC, 1987-88）では、ゴート族の捕虜兄弟が水
平に担いだ梯子に乗ってタイタス（＝ブライアン・コックス）が入場した。
⇒図3（p.49） 5幕2場でも、復讐の神に変装したタモラの登場シーンについ
て類似の問題が見られる。5.2.47注参照。

**1.1.109-11. brought to Rome / To beautify thy triumphs, and return /
Captive to thee and to thy Roman yoke** 「お前の凱旋を飾るためにローマ
へ連れて来られ、お前の捕虜としてお前のローマの軛に繋がれて帰還する」
triumph 「凱旋」ローマへ帰還したのはタモラ母子でなくタイタスだから、
正確にはこの場の状況に合わない。文脈の混乱は、我が子が犠牲に供せられる
と知った母タモラの恐怖・狼狽を映すものか。triumph, and return（Q1）を
Theobald の本文修正（「,」を削除）に従って triumph and return ＝ trium-
phant return と解釈するならば文意は単純になるが、もともと triumph 1 語で
「凱旋」を意味する。主語が曖昧なまま添えられた return は、むしろタモラの
置かれた不条理な状況と釣り合う。

1.1.130. irreligious piety 「神を恐れぬ罰あたりな信心」 撞着語法
(oxymoron)。16世紀は宗教改革に続く新旧両教徒の抗争・流血が多くあった
時代で、この悲劇の書かれた背景・同時代的状況が連想される台詞。陰惨な新
旧抗争・流血事件の例としては、1572年にパリで起きた「聖バルテルミの日
の大虐殺（Le massacre de la Saint-Barthélemy）」が有名。また piety（Lat.
pietas）はタイタスの名に添える形容詞 pius の名詞形であり、ここでも『ア
エネーイス』（10.812）の連想がある。1.1.23 後注参照。

**1.1.136-38. the Queen of Troy / With opportunity of sharp revenge /
Upon the Thracian tyrant in his tent** ギリシャ神話伝説に現れる「トロ
イアーの王妃」とは、トロイアー最後の王プリアモスの妃ヘカベー（Hekabe
/ Lat. Hecuba）のこと。the Thracian tyrant ＝ Polymestor エウリーピデー
ス（Euripides, c485-406 BC）の悲劇『ヘカベー』では、トラキア王ポリュメ
ーストールに息子ポリュドーロス（Polydoros）を殺されたヘカベーが、前者
をその二人の子とともに自分の幕営に招き、子供を殺し、さらに本人の目を抉
って復讐する。オウィディウスでは、ヘキュバ（＝ヘカベー）がポリュメース
トールのみを誘い寄せ、侍女らと協力してその両眼を抉る。子を殺された仕返
しに仇の子を殺すという陰惨な復讐の連鎖は、オウィディウスでなくむしろギ
リシャ悲劇の世界にあることに注意したい。オウィディウスでは復讐者ヘキュ
バが相手の子を殺さない上に、復讐の後直ちに犬に変身して復讐の狂気が止む。

幕営という場が詳しく描かれるのもエウリーピデースの方だ。in *his* tent とあるところがどちらともずれるが、ディミートリアスの古典引用はそもそも常にやや不正確なのでさほど問題ではない。この場面でタモラ親子は、タイタスの率いる敵軍の捕囚となりその首都ローマに連れて来られたばかり。his tent と言っているのも、彼ら親子がタイタスの軍に拘束されている現在の状況に心理的に近い。シェイクスピア自身にギリシャ悲劇の知識がどの程度あったかは不明だが、16 世紀後半のヨーロッパでは印刷技術の発展に伴い、ギリシャ文学の手頃なラテン語訳や希羅対訳本が大学生などを対象に流通している（Hoffman および Leadham-Green 参照）。シェイクスピアの場合でも、機会に恵まれれば、知人や同僚の蔵書などでギリシャ悲劇のいくつかの作品をラテン語訳で読める環境にいたと言える。高等教育を受けている先輩共作者ジョージ・ピールの場合であれば、そのような本で読んだ可能性はなおさら高い。

2. 1. 1-11.　Now climbeth Tamora Olympus' top ... at her frown.　妃となり権力を握ったタモラを語るこの場冒頭のエアロンの台詞は、クリストファー・マーロウの特徴的詩行を彷彿とさせる。Marlowe, *Doctor Faustus*, 3. 1 'Did mount himself to scale Olympus' top ...' フォースタス博士は魔術の力を借りてオリュンポスの高みにまでも飛翔し、宇宙の真理を極めようとする。エアロンは神話的宇宙像（2. 1. 1-8）の中にタモラの姿を写し、世俗の宮廷に絶大な権力を握る彼女の比喩とするスケールの大きなメタファー。様式としてはホメーロス以来の伝統を踏まえた叙事詩的シミリー（Homeric simile）だが、最近の認知言語学ではシミリー（明喩）もメタファーの一種に分類される。マーロウについては 1. 1. 131 および 250 注参照。

2. 3. 2-3.　bury so much gold under a tree / And never after to inherit it　地中に金を埋めて人に罪を着せる策略の例は、オウィディウス『変身物語』でアヤクス（Gk. アイアース）の演説に、ウリュセース（Gk. オデュッセウス）がパラメーデースを陥れるためにわざと金を埋めたという事件への言及がある。*Metamorphoses*, 13. 57-60 'viveret aut certe letum sine crimine haberet; / quem male convicti nimium memor iste fuoris / prodere rem Danaam finxit fictumque probavit / crimen et ostendit, quod iam praefoderat, aurum.'（[パラメーデースは]生きていたであろう、あるいは決して屈辱を受けることなく死ねたであろう。だがあの男[ウリュセース]は自分の狂気が不都合に暴かれたことをひどく気に病んで、彼がダナオイ[＝ギリシャ人たち]の国家を裏切っているという嘘をでっち上げ、有罪だと皆に信じ込ませた。前もって自分で埋めておいた金を[証拠だと偽って]見せたのだ。）inherit「相続する」は「自分のものとして取得する」のメタファー（*OED* inherit, *v.* 2. and 3.）。悪党のエアロンとタモラはこの劇の登場人物の中でも特に子への思いが強く、人間として自然な感覚・欲望の持ち主。4. 2. 91ff 参照。

2. 4. 39.　in a tedious sampler sewed her mind　「手間のかかる面倒な刺繍

に自分の思いを縫い込んだ」 **tedious** = long and tiresome: said of anything occupying time **sampler** = a beginner's exercise in embroidery; a piece of canvas embroidered by a girl or woman as a specimen of skill, usually containing the alphabet and some mottos worked in ornamental characters, with various decorative devices (*OED* sampler, *n.* 3.a. and b.) オウィディウスでは刺繍でなく「織物」(*Metamorphoses*, 6. 571-86)。後者が洗練された技を必要とする技芸であったのに比べ、前者は少女や初心者の女性が習いごととして覚えさせられるお稽古の類。観客にとって極力身近なイメージを用いるのが、シェイクスピア劇における古典受容の特徴の1つ。『夏の夜の夢』でヘレナが幼友達のハーミアに訴える台詞に、手習いの刺繍への言及がある。*A Midsummer Night's Dream*, 3. 2 'Both on one sampler, sitting on one cushion …'

3. 2. 85. SD *Exeunt* ト書き「全員退場」16世紀の芝居の慣習として、場の終わりで退場した人物が直後の場の冒頭で再び入場することはなかった。3幕2場はクオートにはなくF1で初めて加わる場だが、そのF1 (1623) のテクストでは3幕2場の終わりでタイタス、マーカス、ラヴィニア、少年ルーシアスが退場し、続く4幕1場の冒頭で同じ4人が再び登場する。3幕2場が17世紀になってからの挿入であると判断する1つの根拠になる点だが、F1の『タイタス』が実際の上映を反映させたテクストであるとするならば、17世紀に入ってから劇場上演の慣習が変わったことの反映であろうと推測される。例えば国王一座 (King's Men) は1609年に屋内劇場であるブラック・フライアーズ劇場を取得したので、照明用の蠟燭の芯を切る必要から幕間をとるという習慣がシェイクスピア劇にも適用されるようになったという状況が3幕2場の異例な入退場の背景にあるという仮説を、昔清水が修士論文で立てたが、現在ではほぼ定説化している。従って新しい慣習を反映させている3幕2場の挿入は、ブラック・フライアーズ劇場取得の1609年からF1の出版された1623年までの期間のいずれかの年という推測が有力になる。ただし実際の挿入年代については批評家によって微妙な差があり、決着はついていない。　⇒解説9-10頁参照。

4. 1. 「持ち歩ける本」はルネサンス的な本のイメージ。本を読み聞かせることが親子、姉弟、家族の絆を支えとなっていることを、アクションと回想で印象づける場になっている。

4. 1. 0 SD. Q1のテクストでは3幕2場 (F1) を挟まず、3幕1場の終わりでルーシアスが退場した後に、続けて小ルーシアスとラヴィニアが駆け込んで来る形で4幕1場が始まる。3.2.85 SD後注参照。

4. 1. 77. *Stuprum* = dishonour, debauchery「淫乱、恥知らず」(Lat.) 多くの注釈は中世フランス語からの借用語 *stupre* (< L. stuprum) の意味で「レイプ」と解釈しているが、ここは犯人の2人の淫らな性格と蛮行を非難する叫びとし

ての 1 語。Cf. Cicero, *In C. Verrem*, 2. 82 'natum a cupiditate, auctum per stuprum, crudelitate perfectum atque conclusum'（貪欲によって生まれ、淫らな欲望によって育まれ、残忍によって完成され締め括られた）すでにラヴィニアはオウィディウスの本のページからピロメーラがテーレウスにレイプされる物語を示した上で、「レイプされたのか（ravished）」という父からの問いにも身振りで答えており（4. 1. 45-54）、繰り返し「レイプ」という事実を伝える必要はない。マーカスがラヴィニアに敢えて砂に文字を書かせるのは、犯人の名前を知るため。ラヴィニアのメッセージは「淫乱、カイロン、ディミートリアス。」次行でマーカスは lustful sons と言い、ラヴィニアが stuprum の 1 語に込めた意図と怒りを正しく解釈している。英語で連想される類例としては stuprous = corrupt, immoral, lascivious（*OED* stuprous, *adj.*）。

4. 1. 80-81. *Magni Dominator poli ... tam lentus vides?* セネカからの大雑把な引用。Seneca, *Hippolytus*, 671-72 'Magne regnator deum ...'「天の（セネカ：神々の）偉大なる支配者よ、その罪を、何故このように遅く聞き、このように遅く目にするのか。」（Waith） ラテン語引用の問題については⇒解説 15-22 頁。

4. 2. 20-21. *Integer vitae, scelerisque purus, / Non eget Mauri iaculis, nec arcu* 「生き方が純粋で罪に汚れない者は、ムーアの槍も弓も必要なく」（Horatius, *Carmina*, 1. 22. 1-2） ホラーティウス（英名 Horace）の抒情詩集『歌章（*Carmina*）』の中でも有名な一句。続くカイロンの台詞にあるように、シェイクスピアの時代の学校（grammar schools）のラテン語教科書に例文として掲載されていた。*Mauri* は代表的教科書の 1 つ William Lily, *Brevissima Institutio* (London, 1570) での綴り（J. W. Binns / Waith）。ホラーティウスのそれ以外の多くの版では *Mauris*。

4. 2. 62. is delivered = gives birth to a child; is liberated from a state of evil, danger, oppression, etc.; is conveyed and handed over「出産する」「悪い、危険な状態から解放される」「運び届けられる」 続く乳母とエアロンのやり取りでは deliver の 3 つの意味が錯綜し、混乱した滑稽な会話になっている。62 行の台詞では、乳母は初め単純に「出産した」の意味で、あるいは「（悪魔を）産み落として陣痛から解放された」という含みと解釈できる。

4. 2. 72. christen = baptize 「洗礼する」を「刺し殺す」の比喩で使うのは露骨な冒瀆。また異教の古代ローマを扱う芝居にキリスト教の用語・イメージを混在させるのはアナクロニズム。しかしこの芝居が描くのはどの時代にも存在しなかった完全に虚構のローマであり、決して歴史ではない。古代から伝わる詩と悲劇と歴史記述他の諸伝説にシェイクスピア同時代の政治的・文化的関心をも加えて自由に織り成した作品であり、むしろ新しい神話創造に近い。一般に歴史記述と神話創造の境界は曖昧だが、演劇における意図的なアナクロニズムには「歴史」の虚構性・神話性を浮き上がらせる異化効果（Verfremdungseffekt）もある。

4.2.95-96. Enceladus ... band of Typhon's brood テュポーン（Typhon）あるいはテュポーエウス（Typhoeus）は、神々に挑みユーピテル（Jupiter / Gk. Zeus）の雷で打ち負かされエトナ山（またはどこかの火山）の下に埋められた100の竜頭を持つ怪物。エンケラドス（Enceladus）はテュポーエウスに率いられて同じく神々に挑んだ怪物の一人で、ユーピテルの雷に焼かれて同様にエトナ山の下に閉じ込められた。いずれも大地テラ（Terra / Gk. Gaia）の子。All the threatening band of Typhon はその時神々に挑んだ怪物一族を指す。3.1.242-43 注および *Metamorphoses*, 1.182-86 参照。テラは自分の子供のギガンテスたちがヘーラクレースに殺されたのち、さらに巨大なテュポーエウス他の怪物を生む。ただしテュポーエウスの神話はさまざまで、多種多様な伝承がある。

図9 《テュポーエウスを打つユーピテル》黒絵の壺（紀元前540頃）州立古代美術博物館蔵、ミュンヘン

4.3. この場のタイタスの行動が真性の狂気故のものか敵を欺くための佯狂（ようきょう）か、あるいは狂気を演じることの問題をメタドラマ的に問うものか、テクストからはいずれとも決め難い。

4.3.4. *Terras Astraea reliquit* = Astraea has quit the earth（Lat.）*Metamorphoses*, I.149-50 'et virgo caede madentis / ultima caelestum terras Astraea reliquit'（そして天上の神々の最後に処女神アストライアが、殺戮で血に濡れた大地を去った）から。ギリシャ神話でアストライアは正義の女神で、人類史四時代（Golden Age, Silver Age, Bronze Age, Iron Age）の3期めの青銅時代に地上から去る。続く鉄時代が人類史の最後で最悪の時代。シェイクスピアの時代では、エリザベス一世が女神アストライアに擬えられた。

4.3.39. Revenge 「復讐」人格化。英語での revenge, vengeance は、義理・忠義の問題としての日本の伝統的「仇討ち」と違い、もともと専ら「意趣返し、仕返しによる憂さ晴らし」あるいは「復讐心、仕返しによる憂さ晴らしへの渇望」など心理的意味合いの強いもので、狂気に近い。英語史上での人格化は16世紀後半からで、現在では廃れた用法（*OED* revenge *n.* 1.c.）。この劇中で復讐（vengeance）を明確に狂気と割り切る人物は、悪党ながら合理主義者の道化的人物エアロン。解説（22-25頁）、2.3.38 注および5.1.58 注参照。

4.3.44-45. the burning lake below ... Acheron 「燃える」というのは、おそらく冥界のタルタルスを流れる炎の川フレゲトーン（Phlegethon）のこと。*Aeneis*, 6.550-51 'quae rapidus flammis ambit torrentibus amnis, / Tartareus

Phlegethon'（燃え盛る炎の急流すなわちタルタルスのフレゲトーン川がそこ
を囲むように流れ） アケローン（Acheron）も冥界のタルタルスを流れる川で、
その周辺一体の水域を湖（lake）のように想像したものか。（*Aeneis*, 6. 295-
316）

4. 3. 47. the Cyclops' size キュクロープスは『オデュッセイア』他に登場
する単眼の巨人。単数で the Cyclops と言う場合はポリュペーモス（Polyphe-
mus）を指す。オデュッセウスにその1つだけの眼を潰される（*Odysseia*,
9. 105-542）。ポリュペーモスはニンフのガラテーア（Galatea）への片想いで
も有名。

4. 3. 54-55. *Ad Jovem* = to Jupiter ***Ad Apollinem*** = to Apollo ***Ad Martem***
= to Mars 初めラテン語でそれぞれの矢の宛先の神々の名を読み上げるが、
すぐに to Pallas ... to Mercury ... と英語に戻している。古代ローマの雰囲気を
出しながら、シェイクスピア同時代の観客に違和感を覚えさせないよう工夫し
た台詞。

4. 3. 57. Saturn ... not to Saturnine Saturn は神サトゥルヌス（Saturnus）
の、Saturnine は人名サトゥルニーヌス（Saturninus）の、それぞれの英語形。
名前が似ているから「間違えてサターナイナスに届けないように」と注意を促
している。

4. 3. 65. in Virgo's lap 「乙女座の膝に」神話では、正義の女神アストライ
ア（Astraea）が空に登って乙女座になったとされる。狂気を装う（＝演じる）
主人公が性的なジョークを言う類例としては、旅役者による御前興行の場
（*Hamlet*, 3. 2）でハムレットがオフィーリアに言う 'Shall I lie in your lap?'
などがある。

4. 3. 70-75. This was the sport ... for a present マーカスは、「（パブリア
スの放った矢が黄道まで届いて）牡牛座の角の1つを射落とした」というタイ
タスの幻想の台詞を受けて、cuckold のジョークを展開する。兄であり一族の
長であるタイタスが心労のため憔悴して狂気に陥ったと信じているマーカスに
しては、やや不可解な悪ふざけ。嵐の中で狂い始めたリア王が長女ゴネリルと
次女リーガンの裁判を幻想する場（*King Lear*, 3. 6）での、佯狂の家臣エドガ
ーと道化の行動を参照。観客が狂気の見世物を見たがっていたというシェイク
スピアの時代の演劇事情も考慮する必要があろう。

4. 3. 84. Jubiter Q1 では 67 行、79 行、83 行も全て Iubiter（＝ Jupiter）と
なっているが、現代のほぼすべての版で、この 84 行のみ道化が Iupiter（＝
Jupiter）の名を理解できずに Iubiter（＝ Jubiter）と呼んでいるものとする。
Q1 での残りの行の Iubiter は恐らく植字工による誤り。田舎者に限らず、シ
ェイクスピア時代の英国で古典古代の神々は遠い存在。なお、古い綴りで語頭
の I と J の区別はなかった。

4. 3. 94-99. この6行を「劇作家がテクストを推敲・書き換える際に削除する

つもりでありながら削除し損ねた部分（false start）」と見做して削除する現代の版もある（Wells, Taylor 他）。主な根拠は 95 行・97 行の oration「式辞」が 105 行・107 行の supplication「嘆願」と矛盾するという点。しかしこの場の道化とタイタスの会話はそもそもチグハグなもので、道化はタイタスの言葉をまともに理解していない。またマーカスとタイタスの台詞も誠意のあるものでなく、道化の無知をいいことに出任せを言っている場面ともとれる。

4. 3. 105-11.　Sirrah, can you ... Let me alone.　上述（4. 3. 94-99 後注）と同じ理由で、94 行以下 6 行の代わりに 105 行以下 7 行を false start と見做して削除する現代の版（Waith 他）もある。

4. 4. 12.　His fits, his frenzy, and his bitterness?　タイタスの復讐を狂気沙汰だと主張するサターナイナスが、復讐と狂気を連想する言葉を並べ立てる。復讐を狂気と見做す点で、合理主義者の悪党エアロンと無能な皇帝サターナイナスが同じ価値観を持つ。

5. 1. 16.　be avenged on cursèd Tamora　「呪わしいタモラに復讐する」be avenged on = avenge yourself on; take vengeance on　怒りと復讐の対象がローマ軍あるいはローマ皇帝でなくその妃に向けられている。ゴート族がゴート族の女王タモラに反感を抱くようになる理由は不明。女性嫌悪（misogyny）に訴えて戦意を煽る軍人政治家ルーシアスのレトリックか。

5. 1. 21.　a ruinous monastery　ヘンリー八世の時代に起こった宗教改革（首長令 1534 年）で修道院他多くのカトリック系の施設が破壊された。シェイクスピアの同時代的風景で、古代ローマの時代設定としてはアナクロニズム。⇒解説 10-15 頁。

5. 1. 63.　massacres = the indiscriminate slaughters of people　おそらく当時の観客に聖バルテルミーの日の大虐殺（1572）を、あるいはそれを扱ったクリストファー・マーロウの芝居『パリの大虐殺（*The Massacre at Paris*）』を連想させたかもしれない。

5. 2. 0 SD.　*Enter Tamora and her two sons, disguised* 「タモラと 2 人の息子が変装して登場」悲劇の中に仮面劇（masque）風の露骨に芝居掛かった場が劇中劇的構造で埋め込まれ、視覚的にも観客に強く訴える見せ場が始まる。後のタイタスの台詞 on thy chariot wheels（5. 2. 47）から、タモラが戦車に乗って登場したと想像することが可能。ただし第 1 幕のタイタスの場合と同様に、戦車を用いても用いなくても、どのようにも上演可能な柔軟な台本。1. 1. 250 注参照。

disguised　16 世紀までの芝居の約束事として、一般に変装（disguise）は見抜かれないことになっていた。この場でタモラ母子の変装がタイタスにあっさり見破られるという筋立ては約束破りのように見える。しかしタモラが変装で演技するのは復讐の女神あるいは寓意（allegory）で、リアリズムとは程遠い。しかもタモラが自分の変装が見抜かれないと信じるのはタイタスの狂気を前提

としている。もとより正気の相手・観客には機能しないはずの変装のトリック。シェイクスピアが一般に伝統的約束事（convention）を使用する場合、約束に従いつつも、かなり手の込んだ応用を試みる場合が多い。

5. 2. 60-63.　These are my ministers ... of such kind of men　タモラの演じる芝居での2人の息子の役をめぐるタイタスとタモラのやり取り。タモラは、2人が自分の手下（ministers）の神格で、それぞれ（レイプ犯に復讐する神格としての）「レイプ」と（殺人者に復讐する神格としての）「殺人」だと主張する。言い換えれば寓意（allegory）としての Rape と Murder。一方タイタスは初めから2人の正体を見抜きながら、それぞれを Rape および Murder と呼ぶ。その場合 rape = rapist, murder = murderer となり、行為でその主体を表わす換喩（metonymy）であって、タモラの意図する寓意（allegory）とは対照的。なお、そもそも2人を最初に Rape および Murder と名付けたのはタイタスであることにも注意。　5. 2. 45 注参照。

5. 2. 61.　What are they called?　「そいつらは何という名前だ」ここでタイタスが2人の名前を尋ねているのは 5. 2. 45 と矛盾・重複するようにも見えるため、ここを作者の推敲・原稿書き換え時における消去ミスととる解釈もある（Maxwell, Waith）。しかしここはタイタスとタモラが2人の命名をめぐって主導権を争っている場面であり、テクストに問題はない（Bate）。寓意劇を演じようとするタモラに対抗して、タイタスは犯行によって犯人を表わす換喩を用い、この見えすいた芝居の主導権を握る。

5. 2. 203.　Centaurs' feast　「ケンタウロス族の宴」ギリシャ神話。テッサリア地方ラピタイ族（Lapithae）の王ペイリトオスがヒッポダメイアと結婚した折の祝宴を指す。宴のさなか、招待されたケンタウロス一族（Centauri）の一人エウリュトスが酔った勢いで花嫁を奪おうとしたことをきっかけに、ラピタイ族とケンタウロス一族との間で凄惨な戦いと殺し合い（Centauromachia）が起こる。（*Metamorphoses*, 12. 210-535）

図10　《ケンタウロス族の戦い》ミケランジェロ作レリーフ（1492）カサ・ブオナッローティ蔵、フィレンツェ

5. 3. 72.　ROMAN LORD　Q1 ではこの行から *Romane Lord* の台詞とし、F1 ではこの行から *Goth* の台詞とする。Let を Lest に修正してマーカスの台詞が前行から続くものととる Capell の読みに従う現代の版も多い。しかし事件の真相を聴きに集まったローマ市民の代表（Roman Lord）が、コロス（Chorus）の長のような役柄と考えるならばギリシャ悲劇の形に似る。

5. 3. 87-94　My heart is ... hear him speak　前行までを Roman Lord の台詞とし、87-94 のみをマーカスの台詞ととる読みもある。あるいは 66-94 のすべてをマーカスの台詞ととる読みもある。

[編注者紹介]

清水徹郎（しみず　てつろう）

1955年生まれ。東京大学文学部卒業。同大学院修士課程修了。

元東京工業大学講師。元お茶の水女子大学大学院教授。

現在　お茶の水女子大学名誉教授、朝日カルチャーセンター講師。

［共著］『エリザベス朝演劇の誕生』（水声社）、『言葉と文化のシェイクスピア』（早稲田大学出版局）、『シェイクスピアと演劇文化』（研究社出版）、他

［共訳］E・M・W・ティリヤード『エリザベス朝の世界像』（筑摩叢書）

［論文］'The Great Teller of Tales, or πολύμητις: Problematizing the Metonymy of Singing in the Epic Tradition and Shakespeare's *Sonnets*', *Ochanomizu University Studies in Arts and Culture*, Vol. 16., 'Making "blind Homer sing to me": 16th-Century Student Editions of Greek Poems and Marlowe's Art of Imitation', *Shakespeare Studies*, Vol. 50. 、他

〈大修館シェイクスピア双書 第2集〉

タイタス・アンドロニカス

©Tetsuro Shimizu, 2022　　　　　　　　　NDC 932／xii, 226p／20cm

初版第1刷──2022年12月20日

編注者────清水徹郎

発行者────鈴木一行

発行所────株式会社 大修館書店

　　　　　〒113-8541 東京都文京区湯島2-1-1

　　　　　電話 03-3868-2651（販売部）　03-3868-2293（編集部）

　　　　　振替 00190-7-40504

　　　　　[出版情報] https://www.taishukan.co.jp

装丁・本文デザイン────井之上聖子

印刷所────広研印刷

製本所────ブロケード

ISBN 978-4-469-14271-6　Printed in Japan

大修館 シェイクスピア双書 (全12巻)
THE TAISHUKAN SHAKESPEARE

お気に召すまま	*As You Like It*	柴田稔彦 編注
ハムレット	*Hamlet, Prince of Denmark*	高橋康也・ 河合祥一郎 編注
ジュリアス・シーザー	*Julius Caesar*	大場建治 編注
リア王	*King Lear*	Peter Milward 編注
マクベス	*Macbeth*	今西雅章 編注
ヴェニスの商人	*The Marchant of Venice*	喜志哲雄 編注
夏の夜の夢	*A Midsummer-night's Dream*	石井正之助 編注
オセロー	*Othello*	笹山　隆 編注
リチャード三世	*King Richard the Third*	山田昭広 編注
ロミオとジュリエット	*Romeo and Juliet*	岩崎宗治 編注
テンペスト	*The Tempest*	藤田　実 編注
十二夜	*Twelfth Night; or, What You Will*	安西徹雄 編注

大修館 シェイクスピア双書 第2集（全8巻）
THE TAISHUKAN SHAKESPEARE 2nd Series